TENDERLY

With infinite care, Will brushed his mouth over hers. A brief taste, a sampling, nothing more.

And not nearly enough.

He groaned low in his throat and kissed her again, reveling in the sweetness, the softness, the rightness of his action. More. He needed still more.

But Charisma shifted, a sigh escaping her, and he jerked back. What *was* he doing? Her eyes fluttered open but she remained on his shoulder for another minute before awareness dawned.

She sat upright with a gasp. "I . . . I'm sorry. I didn't . . ."

"I don't mind." He didn't mind at all. In fact, he missed her warmth and the gentle weight against his shoulder.

Blinking, she glanced around the car. "Are we home?"

Will firmly believed in fate when the conductor chose that moment to enter. "Colorado Springs next stop."

"Almost." He smiled at Charisma, resisting the urge to touch her again. He had the sinking feeling that if he did, he would never let her go. . . .

BOOK YOUR PLACE ON OUR WEBSITE AND MAKE THE READING CONNECTION!

We've created a customized website just for our very special readers, where you can get the inside scoop on everything that's going on with Zebra, Pinnacle and Kensington books.

When you come online, you'll have the exciting opportunity to:

- View covers of upcoming books
- Read sample chapters
- Learn about our future publishing schedule (listed by publication month *and author*)
- Find out when your favorite authors will be visiting a city near you
- Search for and order backlist books from our online catalog
- Check out author bios and background information
- Send e-mail to your favorite authors
- Meet the Kensington staff online
- Join us in weekly chats with authors, readers and other guests
- Get writing guidelines
- AND MUCH MORE!

**Visit our website at
http://www.kensingtonbooks.com**

A TOUCH OF CHARM

Karen Fox

ZEBRA BOOKS
Kensington Publishing Corp.
http://www.kensingtonbooks.com

ZEBRA BOOKS are published by

Kensington Publishing Corp.
850 Third Avenue
New York, NY 10022

All Kensington titles, imprints and distributed lines are available at special quantity discounts for bulk purchases for sales promotion, premiums, fund-raising, educational or institutional use.

Special book excerpts or customized printings can also be created to fit specific needs. For details, write or phone the office of the Kensington Special Sales Manager: Kensington Publishing Corp., 850 Third Avenue, New York, NY 10022. Attn. Special Sales Department. Phone: 1-800-221-2647.

Zebra and the Z logo Reg. U.S. Pat. & TM Off.

First Printing: September 2003
10 9 8 7 6 5 4 3 2 1

Printed in the United States of America

To Fran Byczynski, Jackie LaForge, and Kim Sheehan, good friends to have at work, and all the engineers at MITRE Colorado Springs. Thanks for the support. You're wonderful! And, as always, to the Wyrd sisters.

One

"Hurry. We're already late." Charisma Sullivan glanced over her shoulder at her dawdling sisters, but didn't wait for them. Waiting for Grace and Belle to get ready for this outing had already taken long enough. Up ahead, she could see the crowd gathered around the visiting lawyer, William Barclay, a candidate for a seat in the Colorado senate.

She resisted the urge to run, hearing her mother's voice in her head. *Young ladies never run.*

Young ladies didn't do a lot of things, most of which were fun. Though her family was wealthy now, Charisma often missed the more casual life they had had when her father had been merely a miner. There hadn't been so many rules and Papa and Mama had rarely fought then.

"Wait for us, Charisma," her older sister, Belle, called out. "You don't want to appear unchaperoned."

Charisma sighed, but paused in the wide dirt road leading to the Colorado Springs Hotel. The only way she'd persuaded Mama to let her attend Mr. Barclay's speech was to have her sisters accompany her. "Please, hurry."

When her younger sister, Grace, tripped over the hem of her gown, Charisma sucked in her breath, waiting for the inevitable disaster, but Grace managed to right herself and finally joined her sisters. "I've missed most of his talk already," Charisma said, spurring her sisters into motion again.

"I don't understand why you should be interested at all," Belle said. "Women have no place in politics. We can't even vote."

"That will change." Charisma felt sure of it. "Mrs. Woodhull said it is only custom, not the Constitution, that keeps women from voting."

Belle shook her head. "Just because Mrs. Woodhull ran for the position of president—unsuccessfully, I might add—does not make her words sacrosanct."

"She has many excellent ideas." Ideas Charisma believed in and strongly supported. Why couldn't a woman make a difference? While living in Leadville, she'd seen how women held their families together while men worked in the silver mines. Women made critical decisions and worked just as hard as the men. Didn't they deserve just as many rights?

Charisma reached the edge of the crowd surrounding the front porch of the hotel. While she could hear Mr. Barclay's voice, she couldn't see a glimpse of him, not even when she stood on tiptoe.

". . . and in conclusion, I believe all individuals have rights, be they simple shop clerks or General Palmer himself." His voice was deep, well-educated, and filled with conviction.

If only she could see him . . .

"Thank you."

Applause rippled through the crowd as he stepped down to shake hands. Charisma's heart sank. She'd missed it.

But she *would* meet him.

Ignoring Belle's protests, Charisma wove through the diminishing crowd toward the front to find a small cluster of young women surrounding someone. Mr. Barclay? Why would so many young women be interested in politics? Most of the young women Charisma encountered in social functions dismissed her "passionate championing" of equal rights for women as "wild ideas."

Unable to proceed any further, she waited for a lull in the female chatter, then raised her voice. "Mr. Barclay, do you think the Leadville Strike of 1880 could have been avoided?"

Several women turned, recognized her, then dismissed her just as quickly. Charisma only lifted her chin. Would Mr. Barclay answer?

"Excuse me, ladies."

She heard him approaching.

"It's just Charisma Sullivan," Edith Wagner said, loud enough for the entire group to hear. "Her father is one of the new silver kings."

"A miner, wasn't he?"

Charisma couldn't see who spoke, but the haughtiness of the tone made her frown. Her papa was every bit the equal to General Palmer or Doctor Bell, both revered leaders in prosperous Colorado Springs.

The gaggle of women parted as a young man stepped out to face Charisma. No wonder they had clustered around him. She found herself unable to stop staring. He was younger than she'd expected, perhaps in his mid-twenties, and devastatingly handsome.

His features were well-defined—an aristocratic

nose and sharp cheekbones with fine lips and a strong chin, but it was his dark brown intelligent eyes that drew her interest as he looked at her.

"Did you ask the question?" he asked.

Charisma blinked, recalling why she'd spoken. "Yes, I wanted your opinion on the Leadville Strike. Do you believe miners have equal rights as well?"

He hesitated, studying her, his expression serious. "I certainly do. They were well within their rights to ask for eight-hour days and increased pay for their dangerous work. However, I also believe the violence they used to get attention for their cause was not the proper way to win sympathy. The citizens of Leadville were justified in asking the governor for help."

He spoke to her as an equal and Charisma's pulse grew unsteady. Most men she'd questioned treated her as a child or simpleton. Emboldened, she continued. "What about unions for miners?"

His gaze held hers for a moment, quizzical at first, then serious. "There are good and bad things about unions, Miss . . ." He trailed off. "I fear we have not been properly introduced. I am William Barclay from Denver."

Though Charisma knew she should wait for someone else to introduce them, she thought it a silly custom when plain talking could make it so much easier. "Charisma Sullivan." She glanced back and saw her sisters approaching, Belle disapproving and Grace clearly awed. "These are my sisters, Belle and Grace."

Mr. Barclay bowed slightly. "I'm pleased to make your acquaintance." His fine eyes rested on Charisma again and she experienced a sudden extra thump in her chest. "You ask knowledgeable questions, Miss Sullivan. Is a member of your family involved in politics?"

"No, but I have an interest in the issues." Charisma saw the corner of his lips quirk upward and she smiled. "Do you believe women should have the right to vote, Mr. Barclay?"

He released a full smile then, and Charisma caught her breath. She was willing to vote for him just based on that smile.

"I believe women are fully capable of understanding the issues and should be allowed to have some choice in our elected officials."

Clever. Charisma tilted her head. "That is neither a yes or a no."

"Exactly." Humor danced in his eyes.

Before Charisma could question him further, Dr. Bell approached. "Time to go, Will." He paused and addressed Charisma and her sisters. "Miss Sullivan, Miss Charisma, Miss Grace. I must say, Mr. Barclay draws more women than our usual orators."

Belle and Grace responded with polite smiles, but Charisma saw no harm in answering him. "I find discussion of these issues very interesting."

He drew back, startled, then smiled. "Admirable. Now, if you will excuse us, ladies?"

He led Mr. Barclay away and Belle placed her hand on Charisma's arm. "You must learn to watch what you say. If Mr. Barclay were not such a good-natured man, you might have offended him."

"By asking questions?"

"It's how you ask the questions." Belle took the sting from her words with a warm smile.

Charisma turned toward home. "No one ever

said I was charming." In fact, they often said the opposite.

She tried to change. In fact, she'd even made a wish to become charming.

Frowning, she recalled the day last spring when she and her sisters had gone to the majestic Garden of the Gods with male escorts, each pleased that they'd finally been invited for themselves. They'd been sorely disillusioned when they overheard the men mention how Mrs. Sullivan had paid them to escort the sisters. Even worse, the men had openly disparaged the sisters in regard to their names. Belle, they'd said, had no beauty. Charisma was far from charming and Grace was . . . simply graceless.

Hurt by these cruel words, the sisters had stood before the pillars of the Three Graces formation and made fervent wishes to receive the embodiments of beauty, charm, and grace to fit their names.

And Belle's wish had come true.

Not that she'd suddenly become beautiful, but she'd learned to dress better and take extra care of her appearance, which had made an amazing difference in how others perceived her. Plus, she'd recently become engaged to Christopher Stanhope, the son of a British lord. No doubt this accounted for the rosy glow that gave Belle real beauty.

Charisma sighed. She'd wished aloud for charm, but thus far hadn't noticed any difference. She tried. She really did, but words often escaped her lips before she could form them into more tactful phrasing.

Besides, that hadn't been her only wish before

the serene red rocks of the Three Graces. She'd also made a silent plea—to make a difference in the world. Though Mrs. Woodhull hadn't been elected president, she had called attention to Susan B. Anthony's and Elizabeth Cady Stanton's movement to get women the right to vote. Charisma doubted she could do anything on that scale, but she firmly believed she could do *something*.

But what?

"What did you think of Mr. Barclay?" Grace asked, breaking into Charisma's thoughts.

For once, Charisma tempered her words before she spoke. "He is an excellent candidate." *And a pleasure to look upon.* She had no difficulty in recalling his face, his expressive eyes and mouth.

"You didn't even hear his speech," Belle said. "How can you know that from a few questions?"

"I found his answers very satisfactory." Charisma glanced at her sister and found a twinkle in Belle's eyes.

"He was extremely good-looking as well," Belle added.

"Yes, indeed." Charisma had to grin. "But should you be noticing that? What about Kit?"

"Oh, Kit is far more handsome."

"To you." Charisma found Mr. Barclay a great deal more appealing.

"Perhaps you will see Mr. Barclay again." Grace pushed a low-hanging tree branch out of her way, then released it, nearly smacking Charisma in the face. Fortunately, Charisma had had years of living with her accident-prone sister and managed to duck in time. She sighed and continued walking.

"Perhaps." The *Daily Gazette* said he planned to

remain in Colorado Springs until the election in November. If so, they were likely to meet at some of the social functions in town.

A shiver of anticipation danced along Charisma's spine. She would not find that a hardship at all.

Will Barclay nodded in agreement with his host's comment, still unable to believe his good fortune. He was actually here in the El Paso Club, the city's exclusive men's organization. "I thank you again for giving me this opportunity, sir."

"I'm happy to do it, my boy. It's up to you to make something of it." Dr. Bell led Will across the room toward the El Paso Club's current president. "Sam, let me introduce you to young Will Barclay. He's running for the senate. Mr. Barclay, Dr. Samuel Solly."

Dr. Solly extended his hand and gripped Will's. "Barclay, eh? One of the Denver Barclays?"

Will accepted the hand, hoping his nervousness didn't show. He really wanted to win this influential leader to his cause. Dr. Solly had come over from England and was now the ranking specialist on consumption. However, more than a doctor, he conceived grand schemes and used his influence to make them happen. Even now, an enormous new hotel was being built at the end of Pikes Peak Avenue. A project conceived by Dr. Solly and financed by General Palmer.

"My family," Will admitted, a fact that could help or hinder him.

"Good people," Dr. Solly added. "I believe your father has supported my sanitariums."

"Yes, sir." Will had counted on the doctor remembering that. "I hear it's been quite successful for you thus far."

"So it has." The doctor waved toward an empty chair. "Have a seat and tell us more about your campaign."

"Thank you." This was exactly the opening he had hoped for.

Will spent the next several hours outlining his platform, drawing a crowd, which allowed him to entertain questions and enter into a rousing debate. By the time Dr. Bell claimed his attention, Will felt certain he'd won the support of several influential citizens. Not a bad start for his first week in Colorado Springs.

"I should warn you Cora is planning a picnic to welcome you," Dr. Bell said as he led Will to the door. "Unless you want to be fighting off all our single women instead of campaigning, I suggest you find a young lady to escort to this affair and other social functions."

Will grimaced. He had no interest in spending time with young ladies at this point in his life. Winning the senate seat was what mattered now. "I am unacquainted with the ladies here."

"I'll find someone to introduce you around. I can probably stall Cora for a few days, but she's determined to show you off. You know how much she loves to entertain."

The men climbed into Dr. Bell's buggy and Dr. Bell turned toward the Colorado Springs Hotel, where Will had rooms. "Perhaps I can find someone for that one function," Will murmured, the image of the young woman he'd met earlier that afternoon appearing in his mind.

He'd found Miss Charisma Sullivan extremely attractive, with her strawberry-blonde hair, creamy skin, and flashing blue-green eyes. Her questions had surprised him. Very few women paid much attention to politics and fewer still asked intelligent questions.

The other women who had cornered him before Miss Charisma arrived had only been interested in his family and fortune, not his views on what the Colorado government should be doing for its populace.

But Charisma hadn't asked about his family at all. During their short conversation, he'd sensed an underlying passion that intrigued him. She'd been very direct—blunt almost. A result of her passion, no doubt.

Will nodded to himself. Perhaps he could find an escort for Mrs. Bell's picnic. After all, it would only be one function. What harm could there be in that?

The Three Graces relaxed on the top of Mount Olympus, sipping their afternoon tea. Aglaia beamed at her sisters. "Now that I have Belle happily engaged and all her wishes answered, you must see to Charisma, Thalia."

"I am looking forward to it." Thalia, the embodiment of charm, set her cup on the table. "Though fulfilling all her wishes should prove to be challenging."

"Does she have more than one?" Euphrosyne asked.

Thalia nodded. "Her spoken wish for charm, of course, and her unspoken wish to make a difference in her society. Plus the wish she isn't even aware she harbors."

"When will you begin?" Aglaia asked.

Thalia stood. "Right away, of course."

A stylishly dressed woman came to meet Will as he descended the stairs at the hotel the next morning. Her dark day gown was obviously of high quality material and cut in the latest fashion. In her late thirties, perhaps, she had black hair twisted into an ornate bun and a welcoming smile that he couldn't help but return.

"I am so pleased to make your acquaintance, Mr. Barclay," she said. "Please forgive my impertinence in introducing myself, but Dr. Bell was unable to accompany me as he'd promised and I dared not wait to speak to you."

Ah, a friend of Dr. Bell's. With all the assistance the older gentleman was providing Will, the least he could do was greet the man's friend. "The pleasure is mine," he said. "But I'm afraid you have me at a disadvantage."

"Didn't Dr. Bell tell you I was coming?" She shook her head. "I see by your expression, he didn't. I must speak with him about that." Her warm smile softened her words. "I am Thalia Papadopoulos. As my deceased husband was very active in Wyoming state politics, Dr. Bell felt I might be able to help you fit in here."

"That is very kind of you." Will struggled to keep from jumping with joy. To have this kind of assistance would be invaluable. "Would you care to join me for breakfast so we can discuss things further?"

"I'm afraid I haven't time right now." She glanced at a small silver timepiece pinned to her bodice. "We are scheduled to be at the Sullivan home within the hour."

Will blinked. The Sullivan home? "I beg your pardon?"

Mrs. Papadopoulos patted his arm. "When Dr. Bell explained your predicament, I knew exactly where to go for help. Patrick Sullivan has three lovely daughters. I'm sure one of them can masquerade as your escort for the duration of your visit."

"Escort?" Will had the horrible feeling he'd lost control shortly after meeting this petite woman. He'd only seriously considered the idea of finding a young woman to assist him late last night. In the bright light of day, he wasn't entirely sure such a thing was necessary. "Please don't go to such trouble. It's only one picnic."

"For now." Mrs. Papadopoulos gave him a knowing smile. "Cora's picnic will only be the first of many invitations you'll receive while you're here. If I may make a suggestion . . ."

"Of course." She was so charming, Will could hardly tell her no.

"You will appear a much more responsible candidate if you are married or, at the very least, settled with one young lady."

Married? Will's collar suddenly felt too tight. "I do not wish to be married." He'd been sadly disillusioned about marriage after seeing the disastrous life his brother and his wife had made for themselves. "Nor do I wish to become involved with any young woman at this time. I need to devote my attention to my campaign."

"Rightly so." Mrs. Papadopoulos smiled. "But I believe we can persuade one of the Sullivan girls to merely act as a companion for you. Provide the façade without the actual involvement."

That would solve one of his problems. "Would a young lady be willing to do such a thing? I thought they all had marriage on their minds."

Mrs. Papadopoulos laughed. "Many do, but I believe you'll find Miss Charisma or Miss Grace are less husband-oriented than most of the young women in Colorado Springs." She led Will outside to the warm summer sunshine. "And Mr. Sullivan much more reasonable about allowing his daughter to accompany you."

They were a block from the hotel before Will realized he still hadn't agreed to this. Mrs. Papadopoulos hadn't allowed him a chance to refuse. He grinned. Definitely a politician's wife.

"I believe you will find it worth your time to appeal to the married women in town during your campaign as well."

"But women aren't allowed to vote." An issue that Will planned to avoid during this campaign.

"No, but they do influence their husbands." Mrs. Papadopoulos's eyes twinkled. "And a charming young man like you can make a very favorable impression on a woman . . . married or not."

Though Will answered with a self-deprecating grin, he had to admit she had a point. His brother wasn't above using his good looks to gain votes or influence ladies. Will's smile faded. In some cases, whether the ladies wanted to be influenced or not.

His newly designated mentor continued, "If you are seen to be involved with only one young lady

during your stay here, then you will have more freedom and spend less time fending off our eligible
females and fathers will worry less."

True enough. "But I won't have much time to devote to any woman. I plan to be busy campaigning.
The election is only a little over two months away."

"Ah, but the right woman will be an asset to your
campaign. She can help you, rather than hinder
you."

The right woman. Like Charisma Sullivan? She'd
been intelligent enough and knowledgeable on the
issues. Plus very pleasant in appearance. If she
agreed to this unusual scheme of no romance, she
could be useful.

"You may be right," he admitted.

Mrs. Papadopoulos only smiled in reply.

Charisma stretched out on her bed, the day's newspaper spread before her. Surely there had to be some
mention of Mr. Barclay's speech yesterday. She
wanted to read more about the intriguing candidate.

But all she found was information on General
Palmer's latest railroad expansion and the upcoming Mendelsohn Quintet performance at the
opera house. Nothing at all on Mr. Barclay. How
frustrating.

Grace bounded into the room, jostling the table
beside the bed as she arrived. "Charisma, we have
company."

Charisma reached out in an automatic gesture
and caught the lamp before it fell, then gave her sister an indulgent smile. "Who is it? Miss Kingsley?"

"No. Guess." Mischief sparkled in Grace's green eyes.

"I can't imagine you'd be this excited about Kit's arrival." Charisma straightened suddenly, her breath catching in her throat. Oh, no. "Don't tell me Aunt Margaret has come for a visit?" Her mother's sour-faced sister always made Charisma feel as if she were six years old.

"Better than that." Grace danced from one foot to another, bumping the table again, and Charisma intercepted a book before it tumbled to the floor. "Guess again."

"Just tell me, Grace." Charisma had to grin at her sister's excitement. This visitor had to be special.

"It's the man from yesterday. Mr. Barclay." Grace revealed the name as if divulging a special secret.

Charisma jumped from the bed. Surely she'd heard wrong. "Mr. Barclay? Are you certain?"

Her sister nodded. "He's accompanied by a woman I've never seen before. They're in the parlor with Papa."

"With Papa?" What would a political candidate want with her father? Perhaps he was asking for funding. Or Papa's support. A former miner and now a mine owner, Patrick Sullivan held considerable sway within the mining community. That must be it.

However, if she happened to pass by the parlor as he was leaving . . .

Charisma snagged Grace's hand. "I suddenly feel the need to visit the parlor, don't you?"

With a giggle, Grace nodded.

They'd only reached the first landing when Belle

met them. "Papa is asking for both of you to come to the parlor," she said.

Charisma exchanged a wide-eyed glance with Grace, then hurried the rest of the way down the staircase. She didn't need another invitation.

She paused outside the parlor doors to draw in a deep breath and glance down at her simple morning dress. It would have to do. She rapped once, then heard her father call for her to enter.

Stepping inside, she found Mr. Barclay at once, looking even more handsome than she remembered in a plain gray suit that made his dark hair and eyes appear even blacker. An attractive woman stood beside him, much older than Mr. Barclay. She had an aura of elegance that made Charisma want to curtsey.

"Yes, Papa?" she asked.

Her father glanced past her. "Where's Grace?"

"She was just behind—"

Grace hurried into the room, lagging behind as usual and filled with exuberance, but her kid-leather boots slipped on the polished wood floor, sending her tumbling into Charisma. Unable to keep her balance, Charisma staggered forward with a gasp, as horrified as she was startled. This was not the kind of impression she wanted to make.

But instead of falling to the floor, she found herself caught and held in Mr. Barclay's arms.

Two

Charisma placed her hands against Mr. Barclay's chest to steady herself, then found herself intrigued by the feel of solid muscle beneath her palm—warm, strong, hard. Heat flooded her body, rising to her cheeks.

Glancing up, she found him staring at her, surprise and something more mysterious lurking in his dark eyes. His hold on her arms tightened briefly, then as their eyes met, he released her completely and stepped back.

"Are you all right, Miss Charisma?" he asked, his tone slightly deeper than she remembered.

She managed to find her voice. "Yes, thank you."

"I'm so sorry, Charisma," Grace said.

Turning, Charisma saw that Papa had kept Grace from harm. Then again, Grace never did get hurt. It was everything and everyone else that suffered from her clumsiness. "That's all right." Charisma glanced at her father, hoping he wouldn't notice her flushed cheeks. "Why did you need us, Papa?"

"I'll be telling you. Sit down now." He placed Grace in a chair and waited for everyone else to sit. Only he and the handsome Mr. Barclay remained standing.

"Seems Mr. Barclay is needing a female escort

while he's in the city," Papa said. "And he's after using one of ye."

One of them? Charisma almost jumped out of her chair. Oh, let it be her.

"Is that wise, Papa?" Belle asked from her position in the doorway.

Charisma sent her a frown. Just because Belle was happily engaged didn't mean she had to ruin any chance for Charisma to spend time with a man. Especially one as handsome and intelligent as Mr. Barclay.

"'Twill make your mother happy. And Mrs. Papadopoulos has agreed to act as chaperone. That takes care of the bother, don't it?"

A wise move on Papa's part and one likely to put him in Mama's good graces.

"What would this involve?" Charisma asked, looking from her father to Mr. Barclay. Would she be expected to campaign for Mr. Barclay?

Mr. Barclay cleared his throat. "I merely have need of a young woman to accompany me to social functions, which I'll be required to attend during my campaign. I . . . ah . . . I am not looking for a wife. She is . . . to fill in a position, much as a sister would if I had one."

Though he was obviously discomfited, his meaning was clear. Charisma didn't mind. While watching Belle and Kit together did make her envious from time to time, she still had to make her mark on the world before she settled down with anyone. *If* she ever did.

"How exciting." Words tumbled from her lips before she thought. "Please, do choose me. I would so love to know more about your campaign."

As Mr. Barclay drew back, startled, and Mrs. Papadopoulos lowered her attention to the wool rug, Charisma realized she'd done it again. But would being tactful get her anywhere? "I'm sorry," she murmured, twisting her hands together on her lap. "Forgive me."

" 'Tis impulsive my Charisma is," Papa added with a wry smile. He motioned toward Grace, sitting nearby. "And this is Grace. Both are good girls, sturdy stock, knowing their manners and such. Their ma insisted on it."

"You make us sound like horses, Papa," Charisma muttered.

"Charisma." Belle's shocked exclamation had Charisma glancing down at her hands, but not before she caught the hint of a smile at the corner of Mr. Barclay's lips.

"It is a difficult choice," he said. "Do you care much for politics, Miss Grace?"

"I'm afraid not," she responded, her gaze fixed on the toes of her boots. "Charisma is the one who's the . . . the suffragette."

"Suffragette?" Mr. Barclay's eyes sparkled as he glanced at Charisma. "Don't tell me you march through the streets demanding equal rights for women?" Humor lingered beneath his words.

"I don't march through the streets," Charisma said, raising her chin. But only because Mama would lock her in her room if she did. "But I do believe women should have the right to vote. They're no less intelligent than men and smarter than some."

She heard Belle's sigh. "Oh, Charisma."

Charisma grimaced. She had probably ruined her chances now. But every word she'd said was true.

"Quite right," Mr. Barclay said. Crossing the room, he extended his hand to help Charisma stand. "I believe we will do well together, Miss Charisma. I have a feeling I will never be bored with your company."

"Oh, Charisma is never boring," Grace added.

She didn't look at all displeased at not being chosen. *Thank goodness.*

Charisma could feel Mr. Barclay's strength and warmth even in his hand, and met his gaze with a broad smile. "I will do my best to support you, sir."

He continued to hold her hand a fraction longer than society dictated as he stared at her. Not that Charisma minded. But she could tell when he realized what he was doing, for he dropped her hand and stepped back.

"Mrs. Bell is holding a picnic this weekend on my behalf. Would you do me the honor of accompanying me?" The twinkle left his eyes and he sounded coldly formal now.

Responding with equal formality, Charisma briefly nodded, though her heart thudded in her chest. "I would be delighted."

"Excellent." Mr. Barclay focused on Papa. "Thank you for your support, sir."

"'Tis the miners I'm doing it for," Papa said. "Don't ye be letting them down."

"I intend to do my best." Mr. Barclay held out his arm toward Mrs. Papadopoulos. "I'm afraid I must depart now. I have several appointments to keep. Thank you again." He paused at the doorway and glanced back at Charisma. "I will call for you on Saturday at nine."

"I'll be ready." She could be ready to go in ten minutes if he asked it of her.

Once Mr. Barclay and Mrs. Papadopoulos departed, Charisma released a shriek and the three sisters ran toward each other for a shared hug. Papa shook his head but grinned as he left the room.

"What shall I do?" Charisma asked. "What shall I wear?"

"Your green flowered muslin, of course," Belle said. "It brings out your eyes. And you must learn to think before you speak, dearest. I thought you had made a cake of yourself, but apparently Mr. Barclay is an understanding gentleman."

Charisma dismissed her sister's admonition. Mr. Barclay obviously appreciated plain speaking. As a lawyer and political candidate, why wouldn't he?

Her dreams took on epic proportions. He would discuss his plans with her and she would actively help him win his senate seat so that he would be immensely grateful to her. And, of course, she would find a cause of her own that would flourish and be lauded by the entire community.

Charisma beamed as she followed her sisters upstairs. She couldn't wait until Saturday.

Will half hoped it would rain on Saturday, but the day dawned bright and clear, the sky cloudless and blue, and the mountains rimming the western edge of the city green and vibrant. All in all, a perfect day for a picnic.

Naturally. He grimaced as he left the hotel in a rented buggy. Now that he'd had time to think, he doubted the wisdom of his arrangement with Charisma Sullivan. Mrs. Papadopoulos had made it sound so reasonable at the time, but now he saw the potential for so many difficulties.

Young, single women were notorious husband-hunters and a husband was the last thing he wanted to be. No doubt Charisma would want all his attention and he had more important obligations, such as winning this election. He couldn't allow anything . . . or anyone to sway him from that goal.

He stopped before Mrs. Papadopoulos's elegant three-story home at the far edge of Cascade Street. Apparently, her husband had done well for himself as a politician.

She answered his knock on the door and joined him immediately. She was immaculately dressed in a fashionable dark summer gown and carried herself with an air of elegance. Her entire being radiated charm.

She beamed a smile at him as he assisted her into the buggy. "Why so grave, Mr. Barclay? It's a lovely day for a picnic."

"I'm afraid I've been embroiled in my own thoughts," Will answered as he climbed up beside her and flicked the reins.

"Having doubts?" she asked.

He glanced at her sharply, but her attention was focused on the homes they passed. It was almost as if she were reading his mind. Which, of course, was nonsense. "I have some," he admitted.

"I'm confident you will find Charisma an asset to your campaign."

Will bit back a sigh. That made one of them. However, he was not obligated to continue to squire Charisma if this charade did not pan out. Recalling that fact lifted his spirits somewhat.

Upon reaching the Sullivan home a short distance down the same street, Will stepped down and approached the front door, his throat dry. He glanced back at Mrs. Papadopoulos, who remained in the buggy, and she motioned him forward.

Straightening his shoulders, he knocked on the door. He was running for the senate. The thought of escorting a mere girl, no matter how attractive, shouldn't panic him.

The butler led him inside the drawing room. Will barely had time to turn before Charisma entered, her younger sister at her heels. Grace bumped a large stand as she passed and Will winced as a large vase filled with fresh flowers toppled.

Without breaking stride, Charisma whirled to catch the vase with practiced ease, murmured a "careful, Grace," to her sister, and bestowed a welcoming smile on Will. His admiration rose. Obviously, she was used to handling unusual situations. Perhaps she would be an asset to him.

Before he could do more than greet her, Charisma touched his arm, the action so forward he blinked in surprise.

"Let us go right away." She glanced over her shoulder. "Before Mama appears."

The hint of apprehension in her voice bumped up Will's nervousness. *Her mother?* Manners dictated he introduce himself. "I should—"

Charisma shook her head. "Trust me. It can wait." She tugged him toward the doorway, and still too startled to respond, he allowed himself to be led.

"Too late," Grace murmured from her station by the door.

Charisma froze, dropping her hand from his arm, and gave him a wry smile. An older woman burst into the room, brushing past Grace, her gaze boring into Will with such intensity he could swear his collar tightened.

"So you're the lawyer running for the senate," she said with such admiration it sounded as if he were the president of the United States.

Will bowed slightly. "William Barclay, ma'am."

"My husband tells me you come from good family." Her eyes glimmered, and her smile held more calculation than warmth.

Though Will could argue that point, he agreed, "Yes, ma'am."

"Mr. Sullivan tells me he gave you permission to escort my daughter to several functions." She didn't give him time to respond before continuing. "Why he didn't ask me, I don't know. Aren't I just as responsible for my daughters' welfare?"

How to answer that? Will glanced at Charisma and found her wearing an expression of despair.

"I assure you I will treat Miss Charisma with the honor and dignity she deserves," he replied finally, unable to keep a formal stiffness from his voice.

"Mama, we have to go," Charisma added, edging toward the door.

Mrs. Sullivan's face darkened. "And why weren't we invited to Cora's picnic? We're related, after all."

That was news to Will. The Sullivans related to the Bells? "It is a small group, Mrs. Sullivan," he answered. "We will most likely be discussing politics."

"Still, I could have acted as chaperone. There's no need to involve Mrs. Papadopoulos."

"Mrs. Papadopoulos has been of great assistance

to me," Will said, which was partially true. Though he'd only known the widow a short time, he felt as if she were a close family member. "I could not offend her by refusing her offer to help in this way."

"Hrrumph, I—"

Charisma stepped forward. "Mama, you don't want us to be late."

Her mother drew back, her frown giving way to anxiety. "No, certainly not. Pray, don't let me keep you."

Will bent over her hand as he passed. "It's been a pleasure to meet you, ma'am."

Once outside, Charisma sent him an apologetic look. "I'm sorry about that. She means well."

"Of course." Will remained noncommittal and assisted her into the buggy beside Mrs. Papadopoulos. After all, Mrs. Sullivan had been a poor miner's wife. She couldn't be expected to understand all of society's ways.

Mrs. Papadopoulos and Charisma exchanged greetings as he set the buggy into motion. He would have to rush now to meet the appointed time at the Bells' home in Manitou Springs. Thank goodness he had been there previously with Dr. Bell and would not go astray on the twisting road.

He found himself extremely aware of Charisma beside him, especially when each jostle bumped her hip against his. She smelled as fresh as the breeze on this brilliant summer day and her blue-green eyes sparkled beneath the simple straw hat perched on her head. Her high-necked gown was covered in a green floral pattern and showed her excellent figure to advantage. He would not be ashamed to have this woman by his side.

"Mr. Barclay."

Charisma glanced at him and his gut knotted. Would it start now? The nonsense that passed for conversation with young women? The latest gossip, the newest fashions, the shows that must be seen?

"Can you tell me about your platform? I would like to know how I can best support you."

He didn't answer right away. He hadn't expected this. "My platform?" he echoed. For an experienced orator, he found himself at a loss for words around this woman.

"You mentioned before that you support better working conditions for miners. Do you believe the Leadville Strike could have been avoided if the miners had had a union in place?"

Will stared at her so long, he had to jerk his gaze back to the road when the horses started to stray. "Please, do assure me you are not some crafty reporter in a disguise." None of the women he knew would have asked such a question.

She laughed in response, which alleviated his worry. "Just interested," she said. "My father's mine is in Leadville, you know, and he prides himself on offering the best working conditions of any mine. Not one of his men were involved in the strike simply because he took the time to listen to them."

"A great many problems can be solved in just that manner," Will said. "Unfortunately, not enough people subscribe to it."

"Do you support primarily the miners, Mr. Barclay?"

"I represent the common man . . . and woman in Colorado." For a moment, Melissa's face flashed in his mind. "Too often they go unheard."

Admiration sparkled in her eyes. "I hope you succeed."

At that moment, hearing her support, he felt certain there was nothing he could do but succeed. Nonetheless, "That is for the voters to decide," he responded. But he planned to do all he could to ensure they voted for him.

"If women could vote, you would be assured of a victory," Charisma added, a mischievous glint in her eyes. She probably remembered how he'd avoided this issue earlier.

Will had to smile. The Libertarian Party supported giving women the vote. However, the Democratic Party, which he represented, did not.

"You are probably correct." Once again, he avoided committing himself and her grin indicated she knew it.

Even with his attention focused on the road, he felt her studying him. He sensed an honest desire to learn about his campaign behind her examination—a difference from most of the other single women, who only viewed him as husband material.

"What made you decide to run for office?" Charisma asked.

Will tightened his hands on the reins as Mrs. Papadopoulos concurred. "I would like to know the answer to that myself," she stated.

He'd fielded this question before. Why should it bother him now? "I want to ensure that the average person—the farmer, the miner, the stablemaster, the salesgirl—has a voice in the senate."

"But don't you yourself hail from a wealthy political family, Mr. Barclay?" Mrs. Papadopoulos asked.

He nodded. He'd dealt with this before, too. "Quite correct. I believe my upbringing will allow me to see both sides of an issue."

"How?"

Charisma's blunt question startled him.

"How can you see both sides," she continued, "if you've never been poor?"

"I have talked to people from all walks of life." He went back to his prepared rhetoric. "I believe I have a sense of what they want, what they need."

"Do you?" Charisma didn't sound accusing, but more questioning. She glanced into the distance, her gaze unfocused. "I remember being poor. We lived in Leadville before Papa found silver in his claim. We didn't have a lot to eat and I only had two dresses, but we were happy—my sisters and I. Even my parents were happy then. At least, they didn't argue so much."

Before Will could address this revelation, she jerked back as if realizing what she'd said. Her cheeks turned a becoming pink. "I'm so sorry," she said, turning her wide gaze on him. "You can't possibly be interested in that."

He was intrigued, actually. Charisma represented both worlds, which could only aid his campaign. He'd been fortunate to have Mrs. Papadopoulos guide him to the Sullivan household.

"I would like to hear more at some other time," Will said. "I want to know all I can about the people I represent."

"An excellent aspiration, Mr. Barclay, and worthy reasons for running," Mrs. Papadopoulos said. "But I am still curious as to what motivated you to declare yourself a candidate? Surely, this type of decision didn't come to you overnight."

Almost that. Will looked away from her shrewd glance, keeping his expression bland. Did she know the entire sordid story, the real reason why he had to do this? How could she? No one knew other than himself, his brother, his father, . . . and Melissa.

Fortunately, Charisma saved him from a response. "Look." She pointed to the gathering of carriages in the distance. "There's Briarhurst. It appears the Bells have kept the party small."

"This enables me to meet each potential supporter." Will guided the horses toward the crowd.

"Of course."

Charisma's answering smile created a knot in Will's gut. She obviously understood his situation— a rare occurrence among most women of his acquaintance.

Upon reaching the Bells' estate, Will exchanged pleasantries and the entire party set off for a high sprawling field in North Cheyenne Canyon.

Along the drive, Will marveled at the magnificence of the Rocky Mountains, looming so close to Colorado Springs. It had only taken minutes to reach the climbing slopes dotted with aspens, a crooked creek meandering beside the road. In less than an hour, they reached a sprawling field beside a lake. The green grass was broken by spots of color where wild flowers stretched their faces to the sun.

Alighting from the buggy, Will assisted Mrs. Papadopoulos and Charisma to the ground. Dr. Solly and another gentleman intercepted them before they'd even found a place to set their basket.

"Ah, there's the young man running for the senate." Dr. Solly extended his hand and Will grasped it firmly, a practiced smile in place.

"Yes, sir. It's good to see you again."

Dr. Solly indicated a man beside him. "Tell Mr. Mason why he should support you, Mr. Barclay, when qualified candidates such as Irving Howbert are running."

"Because I bring total representation," Will answered at once. "The elite and the more common laborer. I believe everyone deserves a voice in what our state does."

"Admirable, but what makes you better suited to provide that voice?" Mr. Mason asked.

Charisma answered before Will could speak. "He actually takes the time to listen to people," she said with enthusiasm. "How many other candidates do that? Really?"

Dr. Solly chuckled. "You have a staunch defender, sir. If Miss Charisma vouches for you, who am I to disbelieve her? Come, let me introduce you to Chumley, Lord Francis Cholmondeley Thornton. Be forewarned, his bark is worse than his bite."

Will took Charisma's elbow and gave her a warm smile as he followed Dr. Solly. This was working perfectly. Mrs. Papadopoulos had been right—a woman by his side did help. Not one of the young women present had tried to divert him from campaigning, which was a godsend.

During the next hour, he met every high-ranking gentleman in Colorado Springs. The fact that several showed an inclination to offer support raised his spirits considerably. By the time he finally sat with the large group to dine, he considered Charisma an asset indeed.

Her presence by his side and her supporting comments only strengthened his cause. Everyone knew her and her family and her father was well-respected, despite his humble beginnings.

In fact, with her assistance Will was becoming accepted as well—a situation far better than he'd hoped. As conversation lingered on individuals with whom he had no acquaintance, he listened and made mental notes to visit them. . . . Until they spoke of Thomas Gardner, a member of the city council and a shopkeeper.

"The poor man just hasn't been himself lately," Cora Bell said with an emphatic nod of her head. "I barely recognized him the other day."

"His work is suffering as well," Mr. Morgan added.

"It's been nearly a year since his wife died. I had expected he would get on with his life by now." Mrs. Morgan sighed.

"It's too bad they didn't have any children. Perhaps then he wouldn't feel so inclined to destroy himself," Mrs. Ellis said.

"Couldn't one of you visit him?" Charisma asked, a frown creasing her brow.

Will glanced at her. Surely someone would have done that already.

"He's not willing to listen." Dr. Solly shook his head. "Too bad. Tom was a good man."

"Perhaps he only needs someone to listen to *him.*" Charisma's voice rose with enthusiasm. "If someone would listen to him, then perhaps he'd listen to you when you tell him his drinking is likely to ruin his career. He'd see . . ."

She trailed off as everyone's expressions changed

to dumbfounded horror. Will stared at her as well. He couldn't believe she had spoken so rashly. Polite society did not mention such things as drinking problems by name. How could she not know that?

He frowned. Perhaps Miss Charisma Sullivan wasn't the asset he needed after all.

Three

"I am so sorry," Charisma said yet again as Will drove the buggy away from the mountain field. It had appeared so beautiful when she'd first arrived all excited and hopeful. Now she never wanted to visit this place again.

Will had been distant since her impulsive words earlier. He'd barely spoken to her and when he had, his tone had been polite but cool.

Why, oh, why, couldn't she have charm? A way of knowing just what to say like Mrs. Papadopoulos, who had smoothed over Charisma's blurted *faux pas* and restored the group's cheerful atmosphere? If only she could have also restored Will's good humor.

He hadn't forgiven Charisma. She knew, already, he had no intention of asking for her company again. She'd lost her chance to do something meaningful before she'd even begun.

She glanced at him, catching her bottom lip between her teeth, as she awaited his response. Anything would be better than his chilly silence.

"It is nothing," he said finally, with far too much formality in his voice, his gaze never once leaving the narrow dirt path.

"You're angry with me." As always, the words escaped Charisma before she thought. "I didn't mean to . . . " She glanced at Mrs. Papadopoulos, seeking guidance. What could she say to change his mind?

"You have a good heart, my dear," Mrs. Papadopoulos said as she placed her gloved hand over Charisma's. "And an impulsive nature. You say what you feel, which, unfortunately, is not always circumspect."

"Maybe I shouldn't speak at all." Charisma wrung her hands together, blinking back the moisture from her eyes. She'd been so excited about this opportunity. Now it was gone.

Mrs. Papadopoulos smiled. "Nothing as drastic as that." She turned to face Will. "If I may make a suggestion, sir?"

He looked away from the road for only a moment. "Yes?"

"I still believe Miss Charisma can be helpful to your campaign."

"I can't agree," he answered in a monotone, not even bothering to glance Charisma's way.

Charisma's hopes sank. How could she blame him? A political candidate had to be twice as careful with his words as everyone else and she certainly hadn't been. She sucked in a shuddering breath. Hadn't her own sisters told her time and again her habit of free speech would get her into trouble?

"I have a proposal for you. What if I tutor Miss Charisma in the dictates and nuances of appearing in society? I have no doubt she will be a quick study." Mrs. Papadopoulos spoke with such assurance that even Charisma believed her. "Did you not find her presence of benefit today?"

Charisma waited, anxious to hear his response, her heart thumping in her chest. He had seemed pleased with her earlier . . . before she let her mouth run away with her.

"There is still Miss Grace." Will cast a dark glance at Charisma. "A trifle clumsy, but I trust she is not as blunt."

"No." Charisma lowered her gaze, trying to disguise her disappointment. "She is very proper." In fact, Grace was the model of propriety. As long as she stood still.

"The decision, of course, is yours, Mr. Barclay," Mrs. Papadopoulos said. "But I beg your indulgence. Mrs. Solly mentioned a dinner party next weekend to which you are invited. Give me that much time and I promise you will see a difference in Miss Charisma."

"A week?" Will lifted his eyebrows. "What do you say to that, Miss Charisma?"

"I . . . I will do my best." She met his gaze, unflinching, and was surprised to see a bright flicker of interest in the depths of his eyes.

He only nodded, then remained silent as he stopped the buggy before her home and assisted her to the ground. As she stood facing him, he continued to hold her hand, studying her.

"Very well." He dropped her hand, addressing himself to Mrs. Papadopoulos. "One week." His gaze returned to Charisma. "Will you attend the Sollys' dinner with me?"

His voice was still overly polite, the hint of coldness lingering.

Charisma straightened. Perhaps she still had a chance to prove herself. "I'll make you proud," she said firmly, ignoring the doubts pricking at her mind.

"We'll see."

"Indeed, we will." Mrs. Papadopoulos beamed at Charisma. "Come to my house tomorrow morning and we will begin."

"Yes, ma'am." Charisma swallowed to ease her tight throat. She would learn to be charming. She had to.

Charisma managed to provide the proper responses to her mother's questions before she fled to her room, but she knew she hadn't fooled her sisters. Therefore, she wasn't surprised when Belle and Grace peeked around the edge of the door.

"Are you all right?" Grace asked, slipping inside the room.

Belle followed, her gaze concerned. "What happened?"

Charisma grimaced. "What you've always warned me would happen. I said something I shouldn't have."

Her sisters sat on either side of her and wrapped her in a mutual hug. "Dear Charisma, anyone who knows you knows you meant no harm," Belle murmured.

"Mr. Barclay does not know me at all." Charisma's voice wobbled, her throat thick with unshed tears.

"Does he no longer want you to help him?" Grace asked, her eyes wide.

"He didn't at first, but Mrs. Papadopoulos convinced him to give me another chance. She is going to tutor me in how to watch what I say."

Belle sighed. "Perhaps she can do it. I know you've never listened to any of us."

Charisma grimaced. "I try, Belle. I do, but it's so ridiculous to talk around something when plain speaking will do." She often found it frustrating to remain quiet when a few well-chosen words would do. But, as she proved today, her words weren't always well-chosen.

"What did you do?" Grace tucked her legs beneath her, tumbling Charisma's pillows to the floor.

"They were talking about Mr. Gardner." Charisma remembered him as a smiling gentleman, who ran the mercantile downtown. Now, the only one she ever saw there was his assistant, Mr. Tate.

"Mr. Gardner?" Belle's brows lifted and she lowered her voice to a whisper. "I have heard it said that he's become lost in drink."

Grace joined the whispering. "Miss Mattingly told Mama that he's wasting away with grief."

"Exactly." Charisma jumped off the bed to pace the floor. "Everyone whispers about these things, but when I said it out loud I was ostracized."

Grace brought her hand to her mouth as Belle groaned. "Oh, Charisma, you didn't."

"I only suggested that someone should go see him, talk to him. Perhaps all he needs is a friendly face." Charisma paused in mid-step. Of course, *she* could be a friendly face.

"No." Belle came to stand beside her. "I know that look. No."

"And why not?" Charisma crossed her arms. This was another good deed she could do. "I will take Mr. Gardner some of Cook's fresh bread. It's the least I can do."

"You can't possibly go there unchaperoned." Belle wore her big-sister-knows-best expression.

"I won't be." Charisma displayed her most brilliant smile. "You and Grace will be with me."

"No, we're—"

"Or I'll go alone." And she would, if necessary. She found it so frustrating that a chaperone was required everywhere she went. Another curse of being a young lady. It had been far easier to roam freely when she'd been ten. She met Belle's frowning gaze.

"You would go alone with no thought to propriety, wouldn't you?" Belle asked.

"If I had to."

"Mr. Gardner is a widower, Charisma. I've heard that even his servants have left him due to ill temper. You can't go alone there."

Charisma didn't respond, but continued to hold her sister's gaze. Feeling a hand slip into hers, she glanced over to find Grace beside her. "I'll go with you," Grace said, so quietly Charisma could barely hear her.

But Belle did and sighed. "Very well. We'll all go, but we'll only stay a moment. Do you promise?"

"I promise." Charisma grinned. How long could it take to explain the situation to Mr. Gardner? He'd been alone in his large house for so long, he'd probably be thrilled to see them and more than willing to rejoin society. Maybe all he needed was an invitation. "We'll go in the morning before I go to Mrs. Papadopoulos's."

It was a perfect plan.

Charisma waited on the long gingerbread-trimmed porch for her sisters to join her. "Must you always walk so slow?"

"Must you walk as if you're in a foot race?" Belle retorted as she and Grace climbed onto the porch. Once again, Grace's frequent trips slowed them down. They paused before the wide front door. "Are you certain about this, Charisma?"

"Very certain." Charisma had played it out in her mind. She would explain the situation to Mr. Gardner. He would rejoin society and tell everyone how grateful he was that she had come to see him.

She rapped sharply on the door, then blinked when it swung open. Had it not been firmly latched? She waited for several moments, but no one came to greet them. Where was the staid butler she'd seen here before?

"Mr. Gardner?" She pushed the door open further.

Belle drew in her breath with a hiss. "What are you doing?"

"What if he's ill or hurt?" Charisma peeked inside, then wrinkled her nose. The interior smelled of spoiled food, unwashed linens, and heavy mustiness. Over it all spread the overwhelming stench of whiskey. "Mr. Gardner?"

Stepping inside, she paused, glancing toward the parlor. All the windows and draperies were closed, despite the heat of the August day. No wonder it felt so suffocating in here.

"Charisma, don't," Grace touched her sister's arm.

"Just one more moment." Charisma raised her voice. "Mr. Gardner?"

Hearing a distant moan, she shot her sisters a warning look, then dashed back to the equally warm and dimly lit salon. She spotted a figure on the divan and rushed toward it. "Mr. Gardner? Are you ill?"

He sprawled on the furniture, his head tossed back. He wore no tie and his wrinkled, dirty shirt hung half-open. His skin was cool and moist to her touch, his breath foul enough to scare off encroaching cougars. But at least he was breathing.

An empty flask sat beside the divan, the fumes still potent though no liquid remained. Charisma lifted the flask between her thumb and forefinger and placed it on a nearby table, the finish ruined with white rings and rancid cigar butts.

"Charisma, what are you doing?" Belle appeared, Grace at her heels, and Charisma released a breath she hadn't even been aware she was holding. Well, it was spooky in here.

"I can't tell if he's sick or drunk," she responded.

"Charisma, you don't call someone drunk out loud," Belle snapped.

"Not even if he is?" She motioned with her head. "Will you open the windows, please? Let some air in here."

The moment Belle pulled open the draperies, Mr. Gardner shot bolt upright, startling Charisma into a gasp. "Close those damned drapes," he snapped.

Belle jumped, then complied, and he turned on Charisma. "Who the hell are you?"

"Charisma Sullivan, sir. I—"

"What the hell are you doing in my house?"

If possible, his breath was even fouler when he was awake. Charisma forced herself not to flinch. "I thought you might be ill."

"Well, I'm not. You can leave now." He swung his feet to the floor, then scowled at her. "Did you hear me?"

"I . . . I . . . yes." Charisma drew in a comforting

breath. "I brought you some bread, sir. I . . . we thought you might be hungry."

"I don't need any food."

Charisma bit her lip to keep from responding to that statement. From the way his clothing hung on his frame, he definitely did need food. "I can give it to your cook for later," she murmured.

"No cook. She left. They all left." He fumbled around for the whiskey flask. "Don't need 'em anyhow." He lifted the flask, shook it, then scowled and tossed it behind the divan.

"I'll just set it here then." Charisma placed the loaf of bread on a nearby table, doing her best to avoid Belle's frantic come-here motion. Facing the man, Charisma forced a smile. "I also wanted to let you know that many people are worried about you, Mr. Gardner. You haven't been in to work or to any social functions in some time."

"A man's got a right to some privacy, doesn't he?" Mr. Gardner prodded the cushions, apparently searching for more whiskey.

"Of course you do, but . . . but . . ." Charisma swallowed hard. "It's not healthy living like this, sir." There, she'd said it. Someone had to. "Your business is suffering."

"Damn the business." He turned his bleary-eyed stare on her, his eyebrows lowered. "The money doesn't mean anything without her."

He was still grieving? After a year? "I know you miss your wife, but—"

Mr. Gardner jumped to his feet, his fist raised. "Don't talk about her."

Charisma stepped back and found a sister by each side. "We need to go," Belle whispered.

"We will." She couldn't just leave the man like this. Couldn't they see he needed help? "I think you need to talk about her, sir. It might help. Mrs. Gardner was a wonderful woman and many people miss her."

"Get out!" He advanced on her, his eyes wild.

Belle and Grace scurried for the door, but Charisma only took one step back. "Don't throw away your life, Mr. Gardner. You're still a young man. You could remarry."

At his growl, she backed away with more speed, not pausing again until she reached the doorway. "Stop for a moment and ask yourself one question, sir."

She waited until his bloodshot gaze met hers. "What would Mrs. Gardner say if she saw you like this?"

He ran toward her with a roar, then slipped on the rug that had bunched up when Grace ran over it and tumbled to the floor. Charisma no longer hesitated. She turned and ran.

The three sisters didn't stop until they were a full block away from the house. Belle leaned against a hitching post, one hand held to her side. "Why do I let you talk me into such things?"

"It could have been worse," Charisma answered. At least, he hadn't harmed them. She refused to believe that he would have even if he had caught them. Though worse the wear for drink, deep inside he still had to have some of the affable Mr. Gardner she used to know.

Didn't he?

"What now?" Grace gasped for breath.

"We leave him alone." They'd done all they could

be expected to. Charisma sighed. So much for making any kind of difference there. "Will you walk with me to Mrs. Papadopoulos's?"

She still had to go to her training. Perhaps there she'd learn enough to be useful to Mr. Barclay and society.

Her sisters left her at the steps of the massive new home, the front porch wrapping around three sides and decorated with swirls. A turret rose out of the back edge of the house, a cupola at its peak. The view of Pikes Peak from there would be wonderful.

Bay windows jutted from the lower level, the interior hidden only by lace curtains. The yard was well-kept, the bushes trimmed, the flowers splurging in one last bloom of color before fall settled in.

Why had Charisma never been here before? In a town as small as Colorado Springs, everyone in upper society made it a point to know everyone else and socialized frequently. Perhaps Mrs. Papadopoulos had recently moved here. For that, Charisma was immensely grateful. Who else would have defended her to Mr. Barclay?

She knocked at the intricate front door, the wood inlaid with stained glass, and waited. This was the right place, wasn't it? Hearing no sound from within, she rapped again only to have the door opened from beneath her hand.

A large man stood there, filling the door frame, his eyes a brilliant blue, his expression devoid of emotion. "Yes?" he asked, in a voice so deep it joined the rumbling in Charisma's stomach.

"Miss Charisma Sullivan." She presented her card only to watch it vanish within his massive paw. "I've come to see Mrs. Papadopoulos."

"This way, please." He didn't look to see if she followed but led the way to a rear door off the hallway. Knocking once, he opened the door and stood aside. "Miss Sullivan."

"Oh, good." Mrs. Papadopoulos came to greet Charisma, taking her hands to guide her into the airy parlor.

The room was beautifully decorated in unusually light colors, the thick Persian rug picking up the colors of the fresh flowers housed in vases throughout the room. Charisma was surprised to find it relatively uncluttered. A walnut settee dominated the room, a gentleman's chair on one side and a ladies chair on the other, all centered around a large oval coffee table.

Mrs. Papadopoulos guided Charisma to the ladies chair. "Please, have a seat. I'll have James bring us some tea."

The imposing man left and Charisma settled into the chair. "My, he's . . . big."

The woman laughed. "So he is, but he's very loyal. I'd be lost without him." She settled onto the settee. "Now tell me, Miss Charisma, have you come to learn?"

"I have." Charisma leaned forward, not trying to hide her eagerness. "And I would be honored if you would call me simply Charisma. I do feel we are going to be good friends."

"I believe that, too. As friends, I insist you call me Thalia. It's so much easier to say, don't you agree?"

"Much easier," Charisma responded with feeling, then froze. She probably shouldn't have said that.

Thalia only lifted one eyebrow. "You have the good grooming and manners of every other young woman in town, but I fear you have more than your share of impulsiveness."

Charisma grimaced. That was true. "I don't always mean to say things. They just pop out. It's not as if I'm lying."

"No, of course not. But you will discover that there are other ways to get your point across besides blunt speech."

"Can you make me charming enough for Mr. Barclay?"

Thalia didn't respond at once, turning her attention instead to the tea tray James set on the coffee table. "Thank you, James." She poured two cups, then handed one to Charisma, clinging to it a moment longer than necessary until Charisma met her gaze. "*I* will have nothing to do with it. Can *you* become charming enough for Mr. Barclay?"

"I'll work hard." She had to change. Somehow.

"The process you need to follow is simple, my dear." Thalia returned to her seat and sipped at her tea. "There are only three things you need to remember."

Only three? She could do that.

"The first is to stop before you say a single word. I fear that will be the most difficult part for you." Thalia softened her words with a warm smile. "The second is to repeat what you intend to say in your own mind. The third is to consider your words carefully. You know when you've said something you shouldn't have. Stop yourself before you say it."

"I need to think about every word?" That would be impossible.

"You can do it. At the very least, you should

practice this at every social situation. If you work on it at home as well, you will progress that much faster."

Charisma wanted to blurt out her disbelief, then hesitated and did as Thalia had advised. Hearing what she intended to say in her mind, she disregarded it and tried again. "Is it possible?"

"If you want it bad enough."

"I do want this." If she could become less blunt, perhaps then she would not only be able to help Mr. Barclay, but she'd find the direction she needed to take in order to make a difference. "So very much."

Thalia placed her cup on the tray. "Then, let us get started." A twinkle danced in her eyes. "I daresay Mr. Barclay will be very surprised when you attend the Sollys's dinner."

Four

Charisma placed her hand over her aching stomach as she inched aside the curtains and peeked outside her bedroom window. Still no sign of Will.

The waiting was unbearable. Part of her longed to see him again. The other part dreaded that even after a week of Thalia's tutoring she wouldn't measure up. Then what? Her chance to make a difference would be gone along with Will's company.

Hearing the soft nicker of a horse outside, she glanced out the window again. He was here! Charisma drew in a deep breath, revealing even more of her already exposed breasts. Mama had insisted her dress, with its deep décolletage, was appropriate for a formal dinner at the Sollys's, but Charisma felt completely out of her element.

"Charisma," her mother called.

"I'll be right there." Charisma swallowed hard and descended the staircase. What if she was overdressed? What if she said and did all the wrong things?

She frowned. This had to stop. She'd never been so uncertain before. Pleasing Will wasn't everything in the world.

Yet the light in his eyes as he spotted her added an extra jump to her heart. "You look lovely," he murmured, bending over her hand.

"Thank you." She allowed him to place her wrap over her shoulders while her mother beamed from the sidelines.

"Have a good time," Mama said, escorting them to the door. "I want to hear all about it, Charisma."

"Yes, Mama."

Will touched her elbow as he led her to the buggy. "Mrs. Papadopoulos tells me you've made great progress."

"I hope so." Charisma couldn't say any more through her tight throat. In fact, she remained silent through most of the journey to the Sollys's luxurious home.

As if sensing Charisma's nervousness, Thalia placed a comforting hand over hers when the buggy stopped before the residence. "You'll do fine," she whispered.

The best Charisma could manage was a weak smile. She'd do her best. Stop. Repeat. Think. How difficult could that be?

Spotting Miss Mattingly inside, Charisma groaned. Very difficult. This would be a true test.

Will marveled at the heightened poise in the young woman by his side. Though quieter than he recalled, she spoke with restraint, her responses appropriate and genteel, despite the brief pauses preceding each sentence. She presented a demure, almost subdued appearance with none of the vivid exuberance from before.

To his surprise, he discovered he missed that. Fool. In fact, she'd stolen into his thoughts far more often than he liked over the last week—usually when he was campaigning. He would imagine what outrageous question she would have likely asked, which had the benefit of making any inquiries he did face seem tame in comparison.

Her behavior now was more of what he needed, what he had to have to garner votes. Yet he found himself watching her, searching for that spark of passion in her eyes.

It remained stubbornly absent until they gathered after the splendid dinner in the large salon and Miss Mattingly approached, the look in her eye a cause for foreboding. Charisma caught her bottom lip between her teeth for a brief moment in a gesture Will found endearing, giving her a quiet vulnerability that made him determined to protect her.

"Miss Charisma, I must have an explanation," Miss Mattingly demanded upon her approach.

"Certainly," Charisma answered with the first spark of life in her words. "Is there a particular explanation you desire or will any one do?"

Will bit back a smile. Miss Mattingly glowered.

"I understand you and your sisters called on Mr. Gardner earlier this week? Is that true?"

"Yes, ma'am. We took him some freshly baked bread."

"Without escorts?" Miss Mattingly's tone implied certain doom, and Will frowned. It did border on improper behavior for the young women to visit a man alone.

"We stayed but a moment." Charisma hesitated. "The lonely man was . . . beside himself upon receiving it. I felt it was the least we could do."

For once the older woman appeared flustered. "Ah, yes, of course."

"May I inquire as to how you learned of our visit?

Were you planning to offer Mr. Gardner a neighborly kindness as well?"

Despite her words, a glint of devilry danced in Charisma's eyes and Will couldn't stop a surge of expectation from overtaking him. He had missed this more than he'd thought. What next?

"Why, Mr. Gardner actually showed up in his store two days ago, looking quite disheveled, I assure you." Miss Mattingly shook her head. "When I expressed my surprise at seeing him, he mentioned that you had visited him. I confess I did not expect three young women to motivate him into resuming his responsibilities."

Charisma hesitated again, a long pause. "Perhaps all he needed was to know his neighbors and friends cared about him."

"Just so," Will added as the sparks in her eyes flared dangerously high. "I am certain others will soon follow your admirable lead."

She sent him a strained smile, then took a step back. "If you will excuse me for a moment."

She fled before he or Miss Mattingly could respond, but instead of heading for the withdrawing room as he'd expected, she darted through the open terrace door into the night. Surely she knew better than to venture into the darkness alone.

Will glanced at Miss Mattingly. She hadn't noticed. Thank goodness. "Thank you for taking such an interest in Miss Charisma and her sisters," he said in an attempt to keep her attention. "I have no doubt they will be pleased to learn their hospitality garnered such good results."

"I had been planning such a visit myself," Miss Mattingly said. "But my schedule did not allow it."

Highly unlikely. "No doubt your visit will be equally fruitful." Will offered her a gracious smile. "Whenever it takes place." He bowed. "If you will excuse me."

He ventured first toward the windows but the interior lights made it impossible to see outside. Ascertaining he was unobserved, he slipped outside.

Charisma paced the stone plaza, muttering to herself. He drew closer until her words became clear.

"Meddling old biddy. I know what she was up to. We didn't do anything wrong."

Will grinned, unable to stop himself. This was the young woman he remembered from before—passionate and outspoken. He stepped toward her just as she whirled around to collide with him.

He caught her shoulders to steady her, instantly aware of her soft breasts pressed against his chest and the close proximity of her lips. Her wide gaze met his, the angry sparks dissolving first into surprise, then warm flames that triggered an answering warmth within him.

He needed to speak, but all he could focus on were her parted lips and the urgent need to taste those lips. "Charisma," he murmured, then caught himself. "I mean, Miss Charisma."

"Charisma is fine." She sounded as short of breath as he felt. "After all, we are friends."

"Yes. Call me Will." He wasn't thinking clearly. *Focus. Focus on something other than her appealing mouth. Her nose. Her pert slim nose as defined and obstinate her opinions.*

This was not helping.

"I . . . I thought you handled Miss Mattingly very well," he choked out.

"All we did was take bread to Mr. Gardner." She spoke quietly, not pulling away. Though she should.

Didn't she realize how tempted he was? He wasn't supposed to be. This was supposed to be a business relationship. Yet he didn't move away either.

"I believe you." If nothing else, he found Charisma to be utterly honest, almost dangerously so at times.

"Thank you."

Voices grew louder inside, jarring Will from his stupor. He jerked away from Charisma. What was he doing? To be found like this could ruin both their reputations. He didn't dare do anything to endanger his campaign.

"Forgive me." He didn't meet her gaze. "You should go inside now."

"Yes, of course." She left the terrace, but he remained, struggling to regain control.

How could he have lost his senses so completely, so rapidly? He shouldn't find her outrageousness appealing, yet he couldn't deny that throughout the entire evening he had missed seeing her defiant spark. Insanity.

His goal remained unchanged. He had to win this election. Stephen could not be allowed into the senate without someone to counter his actions.

Will straightened. As long as he remembered that, he'd avoid all temptation—even that of Miss Charisma Sullivan.

Charisma hurried toward Thalia's house. After her success at the Sollys's dinner party, she was eager to improve even more. Well, successful except for when Will had caught her releasing her fury against Miss Mattingly.

Still, she wouldn't trade that moment for anything. He'd almost kissed her. A kiss wasn't part of their bargain, but she was eager to experience her first one—especially since Belle had told her how delightful she found Kit's kisses.

But Will had remained a gentleman.

Charisma grimaced. *Drat.*

Had her new demure behavior caused his sudden interest? If so, she intended to be extra diligent in her lessons with Thalia.

Not that she was interested in a husband. No, Mama was far more eager for that than Charisma. Especially now that Belle was engaged. But Will was a handsome man and Charisma had never been kissed before.

Would it be sweet and gentle or so passionate it made her toes tingle? She sighed, picturing the brief flare of awareness in Will's eyes the other night.

"No. Please." A woman's pleading cries ripped Charisma from her fantasy.

She turned to see a man slap a young woman across the face with such force that she tumbled from his buggy to the ground. Charisma gasped and rushed forward. What did he think he was doing?

The young woman remained in a heap, her blonde hair hanging loose around her face. As the man stepped from the buggy, she raised her arm as if to ward off another blow.

"Get up," he ordered. "Get up and do as you're

told." When she didn't move, he booted her in the ribs and she collapsed with a whimper.

"Leave her alone." Charisma advanced on him, her fists clenched. *How dare he?* "You have no right to strike her." No matter what male-dominated society might think.

"Stay out of this." He whirled around to glower at her, his eyes red and his face unshaven. The smell of strong spirits surrounded him.

Charisma didn't recognize him, but that didn't stop her. Ignoring his threatening stance, she stepped between him and the cowering young woman. "Don't touch her again."

He raised his arm as if to strike her, but she met his gaze without flinching. Growing up around the silver mines had taught her how to defend herself. "I wouldn't do that if I were you."

His gaze flickered to her clothing and he hesitated, no doubt recognizing that she came from a wealthy family. "I paid for her," he snarled. "She's mine and I'll do what I want."

"You cannot purchase a woman nor does she belong to you." A view Mrs. Woodhull had espoused and one Charisma believed as well. A man and woman formed a partnership. They did not "own" each other.

The man only growled and pushed Charisma aside so he could grab the fallen woman's hair. "On your feet, whore."

Charisma staggered a few steps before she regained her balance, then straightened. Who did he think he was? If she were a man, she'd punch him. Instead she shoved him back, managing to make him release his grip. "Let her go," she ordered.

He swung at her wildly, but she anticipated it and dodged the blow. He might have superior strength, but she wasn't going to abandon this helpless woman.

Spotting a policeman down the street, she waved at him. "Bobbie! Bobbie, help."

Only in Colorado Springs were the police called by the British name of bobbie. She'd remembered to use it, but the policeman showed no sign of hearing her. However, her words spurred her attacker into action. He kicked his victim again, then climbed into his buggy, treating his horses with the same disrespect as he snapped the reins across their backs. "Good riddance," he shouted.

Charisma watched him drive away and sighed with relief. Once she felt certain he wouldn't return, she knelt beside the young woman on the ground who sobbed quietly.

"He's gone," she murmured. "Let me help you."

The woman shook her head, her hair hiding her face. "You don't want to be near me."

"That's nonsense." Charisma wrapped her arms around the woman's frail shoulders. "What's your name?"

"Missy." She offered no surname and Charisma didn't press her.

"Can you stand?"

"I . . . I can try."

Charisma helped her to her feet, shouldering most of the other woman's weight. Not that it was much. Though close to Charisma's height and age, Missy felt like she weighed about half as much.

Once they were standing, Charisma hesitated. *Now what?* Missy needed care and Charisma doubted her mother would be willing to provide that care. But Thalia's home was nearby. She wouldn't turn away someone in need.

"This way," Charisma said. "I'll help you. We don't have far to go."

"Just let me go, miss." Missy spoke so quietly Charisma could barely hear her. "I need to get back."

"You're hurt." Charisma wasn't sure of the full extent of Missy's injuries, but blood showed plainly on the woman's bruised face. "We'll send word wherever you like, but you need to see a doctor."

"I can't afford that." The alarm in her voice was the most emotion Charisma had heard from her yet.

"Don't worry." Charisma could get money from her father if she asked. The important thing was helping this woman.

Missy staggered and nearly fell, lapsing into a near swoon, but Charisma managed to keep her upright. "Just a little further."

Reaching Thalia's house, Charisma rapped hard on the door until James opened it. "She needs help." Charisma staggered forward with Missy's now totally limp body.

"Yes, miss." James lifted Missy in his arms as if she weighed nothing at all—which was close to the truth—and preceded Charisma into the parlor.

Thalia rose to her feet at once. "My goodness, what happened?"

"She's been beaten. We need to call a doctor," Charisma said.

"Of course. James, take her to the Rose Room and send for Dr. Murray." Thalia and Charisma followed close on his heels as he carried Missy upstairs and placed her on the bed, then turned to go.

"I'll be right back with the doctor," he said, then left.

Missy's hair fell back and Charisma gasped at seeing the full extent of the damage to her face. The young woman's lips were swollen and split in two places, bruises covered her cheeks and one eye was swollen completely shut. From the kicks Missy had received, her ribs were probably in even worse condition. "Look at what he did to her."

Charisma should have run for the bobbie and had him arrest the man on the spot, but her concern had been primarily for this woman.

Thalia moved with quiet efficiency as she placed a bowl of water and a cloth on the table beside the bed. "Did you see who did this?"

"Yes, but I don't know who he is."

"Shameful." Thalia sat beside Missy and dabbed at the blood on her face. "Why don't you start on her dress, Charisma? She'll need to be in her chemise for the doctor to do a proper evaluation."

By the time they'd removed Missy's torn, dirty dress and corset, the doctor arrived, James at his heels.

Thalia went to meet him. "Good of you to come so quickly."

He nodded, his smile brief as his gaze lingered on Missy's still figure. "I assume this is the patient?"

"The poor thing has been beaten. I fear she may have several injuries. She's been unconscious for some time now."

Charisma stood to the side, watching in horror as the doctor examined Missy. Her entire body was dotted with bruises that stood out against her pale skin. She was also much thinner than Charisma had suspected with her skin stretched tight over her fine bones.

Curling her fingers tight around the bedpost, Charisma scowled. No one deserved such treatment. If she ever saw that man again, she'd definitely have him arrested.

Missy moaned as Dr. Murray wrapped a bandage tight around her ribs. Charisma stepped forward in an instinctive reaction, her hand outstretched.

"Don't worry, Miss Charisma. She's still unaware." He finished and turned to face Thalia. "As her ribs are cracked, I would advise her to remain still until they heal. I don't see anything more serious that that, which is surprising. She's malnourished, of course, and will require several days rest. Sleep is the best thing for her right now, and later, food."

When Thalia nodded, he glanced back at Missy and frowned. "There is something else you should know."

"Yes?" Thalia asked before Charisma could speak.

Charisma glanced from the doctor to the young woman. What was it? Did he recognize her?

Dr. Murray hesitated, casting a sidelong glance at Charisma. Thalia motioned for him to continue.

"I believe this woman is one of the . . . ah . . . working ladies in Colorado City," he said. "If you like, I can make arrangements to have her returned to her place of employment."

"No." Charisma stalked over to face him. "She's hurt and needs our help. Surely she would not be in her present condition if she had anyone who truly cared about her. You're a doctor. How can *you* even consider sending her away?"

Dr. Murray blinked, his surprise evident.

"Charisma." Thalia's voice held a note of censure as she rested her hand on Charisma's shoulder.

Charisma grimaced. She'd spoken without thinking . . . again.

"Thank you for your consideration, Dr. Murray, but I must agree with Charisma, no matter how outspoken her words. We have a moral duty to tend to this young woman's injuries. There will be time later to return her to her residence."

The doctor's shocked expression gave way to a look of appreciation. "You are a true lady, Mrs. Papadopoulos. I only hope this woman appreciates all you're doing for her."

"We can do no less." Thalia extended her hand. "Thank you again for coming so promptly."

Dr. Murray bowed over her hand with a smile. "I'll check back in a day or two to see how she's doing. For now, I'll leave some laudanum to keep her resting comfortably."

"Thank you, sir," Charisma added, bestowing her warmest smile on him. Would he forgive her earlier outburst?

His returning smile wasn't as wide as the one he gave Thalia, but it was a smile. "Good day, Mrs. Papadopoulos, Miss Charisma."

Thalia escorted him to the bedroom door. "James will show you out."

Once the doctor left, Thalia turned back to Charisma and sighed.

"I know. I'm sorry." Charisma hung her head. "But we couldn't send her away. Not like this."

"Of course not, but there are more tactful ways to achieve the same purpose."

Which Thalia had admirably demonstrated.

Charisma sighed as well. "I just spoke without thinking."

Thalia embraced her. "Your passion is a wonderful part of you, my dear, but it is also what leads you astray. Remember what we discussed . . ."

"Stop and think before I speak." She'd done so well at the Sollys's dinner party, even managing to hold her tongue around Miss Mattingly. "I can do it. I know I can."

"I believe you can as well. You've made wonderful progress, but you can't expect to change completely in only a week."

"I can't expect to." Charisma grinned. "But I want to." She longed to be charming, but it remained an elusive quality.

"Patience, my dear."

Missy moaned and Charisma winced as she glanced down at her. After growing up in a mining camp, Charisma wasn't as naïve as Dr. Murray would like to believe. She knew about working women, though Missy didn't fit Charisma's mental image. The women she'd seen at camp had been full-figured, extremely buxom, and painted their faces.

Missy, on the other hand, was thin to the point of gauntness and wore no adornments. If she was indeed a "wicked woman" as her mother called them, Missy was unlike any Charisma had seen before.

"Shall I sit with her until she awakens?" Perhaps her presence would help somehow. She needed to do *something*.

"Another time, I think." Thalia nodded toward the dainty crystal clock on the bureau. "Don't you have somewhere to be right now?"

Noticing the hour, Charisma moaned. "Oh no. I'm going to miss it again."

Will was speaking in Acacia Park and Charisma had planned to be there for his entire oration this time. She'd never get there in five minutes, not even if she ran.

"Nonsense. I'll have James take you. I'm certain he hasn't unhooked the carriage yet from delivering Dr. Murray. You don't want to keep your sisters waiting either." Thalia called for the butler. "Meanwhile, I'll stay with our new guest. I know some healing draughts that may be beneficial."

"Thank you, Thalia."

Charisma tapped her toe impatiently while James drove as slowly as possible downtown. When they finally reached Acacia Park, she jumped down before he could offer assistance. "Thank you, James."

"Will you be all right, Miss Charisma?" he asked, eyeing the crowd. Men surrounded the platform where Will stood and very few women were in attendance.

"My sisters are here." Charisma spotted Belle and Grace standing off to the side.

"Very well." James smiled and left, while Charisma joined her sisters.

Grace somehow managed to get a twig stuck in her hair and Charisma gently removed it as she greeted them. "Did I miss much?" she asked.

"He's just started," Belle replied, fixing Charisma with a look of boredom. "Though I've barely understood one word in ten that he's said."

"Sssh," Charisma implored. Will was talking again and she listened with pride. She'd missed only a little of his speech and marveled at how he managed to convey integrity and hope with his words: fair working conditions and representation in the senate for all, including a voice for even the shop clerk and housemaid. He spoke with eloquence and passion, stirring a restlessness within her, that need to make a difference. He made it sound possible.

When several men cheered at the end of his speech, she joined in.

"The man is an idealistic fool." A man spoke behind Charisma and she whirled around to see who could be talking so uncharitably of Will.

This man was older, at least thirty, with hard eyes and a once-handsome face that showed evidence of excess. She didn't know him, yet he seemed somehow familiar.

"You are mistaken, sir," she said, struggling to remain polite but unable to let his opinion stand unchallenged. "Mr. Barclay is an excellent candidate for the senate."

He lifted one dark eyebrow, a brief glimmer of interest in his eyes. "You would have our state senate run by fools who believe in pipe dreams? Such a happenstance would be a disaster."

"Charisma," Belle whispered as a warning, but Charisma ignored her sister. This man obviously didn't know much about Will's character.

"Mr. Barclay is offering equal representation. Is that not what our constitution promises?" she retorted.

The man studied her for a moment before he spoke again. "William is a softhearted idealist," he said finally. "He hasn't a chance of winning this election."

"I beg to differ." Charisma held her shoulders stiff. "You speak of Mr. Barclay as if you know him, yet you can't possibly be a friend of his if you speak so." Who was this man? Didn't he see that Will was an outstanding candidate?

"I know him well," the man said. "But we are not friends." He glanced over to where Will conversed with some men, his eyes narrowing. "I'm a candidate for the senate myself."

"That would explain your obvious bias." She couldn't expect Will's opponent to embrace his ideals.

"Oh, my bias goes back further than that." The man smiled but his expression held no warmth. "Will is my brother."

Five

Will shook hands for what felt like the hundredth time, his smile only wavering a little. He'd seen Charisma early on during his speech, then lost sight of her. Knowing her, she was still here somewhere. Though he'd firmed his resolve to remain nothing more than friends, he had to admit he did enjoy her company.

Taking advantage of the lull in well-wishers, he scanned the thinning crowd. There she was. His gut clenched.

With Stephen. What was *he* doing here?

Will wasted no time in reaching Charisma's side. From the way she was glaring at his brother, he assumed Stephen hadn't tried to charm her as he usually did when he met an attractive woman. *Good.*

Her sisters stood a short distance away, their censoring stares aimed more at Charisma. What had she been saying? Was she using her usual blunt speech? No doubt Stephen deserved it.

"What brings you to Colorado Springs, Stephen?" he asked.

"What? No pleasantries?" Stephen lifted a mocking eyebrow. "I'm fine, thank you. So is Abigail."

Will bit back a sigh. Very well. He could play this game. "I'm glad to hear that. Mother? Father?"

"Both well. Mother wants to know when you'll return home."

"Not until after the election. I still have ground to cover here." Besides, Stephen had Denver's county nomination locked up and knew it. Will glanced at Charisma, who gave him a warm smile that added an extra beat to his pulse. "Have you met Miss Charisma Sullivan?"

"We've met but were not introduced." Stephen bowed low over Charisma's hand. "The pleasure is all mine."

Her smile was far less potent than the one she'd given Will. "Sir."

"And her sisters, Miss Belle and Miss Grace Sullivan." Will motioned her sisters forward. The more people present, the less chance of Stephen revealing his true purpose in coming here.

Belle smiled prettily, but Grace managed to spill her satchel of berries all over Stephen's shoes. While she apologized profusely, Will smothered a grin. It was no more than his brother deserved.

Once introductions were completed, Charisma turned to Will. "I didn't realize you had a brother."

"Stephen is married and lives in Denver."

"What brings you here, Mr. Barclay?" Charisma asked with a slight tilt of her head.

Will wanted to cheer her boldness when Stephen sighed. "So we're back to that. I want to see my brother, of course."

No "of course" about it. He and Stephen had never been close, especially since the events of a year ago. His brother had another reason for his visit, which he would no doubt get to in his own time.

Ignoring Stephen's response, Will gave his full attention to Charisma. He much preferred her company. "I'm pleased to see you here. Though I expected to receive pointed questions once again."

"I was distracted." Charisma grinned sheepishly. "Next time, I suppose."

"We need to get home, Charisma." Belle touched her arm. "Cook is waiting for the berries. What's left of them anyhow."

Charisma sighed. "I must go." She nodded toward Stephen. "A pleasure, Mr. Barclay."

"Let me walk with you a moment," Will replied. He'd barely had a chance to talk to her. He touched her elbow, then glanced over his shoulder at his brother. "I'll be right back."

Once they were out of Stephen's earshot, he let her sisters walk ahead, then issued an impulsive invitation. "I've been invited to dinner at Glen Eyrie on Friday. Would you accompany me?"

"To Glen Eyrie?" Charisma's eyes widened. "I would love it. Mama has mentioned several times how lovely the Palmers' home is."

"Excellent. I will confirm with Mrs. Papadopoulos and call for you around seven." They would have plenty of time to talk during the drive to the Palmer estate tucked away in Queen's Canyon.

"I look forward to it. Thank you." Charisma squeezed his arm once, then darted off to join her sisters, giving him a slight wave before they turned toward home.

Will took a moment to anticipate the event. If Charisma behaved as well at the Palmer home as she had at the Sollys's, he would be fortunate indeed. That is, if he could keep his thoughts on the campaign instead of straying to her appealing lips.

Forcing that image away, he returned to where Stephen waited. His brother wore a smirk that had Will clenching his teeth.

"Pretty thing. Didn't take you long to find company."

"The lady is a friend, nothing more." No matter how much Will kept thinking about tasting those lips. "Would you care to join me at the hotel for a drink?" Will asked, already knowing his brother's response.

"Thought you'd never ask." Stephen slapped Will's back in an overly hearty gesture. "Lead on."

Once they had their drinks before them, Will waited for Stephen to get to his real reason for coming all the way from Denver. He didn't have to wait long.

Stephen drank, then set his glass on the table with a thump. "I want you to drop your candidacy."

"No."

His brother's eyes widened and his jaw dropped. Obviously he hadn't expected such a direct answer. Will almost grinned. Charisma was right. Sometimes plain, blunt speech was best. "Anything else?"

"I'm serious, William. You don't have a chance of winning this election, especially in this county. All you're doing is confusing the issue. We have the same last name. Folks will confuse your ridiculous platform with mine. They won't know who is who."

"And that's the real issue, isn't it? You're afraid I'll receive some of your votes." Will hoped he would. Though they were running in different counties, if he could gather votes from people who believed in the Barclay name he had a better chance of winning.

His brother scowled. "Look, you're not qualified for this. I'm the one who's worked his way through the levels of government. I've earned this."

"You've earned what our father's name would get you." Only two years older than Will, Stephen hadn't worked overly hard to get to his current position as a Denver councilman. Their father's political career had eased the way considerably. "Now it's my turn."

"You're being foolish. You're not cut out for this. Go back to studying your books and defending people in need."

"I *am* defending people in need." Will clasped his glass so tightly, the cut crystal edges dug into his palm. "Something you'll never do."

Color infused Stephen's face. "I represent my constituents."

"Only if they're wealthy. What about the poor, the miners, the shop clerks?" Will paused and leaned forward. "What about Melissa?"

"For God's sake, it's all about her, isn't it? She was nothing, I tell you. Nothing."

Will resisted the urge to wrap his hands around his brother's throat. Instead, he sat back, calmly took a drink, then met Stephen's gaze. "Which proves my point." He pushed away from the table. "I think we're finished here, Stephen. Nice of you to stop by."

He left the room, not bothering to look back. Will might not have the political experience of his father or his brother, but he did have integrity and a sincere desire to help people. He had to win. To allow Stephen in the Colorado senate unchecked would be disastrous.

For everyone.

* * *

Charisma couldn't believe how fast Missy's condition improved. By Friday morning, the young woman was up and about, wearing an altered dress of Charisma's and sitting with Thalia in the parlor when Charisma arrived.

"You should give Dr. Murray the recipe for your draughts," Charisma told Thalia as she sat in the vacant ladies chair. "It's worked miracles for Missy." She smiled at the young woman. "You look so much better."

The bruises were mostly gone now with only a hint of yellow around one eye. Now that Missy had rested and eaten regularly, she'd blossomed, revealing that she was actually an attractive young woman.

"I feel so much better, too," Missy said. "I can't thank either of you enough." She hesitated and plucked at her dress. "But I do need to return to Colorado City today. I have friends who must be worrying about me."

Charisma frowned. "Friends would not have allowed you to go with that man you were with."

Missy dropped her gaze to where her folded hands rested in her lap. "They had no choice."

"If you'll tell me his name, I'll have him arrested." They'd been over this before and as Charisma expected, Missy shook her head. "Please, Missy."

"It's not important."

"It *is* important. He could have killed you." Just remembering the event made Charisma clench her fists.

"There are people who would say I deserved it."

"Those people are wrong." Even if they included Charisma's mother.

Though Missy, Charisma, and Thalia had not openly discussed Missy's profession, she had not hidden it from them either. Now that Charisma knew Missy better as a person, she felt even more strongly about equal rights for women. Missy did not deserve to be treated as she had, no matter what her profession.

Charisma hesitated, actually taking the time to think before she spoke again. "If I may be so bold, how did you get into this . . . your . . . line of work? I can't believe you . . . enjoy it."

"I hate it." The words erupted from Missy with such vehemence that she paused, as if surprised at herself. "I had no choice," she continued in a quieter tone. "I used to be an upstairs maid. I . . . I was . . ." She sucked in a deep breath. "My employer fired me without any references. I have no family and I couldn't find any other work." She looked from Charisma to Thalia, her gaze beseeching. "I was starving."

"And you did what you had to to survive." Thalia placed her hand over Missy's. "Completely understandable. And if you wish to return home today, I will have James bring the carriage around."

"I want to go with her," Charisma said, rising to her feet, her voice firm, ready to face Thalia's disapproval.

"Colorado City is not the best of places for a young woman," Thalia said.

"I want to see where Missy works, who her friends are, what I can do to help. I'm eighteen, Thalia. I don't want to be sheltered forever." A woman who intended to make a difference in the world could not shy away from the seedy side of things.

"Remember that I grew up in a mining camp," Charisma added. "I've already seen things most other young women here haven't. I've been around the poor, the working women, the miners."

Thalia sighed, no doubt recognizing that she couldn't sway Charisma. "Very well. Then I will come along as well." She smiled at Missy. "You shall have a very proper escort, my dear."

Missy gave them a half smile. "Thank you."

In a short time, they were on the road to Colorado City. Charisma frowned, noticing that the closer the carriage drew to the city, the paler Missy became.

"Are you certain you want to return?" Charisma asked. "I'm sure we can find employment for you in the Springs."

"Do you know of something?" A touch of eagerness brightened in Missy's tone.

"Not right now, but if—"

Missy shook her head. "I cannot be more beholden to you and Mrs. Papadopoulos than I already am. But if you do find something . . ."

"I will make it a point to let you know." In fact, Charisma intended to start searching immediately.

But for now, her gaze was caught by the bustle of life along Colorado Avenue, the main street in Colorado City. Saloons and taverns lined the dirt road. She quit counting after eight. Bawdy music flowed from one of the saloons, a lively tune that had her tapping her toe for a moment.

Wagons and horses filled the street, carrying miners and railroad workers. Women of all ages scurried across the road, all different, yet all wearing the downtrodden expression of weariness.

Once they turned onto Cucharras Street, Charisma knew they'd reached the area where the working women dwelled. An aura of potent hush hung over the saloons and houses as if waiting for night when the street would burst into tawdry life.

Missy directed James to stop before a small plain blue house with nothing to distinguish it as a house of ill repute except for the single feather boa dangling off the upper porch. After James assisted Missy from the carriage, she turned back to smile at Thalia and Charisma. "Thank you truly for all you've done."

Charisma pushed herself to the carriage door. "May I come inside?"

Missy's eyes widened. "I don't believe you should be here, Miss Charisma."

"I agree." Thalia placed one gloved hand on the door, holding it closed.

"I'm curious." Which was true, but even more Charisma wanted to ensure Missy wouldn't be returning to the horrible man who beat her. "I won't stay long."

Missy glanced past Charisma to Thalia, mutely asking for advice. Thalia sighed, then released the door and motioned for Charisma to continue. "Very well. We'll only stay a moment. James, please accompany us."

To Charisma's surprise, the interior of the house resembled the drawing room and hallway of most houses she frequented, though the furniture was more worn, the carpet a trifle threadbare, and the paintings fewer but far more interesting with most of them featuring women in various stages of undress. She was jerked from her scrutiny as a young woman clad in a silk robe ran down the staircase to throw her arms around Missy's neck.

"Missy, I've been sick with worry about you. Where you been? After that man dragged you out, I fetched Clyde to help, but you were gone." Her brown curls were tousled as if she'd just arisen from bed and she was equally as thin as Missy, her shoulder bones sharply defined through the thin robe.

"He . . . he took me to Colorado Springs. He wanted me . . . to do things." Missy squeezed the other woman even tighter. "He . . . he hit me."

"He beat her nearly senseless," Charisma added, drawing the young women's attention. "Mrs. Papadopoulos has been caring for her until she was well enough to return."

Missy waved a hand at the young woman. "This is my friend, Patsy. Patsy, Mrs. Papadopoulos and Miss Charisma. I owe them my life."

"You owe us nothing, my dear," Thalia said. "Your return to good health was payment enough."

Patsy broke away and dropped a sloppy curtsey before Mrs. Papadopoulos. "I owe you, too, ma'am. I been worried sick over her."

"It's Missy." Another woman, slighter older than Missy and Patsy, thundered down the steps, a smile lighting her tired face. "You're alive."

"Esther." Joy filled Missy's voice as she turned to the woman.

Esther, too, embraced Missy. "I feared for you. I knew that man was evil. He kissed like he was evil."

Charisma started. "You can tell about a man from his kiss?"

"Of course." Esther glanced at Charisma, her gaze traveling the length of Charisma's summer dress. She nudged Missy. "Landed on your feet, didn't you?"

"They saved my life," Missy said.

"Well, then, I'll tell you my secret about men and their kisses." Esther drew closer to Charisma, lowering her voice. "A man's kiss tells you plenty about him—if he's gentle or rough, kind or mean, trustworthy or an out-and-out liar."

"It tells you all that?" Why hadn't Belle told Charisma any of this?

"Never been kissed, have you?" Esther asked.

Charisma shook her head, heat rising into her cheeks.

"You'll see what I'm talking about one of these days. You'll see." She swung back to Missy. "Better go tell Mamie you're here. She's been worried about you."

"And we need to take our leave as well," Thalia added. "Take care of yourself, my dear."

"Thank you, Mrs. Papadopoulos, Miss Charisma." Gratitude filled Missy's eyes as she waved good-bye.

Charisma remained quiet during the ride back to the city, responding to Thalia's few questions with monosyllables. She'd actually been inside a brothel, though it hadn't been nearly as mysterious as she'd expected. However, the women were interesting. Her thoughts drifted to Esther's advice. *A kiss holds all that information? Amazing.*

What would Will's kiss say? She smiled, imagining it. Since she was going to see him soon, she intended to find out.

* * *

Will found Charisma an eager listener during the trip to Glen Eyrie on Friday as he confided the steps he'd taken to ensure he was named the El Paso County Democratic candidate for the Colorado senate. True, a Democrat in this county was as rare as a four-eyed jackrabbit, but he was earning some support. His platform, not to mention his family name, was helping.

To be honest, Charisma's presence by his side had swayed some opinions as well. Many folks in Colorado Springs would just as likely refuse to even talk to him, but she provided a link through which he could meet them—such as this dinner with General Palmer. He intended to make the most of it.

"The Republican County Convention is going to be held at the courthouse meeting hall tomorrow night," Charisma said, interrupting his reverie. "What do you expect to happen?"

"It's just a formality. Howbert has the senate nomination. He has solid backing here." Will grimaced. "A *lot* of backing." Backing he would have to overcome in order to win.

And he would win. Somehow.

"Your name is well-known, too, Mr. Barclay," Thalia added.

"True, though Barclays have always been Republican candidates." A fact his father threw in his face often.

"Why are you running for the Democratic candidacy then? Especially here?" Charisma asked.

It was a good question. And it deserved an honest answer. "A couple of reasons. I support the Democratic platform. It ties in with my personal views. But the main reason is because I have no chance of winning the Republican nomination. With my brother running in Denver, and Parrish and Howbert fighting it out here, I would be brushed aside."

Charisma nodded, her expression thoughtful. "Whereas here there are no other Democratic opponents."

"Exactly." Will grinned. He was pretty much guaranteed the candidacy—if the Democrats here even selected candidates. He'd heard rumors that many of them were not planning to select a candidate, because they didn't think he'd stand a chance against the Republicans. He had to convince them otherwise.

Rounding a curve along the road to Glen Eyrie, Will noticed a jutting turret peeking above the trees and motioned for Charisma to look. "Is that it?"

"Yes. It's a magnificent place, even if Mrs. Palmer doesn't like it. Mama would take it in a moment." Charisma leaned forward. "It was just remodeled last year and Mama says it has twenty-two rooms."

Will nodded. His own family's home was equally as large, but not nearly as impressive. General Palmer's home nestled among the pines and scrub oak that filled Queen's Canyon, appearing as majestic as any Tudor castle.

An eagle soared overhead as he pulled the buggy to a stop and handed the reins to a stableboy. Glen Eyrie. Valley of the Eagle's Nest. Now he understood where the name for the Palmer's home originated.

General Palmer himself met them at the door

and shook Will's hand firmly. "I've only been home a couple of days and already I've heard your name bandied about by several of my friends, young Barclay. I'll enjoy a chance to talk with you."

"It will be my pleasure, sir," Will said. If he could convince the founder of Colorado Springs to back him, he would win this election easily . . . even as a Democrat. "I believe you know Miss Charisma and Mrs. Papadopoulos."

"I am very familiar with Miss Charisma." The general gave her a welcoming smile, then took Mrs. Papadopoulos's hand. "But I'm afraid I haven't had the honor, madam."

"The honor is all mine," she replied. "I must admit I am overwhelmed by your lovely home. It's exquisite."

General Palmer beamed. "Please, come in, and let me show you around. This is only a temporary home until I can build the castle I promised Queen, but I find it very comfortable." He led them inside. "Especially after so much traveling."

"I heard you'd been to Europe," Charisma said. "Did you have an enjoyable trip?"

A flash of pain crossed the general's face. "It sufficed. I was able to spend time with my wife and daughters."

"And is Mrs. Palmer well?"

Will sent a quick glance toward Charisma. He'd been told that Mrs. Palmer had returned to England because of a heart condition. What if she wasn't well?

"She was very well, thank you." He paused and waved toward a large chandelier hanging in the hallway, his pride obvious. "Did you notice my new lamp?"

Will blinked. "Is it electric?" There were no candles, no oil that he could see, only bulbs glowing with a bright light.

"Yes, indeed, I just had electricity brought in over the past few months. Fascinating, isn't it?"

"It's wonderful," Charisma exclaimed. "The light is so much brighter."

"Look how it stretches to illuminate this entire area," Mrs. Papadopoulos added. "You are to be commended, sir."

After a tour of the incredible house, General Palmer seated them in the parlor, then left to retrieve more guests and returned with a middle-aged couple. "May I introduce William and Helen Jackson?"

With introductions made, the group drifted into easy conversation with no talk of politics. Will understood at once that any interrogation on his views would take place after the meal when the men retreated for a cigar. Which left him that much more time to worry about it.

Glancing at Charisma, he found her staring outside. "Do you see something interesting?"

She flushed and returned a beguiling smile, then directed her answer to General Palmer. "I've been noticing the gardens. Would I be permitted to stroll through them, sir?"

"Certainly. Would you like me to escort you?"

"Please, do not bother. I don't wish to interrupt your conversation. I can see you are very comfortable just as you are." Charisma stepped toward the door and Will jumped to his feet, speaking before his brain had completely realized he intended to say anything.

"May I accompany you, Miss Charisma?"

"I would enjoy that." She darted a glance at Mrs. Papadopoulos, who waved them away, apparently more interested in continuing the conversation with others closer to her own age than joining them.

Will hesitated only a moment before joining Charisma. The gardens were in plain view of the house, easily seen from the window. The two of them alone was not likely to cause any concern.

Once outside, Charisma grew strangely silent, pausing on occasion to remark over the blooming columbines. Was she nervous? Surely she felt comfortable enough around him by now.

"Is there a problem?" he asked.

She hesitated. "No. Yes. Well, maybe."

"Can I be of assistance?" He found her indecision at odds with the young woman he knew. Of all the women of his acquaintance, Charisma always appeared to know her mind.

"You could." She walked a few more steps, then paused, not turning to face him. "But I'm not sure that you will."

"I would be glad to help if it is within my power." Weren't they friends? He felt obliged to assist her in any way he could.

She strolled a short distance further, then turned to face him, the determination on her face giving him a slight touch of unease. "I want you to kiss me," she said.

"What?" Will stopped, unable to take another step. Had he heard correctly? Charisma was bold, but surely not this bold. Yet his gut twisted at the thought of tasting those delectable lips.

"I know it sounds crazy, but someone told me I would know all about a man if I kissed him. If . . . if I am to support your candidacy, I need to know all about you. And I know you wouldn't kiss me on your own because you're a gentleman, but I really want to know so I have no choice but to ask." Her words tumbled over one another until she paused to draw in a deep breath. "So, would you kiss me?"

"I cannot." To do so would be disastrous. She would expect more from him than he was willing or able to give. This was supposed to be a platonic partnership.

"Of course." Disappointment crossed her face and he took an involuntary step closer, wanting to pull her into his arms. "I understand," she continued. "After all, you made it quite clear you don't see me as a woman. I can always find someone else. Alexander Drake has been trying to get me to kiss him since I first arrived here. He might possibly be willing."

Not see her as a woman? That's the one thing he'd failed miserably at doing. If he concentrated on her intelligence, he could distance himself, until the appeal of her dancing eyes and full lips enticed him once again.

A stone dropped into his gut at the thought of another man holding her, kissing her. "That would not be wise," he said.

She continued to ramble as if she hadn't heard him. "But Alex doesn't appeal to me at all. I even punched him in the stomach when I was twelve. Perhaps I should ask Mr. Edwards. He has smiled at me once or twice and he's very appealing."

Will had met the "appealing" Mr. Edwards and didn't share her opinion of the man. From the little Will knew, Mr. Edwards was nothing more than a remittance man, sent off to America to live while bankrolled by a wealthy father. "I don't think that's a good idea." She would not be kissing Mr. Edwards.

She shouldn't be kissing anyone.

Except him.

She was still blathering when he crossed to her and held her shoulders. "Charisma," he said firmly. "Be quiet."

She stopped in mid-sentence, her enticing lips parted, her eyes wide with surprise.

And—Lord help him—he kissed her.

Six

Esther had told the truth. Charisma found Will's kiss strong and passionate—qualities she'd already seen in him. As he deepened the kiss, his lips moving over hers, he wrapped her in his arms, and she forgot to think about anything at all.

All she could do was experience the tumult of sensations exploding inside her, a longing she'd never experienced before, an ache that wanted . . . something. And the feel of Will's lips against hers was pure heaven. No wonder Belle hadn't been able to adequately describe it. There were no words for it.

She murmured in protest when Will raised his head and eased her out of his hold. Though his breathing was equally as erratic as hers, she recognized the familiar light of responsibility in his eyes.

"I beg your pardon," he said, his voice husky. "I shouldn't have done that."

"I asked you to," she told him. In fact, she was tempted to ask him to kiss her again.

"Regardless, as a gentleman I should have known better . . . behaved better." He stepped away from her and motioned toward the house. "I believe we should go inside."

Charisma grimaced, but brushed past him. "Yes,

of course." At least the thick spruce she had to skirt
had hidden them from the parlor window. Will's
flawless reputation . . . and hers . . . were secure.

Their return was barely acknowledged since the
remaining group members were deep in conversation about the upcoming performance of *Uncle
Tom's Cabin* the following night at the opera house.
"I managed to procure excellent seats," Mrs. Jackson said. "I can't wait to see it."

Charisma wanted to see the play as well. Would
Will ask her? Unlikely, especially since he spent the
remainder of the night staying as far away from her
as possible. Even Thalia noticed, pausing by
Charisma's side after the men departed for their
port and cigars following dinner.

"Did you and Mr. Barclay have a disagreement?"
she asked.

"No." *Not a disagreement.* More like an agreement
since his response was equally as fervent as hers. He
obviously regretted that action now, but Charisma
didn't. Will's kiss had been all she'd expected and
far, far more.

"He appears rather aloof tonight."

"He is probably nervous about winning General
Palmer's support." Which was true, though he
hadn't admitted that to her. She knew how important the general's opinion was to him.

"That must be it."

But Will remained silent during most of the journey back to the city until Charisma could stand it
no longer. "Did your discussion with General
Palmer go well?" Will had been smiling when he'd
emerged from the smoking room.

"As well as could be expected. The general was

very tolerant of my position and promised to make several important introductions, but he would not endorse me as the county's candidate for the senate."

In all honesty, Charisma had not expected General Palmer to endorse Will, though she'd hoped for it. "That is not all bad then, is it?"

"Not all bad," Will admitted. "I will just have to work harder to convince others that I am the best candidate."

"Anyone who's heard you already knows that," she said impulsively.

He sent her a dry look. "I fear not all."

Charisma longed to touch him, to reassure him. But he did not want her touch. Not now. Had her desire for a simple kiss ruined their friendship?

She grew warm remembering the incredible sensations his touch had created. Not a simple kiss, after all. All she could think about was kissing him again. Of course, for that, she'd need an opportunity.

She brightened. "Have you heard that the Bee Line excursionists are hosting a dance at Manitou House Saturday week? They've invited the entire area." Would he ask her to accompany him to this event? "I expect everyone who is anyone will be there."

"I have heard about it." He said no more and she bit her lip.

That made his position very clear. She *had* ruined their friendship.

When he later escorted her to her door, she caught his arm before he could turn away. "Will, I'm sorry."

Pausing, he glanced at her, his gaze penetrating even in the night darkness.

"I'm sorry if I offended you," she added. "I was merely curious."

His gaze dropped briefly to her lips and her breath caught in her chest. "I hope you have managed to satisfy that curiosity," he said, no emotion coloring his words.

"I . . . yes." What else could she say? That she wanted more? That his kiss had awakened a longing she hadn't even known existed?

"Good night then."

She watched him walk back to the buggy before stepping inside. He wasn't going to invite her to the dance. She knew it. In fact, no matter how charming she became, he wasn't going to come near her again.

Still, she managed to smile for her mother and sisters and amuse them with her story of the evening. Only after she reached the comfort of her bedroom, did she allow a single tear to fall.

When would she learn to control her impulsiveness?

Will hesitated outside Manitou House. Already the hotel was filled with people, the chatter and music drifting into the night. All of Colorado Springs society would be here tonight. That fact behooved him to attend.

But should he?

He'd already decided not to bring Charisma. In fact, he was better off without any young woman by his side. It was too dangerous. They all wanted what he wasn't prepared to give—his freedom.

Still, he hadn't been able to dismiss the intense

pleasure of kissing Charisma either, the way she'd felt so soft against him, the movement of her mouth beneath his. He hadn't wanted to stop. In fact, he'd wanted more—far more—than he had any right to ask of a respectable lady.

Thank goodness, he'd come to his senses in time. He'd stick with his initial plan of remaining solo and spending time with the influential gentlemen of the city. If he could win their support, he had a chance.

That was what mattered.

Not these traitorous thoughts of holding Charisma.

Scowling, he entered the hotel and was immediately swallowed into the party crowd. Several young couples danced on the smooth wooden floor while older ladies and gentlemen talked in groups around the side. He recognized Dr. Bell and Mr. Solly and turned to join them.

He'd only taken six steps when an attractive blonde appeared at his elbow. "Good evening, Mr. Barclay."

He paused to glance at her. Had they met? She appeared familiar and he struggled for her name. "Miss . . . Caulfield?"

At her beaming smile, the tightness in his chest eased. Good guess.

"Are you alone tonight?" she asked, stepping even closer to his side, fluttering her eyelashes so rapidly he wanted to blink.

He fought the natural instinct to take a step away. It would not do to insult the lady. "Tonight, yes."

"Does that mean you're no longer squiring Charisma Sullivan around town? No one has seen the two of you together since . . . well, since last week." Her gaze held him trapped as she inhaled deeply, raising her partially exposed bosom. She fluttered her fan in an obvious attempt to draw his attention to that flesh. "I find that excellent news indeed."

"I . . . I . . ." He struggled to clear his throat, his collar suddenly too tight, the air unable to provide sustenance for breathing. "I have been busy."

"Not too busy for a dance, I hope." Before he could answer, she tucked her hand through his elbow and led him to the dance floor. "I just know you'll dance divinely."

He restrained a grimace and escorted her through the steps, making inarticulate responses to her inane chatter on the weather, the fashions, the people in attendance. When the dance finally ended—eons later—he was surrounded by several other young women with no chance of escape. Dear Lord, he was doomed.

Going through the steps of his fourth dance, he bit back a sigh. Mrs. Papadopoulos was correct. He needed a permanent escort. At this rate, he'd accomplish nothing tonight.

Worse yet, none of these women saw him for Will Barclay, the idealist, the humanist. They saw the Barclay name, the family wealth, the politician. Not one of them expressed the slightest interest in his campaign.

As he swung away in the dance movement from his latest partner—a Miss Everly—he caught sight of Charisma by the wall and stumbled. Though he recovered quickly, he couldn't look away. He hadn't expected her to be here since he hadn't invited her.

Foolish idea. The invitation had included all the young people in town. Why wouldn't she attend?

She turned and met his gaze, as if she'd felt him staring at her. He felt her flinch from across the crowded room, then she gave him a wan smile and turned back to her sisters and Belle's fiancé, Kit Stanhope. Obviously, he had escorted all three sisters tonight.

Will grimaced. If he'd been wise, he would have invited Charisma to accompany him instead of panicking. So, she stirred his senses. That was completely normal. She was an attractive, intelligent woman. He should be able to maintain a friendship with her without any more kisses.

As soon as the polka finished, Will bowed to his partner, then headed toward Charisma, not daring to look to either side. Unable to slow his approach, he stumbled into her, and she glanced at him in surprise.

"Mr. Barclay?" Surprise and a new coolness layered her voice.

"Please tell me you have this dance open." He spotted Miss Caulfield approaching and took Charisma's hand. "Save me," he whispered.

Her lips lifted in a half-smile, and she wrapped her arm through his, stepping toward the dance floor just as Miss Caulfield reached them. "I'm afraid I have this dance," Charisma said, not giving the other young woman a chance to speak.

On the floor, the music signaled a waltz and Will placed his hand on Charisma's waist as he led her smoothly through the steps. She followed him effortlessly as if she'd danced with him often instead of this being their first dance. An opportunity he would have otherwise relished except for the tension between them. For a long time, she didn't speak, her gaze avoiding his.

Will swallowed. What could he say? "I—"

She lifted her gaze, a hint of fire burning deep within and he experienced a sensation. "I thought you no longer wanted my company."

Trust her to be blunt. "I made a mistake. I am far safer with you than the lions out there."

Her grin emerged. "Lions?"

"Lionesses, then. I feel as if I am the fresh kill tonight."

She laughed and he found himself holding her just a little closer as they whirled around. "That is your fault for being such an eligible gentleman," she said, humor dancing in her eyes.

"Clearly my fault." He returned her smile, at ease for the first time all evening. His attraction to her was a problem, but he trusted her as well and that was worth far more.

The waltz finished far sooner than any other dance during the night, and he led her to the side. They'd barely reached the edge when Charisma touched his arm and gave him a coquettish smile that made him blink in surprise. What was she doing? Had he been mistaken about her?

"I am parched, Mr. Barclay. Would you be so kind as to fetch me a cup of punch?"

Though puzzled, he agreed. "It would be my pleasure." Turning, he spotted Miss Adamson only a couple feet away. Ah, that's what Charisma had been doing—rescuing him again. He paused to shoot her a thankful grin, then made his way to the punch table.

Returning with her drink, he saw no sign of the young women who had hunted him since his arrival. "Did you frighten them all off?" he asked, hopefully.

Her smile held a touch of mischief. "Me? I merely told them you were otherwise engaged for the remainder of the evening."

"Brilliant." He sat in a chair beside her. "Please tell me that you will forgive me for my rude behavior this week."

"If you will forgive me for my impetuousness."

"Agreed." The tight band around his chest eased. Until that moment, he hadn't fully realized how important her forgiveness was.

She sipped her punch. "Wasn't the Democratic meeting this afternoon? Did you receive the nomination?"

Recalling the afternoon's events, he scowled, and Charisma reached out toward him. "You did get the nomination, didn't you?"

Her rising anger echoed what he'd felt earlier and he took her hand. "I received the nomination, but I had to convince them to do so." He shook his head. "This is such a Republican stronghold that Mr. Harrison was disinclined to even nominate candidates for the open positions."

"That's not fair."

He had to grin. "Fairness and politics aren't close acquaintances. I finally managed to persuade him and the others that with my family name and platform I had an even chance of winning the election for the county's senatorial seat."

"Better than even." She gave his hand an encouraging squeeze.

Her unflagging support warmed him. "That remains to be seen. In any case, I am the only Democratic candidate to come out of that meeting. The other positions have been left to the Republicans."

"Then you must do all you can to persuade everyone you're the best candidate." She stood. "Come, Mr. Ingalls is here tonight. You must meet him and convince him of your cause."

As she led him across the room, Will vowed not to be so foolish as to throw away her friendship again. What other woman would not only support him so fully, but also understand the aspects of what it meant to be a candidate?

By the time the event faded away in the early hours of the morning, he had met and talked with several of Colorado Springs' prominent citizens. Though some had dismissed his candidacy as folly, others had listened. He was making progress.

Charisma had remained by his side, silent except for when she performed introductions. She yawned now as he escorted her outside to join her sisters and Mr. Stanhope.

"Bored?" he teased.

"Not at all. I found it fascinating. You did well tonight."

"Thanks to you." Will paused to face her. "Would you be willing to accompany me on a mountain picnic tomorrow?"

"A picnic? I haven't heard of one."

"There is nothing planned. This would be you and me . . . and Mrs. Papadopoulos, of course." He knew the action was foolish, but he wanted to spend some time with her. Just her. Her chaperone was a necessary accoutrement.

Charisma hesitated, her eyes shining in the dark. "I would love it, Will, but your time would be better spent furthering your platform at this point."

She was right, though he couldn't deny a sense of disappointment. He cupped her cheek, the softness of her skin tantalizing. Her full lips beckoned him. "Another time, perhaps." His words sounded raspy as he forced them from his tight throat.

"I would like that." Her breathing quickened as she met his gaze.

For several long moments, neither of them spoke. He drew closer, drawn by the inescapable urge to sample her sweetness again. She didn't move.

"Charisma, we're waiting."

At the sound of Belle's voice, they jerked apart, Charisma blinking as if startled. Will managed a rueful grin. "Good night, Miss Charisma."

Her slow smile added to the heat already flowing through his veins. "Good night, Mr. Barclay."

He watched her carriage until it was out of sight, then shook his head to clear it. This attraction was dangerous, but he would learn to handle it. Far better the danger he knew than that posed by the other single females in this city.

He would smother these passionate urges until they passed. Charisma was only a friend.

Yet doubts lingered as he made his way to his buggy.

Wasn't she?

Charisma hurried toward Thalia's home, eager to relate the previous night's events. The evening had turned out far better than she had expected when she'd let Belle persuade her to attend. Her original inclination had been to remain home and mope, but her sisters had refused to attend unless she accompanied them.

Thank goodness she had agreed. Now she and Will were friends again. She couldn't stop smiling. He didn't hate her after all. She recalled those special moments at the end of the night when she could have sworn he'd wanted to kiss her. Perhaps he even liked her more than a little.

Well, of course. She grinned. Friends liked each other. And no matter how much she desired another heavenly kiss, she would not be so forward as to ask again. She'd learned that lesson.

"Miss Charisma."

Hearing her name, she turned to see Mr. Gardner approaching in his buggy. Her chest tightened and she judged the remaining distance to Thalia's house. Could she run that far if necessary?

"Good morning, Mr. Gardner," she replied as he stopped the buggy beside her.

He appeared far improved from the last time she'd seen him. His face was clean shaven and his clothing neat. His eyes held a clarity previously missing and the smile he beamed at her reminded her of the days when her family had first arrived in Colorado Springs. He'd been one of the few to treat them warmly. Charisma had always enjoyed their visits to his mercantile.

"I wanted to talk to you." He held the reins loosely in one hand and leaned down. "I need to apologize for my behavior at your last visit. I wasn't myself."

Charisma wouldn't argue that point. He'd been a stranger blinded by grief and drink. "I accept your apology." She paused to consider her next words. "I hope things are better now."

"Better." He grimaced. "I am facing life again, which is not as difficult as I expected it to be. Work helps." He hesitated. "Thank you for your boldness, Miss Charisma. For saying what everyone else was too polite to say."

She didn't respond. What could she say to that? Few ever complimented her runaway tongue.

"You were quite correct. Mrs. Gardner would have been ashamed if she'd seen me." He glanced skyward. "And I trust that she does watch over me from time to time."

"I'm sure she does." Charisma smiled warmly. "I am so glad you have joined us again."

He chuckled. "Yes. Now I only have one problem left."

"What is that?"

"All my servants left while I was . . . er . . . not myself. The bulk of them have found other employment already. I have discovered I will quickly starve if I survive on my cooking much longer. And the state of my household is appalling. I'm ashamed I let it deteriorate so much."

For a moment Charisma didn't speak. This was the answer she'd been seeking. "Oh, Mr. Gardner," she blurted. "I know someone who would be perfect as a housekeeper."

"Do you? That's wonderful. Could you bring this person to my home later today? I am in desperate need."

"I will do my best." Charisma clenched her hands together to keep from crying out in glee. What a perfect opportunity for Missy.

Once Mr. Gardner continued down the road, Charisma ran to Thalia's house. They needed to go to Colorado City and fetch Missy at once.

Reaching Thalia's house, she rapped on the door, then paced while she waited for James to answer. They had to go at once. This opportunity could not be missed.

When no one answered after a minute, Charisma frowned and rapped again. Thalia was always home. At the very least, Charisma expected James to respond.

But still no one answered.

Perhaps James had taken Thalia somewhere. Though she rarely mentioned friends, Charisma knew she must have some. Evidently, she'd gone visiting.

Charisma frowned. Now what? If she waited for Thalia to return, the hour could grow too late. Yet she had no hope of persuading her sisters to go to Colorado City. They would be scandalized.

Returning to the walk, Charisma directed her steps toward downtown. She *had* to get this message to Missy as soon as possible. Besides, it was daytime. The city didn't become dangerous until dark.

If she went straight there and back, what harm could there be? Charisma hesitated only for a moment. She had no choice. This was too important to Missy's future.

With that thought in mind, she waved down a passing hansom cab.

Seven

Charisma arrived at the small house on Cucharras Street and glanced around before stepping out of the cab. As when she'd been there previously during the day, the street was quiet with little signs of life. Good.

She turned back to the driver. "Please wait for me. I'll only be a few minutes."

"Are you sure you want to go in there?" he asked. The older man had obviously taken a grandfatherly interest in her. His concerned gaze flicked from Charisma to the house. "It's not right, miss."

"I must." Charisma forced a smile. "I will be right back."

No one answered her knock at first, then a voice rang out from the upper level. "Go 'way. We ain't open till night."

"I need to talk to Missy," Charisma called.

Missy poked her head out of an upstairs window. "Miss Charisma? I'll be right there." The door opened moments later and Missy peeked outside, her face pale. "What are you doing here?"

"I found a position for you." Charisma couldn't keep the excitement from her voice. "You need to dress quickly and come with me."

Missy's eyes widened. "You found me a position?"

"As a housekeeper. Yes."

Still, the young woman hesitated. "At a good house?"

"Yes." As long as Mr. Gardner wasn't drinking. "I'll explain on the way." Charisma glanced back at the cab. "Please, hurry. I have the hansom waiting."

Missy left the door open and dashed upstairs, calling out her news as she went. Charisma smiled and slipped inside to wait. By the time Missy returned, a small bag in her hand, several other women had joined Charisma, buzzing with questions.

"A position?"

"Where?"

"With who?"

"What kind of position?"

Charisma laughed. Their enthusiasm was contagious. "It's a position as a maid for a respectable gentleman in Colorado Springs. He also needs a cook. Do any of you have experience as a cook?" Perhaps she'd be able to help out more than Missy.

"I do." An older woman stepped forward, a look of hope in her faded blue eyes. "Nothing special, but good solid food."

"And what are you doing here if you can cook?" Patsy demanded.

The woman flushed. "I burned the dinner once—just once—and the mistress threw me out with no recommendations. Where was I to go?"

Charisma glanced at Missy, who nodded. "Then you can come, too." Charisma waved at the woman. "But hurry, we must leave soon." She didn't want to be here when night came and their customers arrived.

Esther sighed and hugged Missy. "Be sure to let

us know how you're doing. Don't let him treat you bad."

"I won't." Missy turned from Esther to Patsy and hugged her friend. "I wish you could leave here, too."

"I don't have the skills you do," Patsy said.

"You could be taught," Charisma added. How much was there to becoming a maid? Charisma had done her share of keeping her home clean until her father's mine had changed her family's fortune.

"Would you?" Patsy asked.

"Would you teach us?" Esther added.

Charisma hesitated. It would mean returning here. Yet if she only came during the day, she'd be safe enough. Even better, this would give her the opportunity to make a difference. If she could find good positions for all these women, they could leave this unsavory profession. "Yes," she said. "I'll teach you."

Esther's eyes lit up. "When?"

"Soon. I'll come back. For now, we really must leave."

"What's this about leaving?"

Charisma whirled around at hearing the demanding tone. A woman appeared in the doorway to the room, resembling Charisma's former image of a working woman. Well-rounded, with bright red hair and a robe that barely covered her assets, the woman descended on Charisma and Missy, her hard eyes glittering. Evidently, she was the authority in this place.

Charisma refused to be cowed. "I have found respectable work for Missy. Surely you won't deny her that opportunity."

Though the woman was shorter than Charisma, she was much larger with an aura of power surrounding her. "You can't steal one of my girls."

"I'm not stealing her. She has the freedom to choose her profession, and she prefers this." Charisma stood as tall as she could. "Women do have rights, you know."

"The only rights women have are what men give them." The woman came to stand toe-to-toe with Charisma. "And the only right that men give them is to lie beneath them."

Heat filled Charisma's cheeks as she grasped the woman's meaning. "Then we know different types of men, don't we?"

The madam laughed. "All men are the same. You're just too naïve to know it."

Missy touched the woman's arm. "Please, Mamie."

Mamie's gaze softened as she glanced at Missy. "There's no guarantee this employer will treat you any better than the last."

"I won't let him mistreat me," Missy said, her voice firm.

"Neither will I," Charisma added. Mr. Gardner had never been prone to violence and now that he wasn't drinking, he was much more amiable.

"Go then, girl." Mamie brushed off Missy's hand. "But know you'll always be welcome here."

"I know," Missy replied.

Charisma eased out the breath she'd been holding. *Thank goodness.* "We must go, Missy."

The older woman who'd claimed to be a cook joined them at the front doorway. "Naomi, too?" Mamie asked.

"Yes." Charisma ushered Missy and Naomi outside, forming a barrier between them and the madam. "Shouldn't she have a choice, too?"

Mamie sighed. "You'll see. They'll be back."

"No, they won't." Charisma would do everything in her power to ensure that. She gave Esther an encouraging smile, silently promising to return, then followed the other women.

The driver had waited as requested and, within moments, the little house and Cucharras Street had receded into the distance. Charisma eased a sigh. She'd succeeded. Thus far.

She quickly explained Mr. Gardner's situation to Missy and Naomi.

"Does he have a bad temper?" Missy asked.

"He might." Charisma had no way to tell if Mr. Gardner would manage to stay away from the bottle or how volatile his temper might be.

Missy nodded, staring into the distance, her lips pressed together. Though her outer bruises had faded, how much scarring lingered inside? Could she do this?

Charisma examined the women with a critical eye. They could not face Mr. Gardner as they were in their present apparel. Their dresses proclaimed the trappings of their former profession, revealing far more bosom than even Charisma's evening gowns. "We need new clothing for you."

When they reached the Springs, she directed the driver to stop near her home and paid him a handsome tip, glad she'd saved her spending money—though she'd never thought she would need it for something like this.

Now to smuggle the women inside her home.

Charisma's heart raced as she peeked inside the front doorway. *No one in sight. Good.* She motioned both women inside and directed them upstairs to her room. "Quiet."

Just before they reached the safety of her bedroom, Belle appeared in the hallway, her eyes going wide. "What—?"

"Sssh." Charisma grabbed her sister and pulled her into the bedroom as well, then closed the door as quietly as possible. Why did it have to be Belle?

"What are you doing now?" Belle demanded. "Who are these women?"

"Missy and Naomi. They're . . . friends of mine."

"Friends?" Belle eyed Missy and Naomi's clothing with a dubious eye. "What's going on? The truth now."

Charisma sighed. She'd never been able to hide anything from Belle. "I've found respectable work for them, but they need new clothes before I present them to Mr. Gardner."

"Mr. Gardner?" Belle's eyebrows shot up. "Start at the beginning, Charisma, and don't leave anything out."

In as few words as possible, Charisma related how she'd encountered Missy and the timeliness of Mr. Gardner's request. "I *have* to help," she finished. "And I believe I can in this instance."

Belle sank onto the bed, shaking her head. "I thought you were learning how to be charming."

"Charming has nothing to do with doing what's right." Charisma sat beside her sister. "Will you help me?"

"I'll help." Belle glanced at Missy and Naomi,

who had remained silent during Charisma's explanation. "What do you need?"

"Can you get one of Mama's day dresses? I think it will fit Naomi. And I'll get one of mine for Missy. Then we have to fix their hair."

"One of Mama's dresses?" Belle frowned. "What if she misses it?"

"Take an old one. She has so many, she'll never notice."

Belle left the room, muttering beneath her breath, leaving Charisma to focus on a dress for Missy. "I have just the thing."

In less than a half hour, she and Belle had both women dressed and their hair styled. "I don't believe it." Belle examined the women. "They look so different, so proper."

Charisma grinned. "That's because the inside was never a problem. Only the outside."

"I can't believe it's me," Missy murmured, touching her hair and gown with a tentative hand. She straightened her shoulders and her chin rose with confidence.

"This is how it should be," Naomi said. She nodded at her reflection. "Now, where do we go, Miss Charisma?"

Charisma had to admit the transformation made all the difference. Mr. Gardner would be pleased to hire them now.

Yet when they reached Mr. Gardner's door, she swallowed hard to remove the sudden lump in her throat. Would he employ both women? He had said he was desperate. Desperate enough to take two women without references?

Mr. Gardner answered the door himself and

smiled a warm welcome. "Miss Charisma, a pleasure." His gaze darted to Missy and Naomi. "Is this the help you mentioned?"

"Yes. May I present Miss Missy . . . Smith." Realizing she didn't know either woman's surname, Charisma quickly invented them. "And Miss Naomi Anderson. They have experience as a maid and as a cook, respectively."

"Do they? Excellent." Mr. Gardner led them inside, then paused in the hallway. "Do they have references?"

Missy paled and Charisma hurried to reply. "Their . . . ah . . . their previous employer died suddenly and so did not provide references. I will vouch for them, though."

Mr. Gardner hesitated, watching her, and Charisma held her breath. Would he believe her? Her sisters had told her often enough that she made a terrible liar.

Finally he nodded. "If you vouch for them, Miss Charisma, who am I to doubt you? Miss Smith, I would like you to become my housekeeper. I prefer a clean, orderly home, and to be left alone in the evenings."

Missy curtsied. "Yes, sir."

"And Miss Anderson, I am a man of simple tastes. Hot food and enough of it will satisfy me."

Naomi smiled. "I can do that, sir."

"Very well. Let me show you the servants' quarters on the third floor and you can start at once. I'm starving." He paused to bow to Charisma. "Thank you, Miss Charisma, for once again providing the answer to my problem."

"I'm certain you'll be satisfied with their performance," Charisma said, catching Missy's gaze. The new housekeeper returned a shaky smile.

"As am I." He held open the front door. "If you come across a good butler, I am in the market for one of those as well."

Charisma grinned. "I'll see what I can do."

She hurried toward home. If Mama knew she was roaming the streets unescorted again, she'd be polishing silver for a week. Still, she paused by Thalia's house, but the door remained unanswered, the interior dark in the gathering dusk. Perhaps she had gone out of town. Charisma couldn't expect the woman to be at her beck and call.

But she did so want to share her good news.

She had made a difference. If all went well, Missy would have a much better life than the one she had left. Naomi, too.

Now all Charisma had to do was figure out a way to tutor the remaining women in skills that could earn them a respectable profession. She knew all about cleaning, but her cooking knowledge was slim and her stitchery less than perfect.

Perhaps she could persuade Belle . . . No. Charisma discarded that idea at once. Though she'd convinced Belle to help today, her older sister would never agree to go into Colorado City, especially to a house of ill repute. Charisma would have to do the best she could on her own.

"Charisma."

She recognized Will's voice and glanced up to see him approaching, his long strides quickly covering the distance between them. In the fading sunlight, he looked tall, strong, and extremely handsome.

Her stomach knotted, though she presented a warm smile.

"What are you doing out alone?" he asked. "It will be dark soon."

"I'm on my way home." On this main street, she felt safe enough to walk the two blocks remaining to her home.

"Let me escort you."

"I would enjoy that." And this would please Mama very much.

They walked some time in silence while Charisma debated what to say. They were friends again, weren't they? So, why did she suddenly feel so tongue-tied?

"I spoke today, outside the courthouse." Will broke the silence first.

"Excellent. Did you do well?" Surely anyone who heard him speak, who listened to his platform, would be persuaded to vote for him.

He shrugged. "As well as could be expected." After a moment's hesitation, he continued. "I had hoped to see you there. I sent word to your house of where I would be."

"Did you?" And she had missed it. "I would have been there, but I had an obligation . . . to a friend."

"Of course. I cannot expect you to build your life around mine." He stopped to face her, a last single ray of sun adding a sheen to his dark hair. "However, I do have a request."

"Yes?" Charisma couldn't deny the sudden rush of excitement through her veins.

"The Democratic Convention is in Denver on Thursday. If Mrs. Papadopoulos and your parents agree, would you accompany me?"

"To the convention?" Charisma's voice squeaked.

To see the government actually in action? "I . . . I would love it." Impulsively, she threw her arms around his neck in an enthusiastic hug.

He eased her away from him, a flame flickering in his eyes. "We are in a public place, Charisma." Though his voice held a note of warning, he also sounded much huskier as well.

"I'm sorry." But she couldn't wipe the grin from her face. "But to go to the convention. To Denver. How wonderful!"

He grinned. "I will talk to your father and Mrs. Papadopoulos tomorrow then. If she is willing to accompany us and your father is willing to let you go, I will make the train reservations."

"Oh, they must agree. Will Mr. Chaffee be there? And Mr. Grant?" She could actually see the personages she'd read so much about in the *Daily Gazette*.

"Mr. Chaffee is a Republican so I very much doubt as he will make an appearance. But if Mr. Grant receives the nomination for governor as expected, he will be certain to put in an appearance."

"How exciting."

Will laughed. "You are amazing, Charisma. Most young women won't even admit to understanding politics, let alone profess an enthusiasm for them."

"Is that a bad thing?" Her smile faded. "I cannot change who I am."

"Nor should you." Darkness hid his expression as he touched her cheek, his thumb brushing her lips. Charisma's breath caught in her chest, her heart racing. "Your enthusiasm revitalizes my own."

"I . . . I'm glad." She had to force the words from her dry throat.

"So am I." He moved his thumb once more over

her lips, then dropped his hand and offered his arm. "Come, we must get you home."

Though disappointed, Charisma nodded. At least she had something to look forward to. *A trip to Denver. With Will. To visit the convention.*

It promised to be a day she would never forget.

"I fear you're making a mistake, Thalia." Euphrosyne rose gracefully from her chair to face her sister.

"I agree," Aglaia added, her beauty momentarily marred by her frown. "Why did you let Charisma venture into Colorado City alone?"

Euphrosyne nodded, her expression unusually serious. "You are most fortunate that no harm came to her."

Thalia only smiled and continued to watch the entertaining dance of the muses. Once they finished, she clapped with enthusiasm.

"Did you hear us?" Aglaia asked.

"I heard you." Thalia paused. "Charisma wants to make a difference. She must be allowed to do so."

"Not if it puts her in danger." Euphrosyne took a seat beside Thalia. "We agreed never to do that."

"She is not in danger. Not yet."

"Then you must ensure she never goes alone again," Euphrosyne said.

"It will all work out for the best." Thalia gave her warmest smile. "You must trust that I know what I am doing."

"You are dealing with mortals, my dear sister," Aglaia added. "They are most unpredictable."

"True. Very true. And I will do my best to keep

Charisma safe, but some things must be allowed to unfold." She stood. "How else can she discover the answer to her true wish?"

Both of her sisters scowled at her, but Thalia ignored them. "Come, Heracles," she called to her half brother. "It is time for us to return." Her eyes sparkled. "I am most interested in this upcoming trip to Denver."

Eight

"You're going to hurt your neck if you keep doing that."

Charisma grinned at Will's remark as they walked through downtown Denver. "There's just so much to see. I've never been here before."

Colorado's capital city bustled with life and a very different energy than that of Colorado Springs. Charisma had never felt so alive. She examined the new buildings, the paved roads and passersby with enthusiasm, noting that a majority of the crowd was heading in the same direction. The auditorium where the Democratic Convention would take place was crowded when Will, Thalia, and Charisma arrived.

"Here." Will managed to locate empty seats and guided them there, his hand on Charisma's elbow. Charisma's excitement, already built to a new height, surged a little more as she settled into a chair. She beamed at Thalia as the woman sat beside her.

"Isn't this exciting?" she asked.

"I find it very interesting," Thalia replied, with a smile and considerably less enthusiasm than Charisma.

Charisma had to squint to make out the features

of the man at the podium, but when he spoke, calling the meeting to order, she had no difficulty in hearing his booming voice. She listened to every word, still unable to believe she was actually here in Denver . . . at the convention . . . with Will by her side . . .

She glanced at him from the corner of her eye. He was focused on the speaker, jotting notes on a small tablet. Pride swelled in Charisma. He would be an outstanding senator. How could anyone doubt that he cared about the people he wanted to represent? With a smile, she returned her attention to the discussion of the platform.

When the talk turned to the subject of restoring the silver dollar as the primary currency, she had to bite her tongue to keep from jumping into the conversation. Her father's fortune had come from silver. Keeping its value was important.

To her relief, the delegates were in agreement and the restoration of the silver standard was added to the platform. Will would have her father's vote, for sure, and the other silver miners' votes as well.

When they broke for lunch, the entire crowd was rejuvenated and the talk enthusiastic. Charisma smiled at Will as he led her and Thalia outside.

"They have some outstanding ideas," Charisma said.

Will nodded. "I imagine even many Republicans would support our platform. I particularly like the part about reserving homesteads for actual settlers. Too often the land isn't there for the people for whom it was intended."

"Exactly," Thalia said. "These promises should help garner you votes."

"I hope so." Will pointed to a building partway down the block. "There is a good place to eat just ahead. Shall we?"

"That's fine," Thalia said while Charisma nodded, not caring about where she ate so much as what was to come next.

"When will they declare Mr. Grant as the candidate for governor?" Charisma longed to see the man she'd read so much about.

Will grinned. "Shortly after we resume."

"Will we see him?"

"I would assume he'll have to make a speech." Will paused to touch her chin with his finger. "You will see him."

Charisma's smile broadened. "Good."

They were shown to a table at once, barely managing to beat the crowd in their wake. Charisma found it difficult to remain still, the energy of the convention coursing through her veins. What an incredible day.

"I can't thank you enough for asking me to come," she said.

"Believe me when I say the pleasure is mine." Good humor danced in Will's eyes. "I have never found a convention as stimulating as I have today."

"I agree," Thalia said. "You bring a natural enthusiasm with you, my dear."

"There is history being made here. It *is* exciting." Charisma extended her arms, almost smacking a passing waitress in the process. "Oh, dear. I'm sorry." If she wasn't careful, she'd be as dangerous as Grace.

The waitress gave her a tight smile and kept walking while Will chuckled and directed Charisma's attention to the menu. "Perhaps you should make your choice. If we return early, we can obtain better seats."

Charisma turned her attention to the menu, then looked at Will with a smile, but her smile faded as she spotted his brother approaching.

"What is it?" Will asked. Following her gaze, he glanced over his shoulder, then grimaced. "Stephen."

"I thought I'd find you here." Stephen settled into an empty chair without waiting for an invitation. "Miss Charisma, we meet again."

She nodded in his direction. "Mr. Barclay." Though her traveling suit covered her chin to toe, his gaze lingered on her in such a way that she felt undressed. She shifted uneasily and focused on Will instead. Even when he looked at her with heat in his gaze, he never made her feel unclean—only special.

Will performed the only remaining introduction. "Mrs. Papadopoulos, my brother, Stephen Barclay."

She extended her hand. "It is a pleasure to make your acquaintance, sir."

Stephen touched his lips to her glove. "The pleasure is all mine."

"And how am I so honored with your presence?" Will's voice held a note of sarcasm that brought a twitch to Charisma's lips. Apparently he held no fondness for his brother either. "I cannot imagine you're interested in the Democratic proceedings."

"Why not?" Stephen displayed a cocksure grin. "Shouldn't I be familiar with the enemy?"

"Of course."

"However, I do have another reason for finding you."

Charisma wasn't surprised and judging from Will's expression, neither was he. "Yes?"

"Mother and Father request your attendance at supper tonight." Stephen glanced at Charisma and Thalia. "Your lady friends are welcome as well."

The tone of his last statement had Charisma pressing her lips together to keep her angry retort in check. Glancing at Thalia, she found the woman giving her a reassuring smile.

"I'm afraid we intend to catch the night train back to Colorado Springs," Will said.

"There's an even later train." Stephen dismissed Will's excuse with a wave of his hand. "You can't deny Mother a chance to see you. It's been months."

Will grimaced, then nodded. "Very well. I would like to see Mother. We will join them after the convention."

"Good." Stephen stood and bowed. "Ladies, I look forward to seeing you later." His gaze flickered to his brother. "William."

Will only nodded, his expression tight. What was he thinking? Charisma wondered. Was the thought of a meal with his family that unpleasant?

Somehow, Charisma managed to bite back her words. Will didn't owe her any information about his family, no matter how strong her curiosity. In any case, if they went to dinner tonight, she would see for herself. For now, she would concentrate on making the rest of the lunch more cheerful.

The afternoon session of the convention flew by for Charisma. As Will had promised, James B. Grant was put forth as the Democratic candidate for governor and easily approved by the elected delegates. Mr. Grant himself appeared to make an acceptance speech that left Charisma in a state of euphoria. If only she could vote . . .

Afterward, the crowd outside was enthusiastic, with the delegates believing their candidate had an excellent chance of winning the governor's position. Charisma bubbled with excitement, until she caught a glimpse of Will's face. He rarely looked so torn.

She touched his arm. "What's wrong?"

"I should not have accepted my parents' invitation to supper. I know better than to let Stephen do that to me. Now I'll have to meet with Father again."

Father? He'd only mentioned his mother earlier. Of course, if his father was like his brother, she understood his reluctance somewhat better. Though she had nothing to base it on, Stephen Barclay made her uneasy.

"Don't you want to visit your parents?"

"I'd like to see my mother again." Will gave Charisma a dry smile. "In any case, I did agree. Come, we can catch a street car to their home."

The horse-drawn street car gave Charisma the freedom and time to gape at the bustling crowds, the modern buildings, the tree-lined magnificence of Broadway, and the rippling water of Cherry Creek. Before she was ready, Will was leading her and Thalia onto the street.

He walked only a short distance, then paused before a huge Italianate-style home. Charisma bit back her gasp. She had thought many of the houses along Cascade and Nevada Streets in Colorado Springs were impressive, but this structure reminded her of a castle.

"Is this your home?" she asked, unable to keep the awe from her voice.

Will grimaced. "My parents' home." He hesitated, his hand resting on the iron fence surrounding the estate. "Would you be upset if we did not attend this dinner?"

Charisma swallowed her eagerness to see the interior and left the question for Thalia to answer. The older woman would be much better with the finesse required than Charisma.

"We are willing to do whatever you prefer," Thalia answered.

Charisma shifted her weight from one foot to the other. What would Will make of that answer?

"That's not much help." Will sighed. "But I am anxious to see my mother. Besides—" He grinned and tugged a stray lock of Charisma's hair. "Charisma is about ready to burst."

"I am curious," she admitted. "This place is magnificent."

"It is one of the finest structures in Denver, as my father will be happy to tell you." Will opened the gate and motioned the women forward. "This way, please."

His knock at the heavy wooden door was answered by a starchly polished butler, whose expression appeared frozen into permanent sourness. "Good evening, Master William." The butler stood aside and held open the door. "Your parents are waiting for you in the drawing room."

"Thank you, Henry." Will touched Charisma's elbow and moved toward a closed set of mahogany double pocket doors inset with oval beveled glass. Thalia walked beside them. He hesitated only a moment, then flung open the doors and stepped inside, leaving Charisma and Thalia outside. "The prodigal son returns," he announced.

A middle-aged woman stopped in mid-sentence, her open mouth transforming into a brilliant smile. Despite the gray streaking her dark hair, her expression contained youthful exuberance as she crossed the room and threw her arms around Will's neck. "William. It's about time."

"It's good to see you, too, Mother." Will enveloped her in a warm hug, bringing a glow to his mother's face that made Charisma long for an equal embrace.

Heat warmed her cheeks at the thought, and Charisma glanced away to find a man seated across the room staring at her. She had no doubt he was Will's father—the nearly black hair and dark eyes were the same, though Charisma saw more facial resemblance to his mother.

Will finally drew back and waved Charisma and Thalia forward. "Mother, please allow me to present Mrs. Papadopoulos and Miss Charisma Sullivan. Ladies, this is my mother, Mrs. Barclay, and my father, Mr. Barclay."

As he spoke, he extended his hand to the stern-faced man. "Father."

"William." For a moment Charisma thought the elder Barclay would refuse to accept Will's hand, but he finally exchanged a quick, solid handshake. Mr. Barclay's dark gaze then centered on Charisma. "Ladies."

"Mrs. Barclay. Mr. Barclay." Thalia gave a warm, encompassing smile. "I cannot tell you how honored Miss Charisma and I are to be included in this generous invitation. I do hope you didn't go to any extra trouble on our behalf."

Mrs. Barclay returned the smile. "It is no trouble at all. Please, come in. Be seated. I imagine Stephen and Abigail will be here soon."

"Stephen is coming?" Will didn't sound pleased.

"I insisted," Mr. Barclay said. "After all, we have a lot to discuss now that you've seen fit to grace us with your presence."

From the way Will pressed his lips together, Charisma doubted he wanted a part in those discussions. In fact, the animosity in the room was clearly evident. Even ever cheerful, good-hearted Grace would have noticed it.

"You have a lovely home," Charisma said, intent on changing the subject.

"Thank you." Mrs. Barclay brightened. "Would you like to look around?"

"I'd love to." Charisma planned to take many mental notes so that she could describe this incredible place accurately to her sisters. She eagerly followed Mrs. Barclay out of the room, Thalia joining them.

Before Will could take a step toward them, his father spoke. "Stay, William."

Charisma glanced back to catch Will's grimace. She sent him a smile of encouragement, but he merely nodded and turned back to face his father.

Will dreaded the moment the ladies were out of earshot. He already knew agreeing to come to supper was a mistake. He didn't need to hear his father's next words to know that his opinion hadn't changed since their last exchange nearly a year ago. Unfortunately, that wasn't going to stop his father from expressing it.

"I hope your presence here means you've changed your mind."

"It doesn't." Will met his father's unflinching glare with one of his own.

His father stood, something he didn't usually do around Will, since Will was more than two inches taller. "Your quest is foolish and a waste of time. You should be giving all your support to your brother's campaign instead of trying to win a Democratic seat in a Republican county. It's heresy. You were raised a Republican."

Resisting the urge to roll his eyes, Will responded with the same words he'd used many times before. "I don't think Stephen is the best candidate for the senate."

"And you're better?"

"Better than Stephen." Will had no doubt of that. What he lacked in political knowledge, he made up for in ethics. That had to count for something.

"You're not trained for political office. You don't have the contacts, the knowledge." Father shook his head. "You're making a fool of yourself and reflecting badly on the family name."

"I'm learning every day and making numerous contacts. I've even met with General Palmer."

That made Father pause for a moment. "And is he supporting you?"

Will wanted to lie, but refused to do so. "Not yet. But he has been very amiable."

"Amiable doesn't bring in votes." The older man paced the floor and Will's heart sank as he recognized the signs. Father's anger was nearing the breaking point. "All you're doing is damaging your brother's campaign. Folks may mistakenly read your ridiculous platform as his. You could cost him votes."

"Good." That was the point. Will didn't care so much that he won so long as his brother didn't. Well, that wasn't entirely true either. He was beginning to care about having the opportunity to make good on his campaign promises.

His father whirled around, his eyes blazing. "Your brother has never done anything to you to deserve such disrespect."

"Not to me," Will said flatly.

"So you care more about that . . . that girl than your own family."

"What he did was wrong. What *you* did was wrong. You know it as well as I." Will clenched his fists, his anger as easily riled now as when he'd first learned of what his brother had done.

"What I know is that you are nothing but a bleeding heart. You have no right to join the senate."

Will kept his expression neutral. His father's words were actually losing their sting. Of course, it helped that Will had people who did believe in him . . . like Charisma. Her unwavering faith meant more than any insults his father could throw.

"That's your opinion," Will said.

"I—"

"Am I interrupting?"

Will and his father turned as Stephen and Abigail appeared in the doorway. A smirk played around Stephen's lips but his expression exuded concern.

"Not at all." Will managed a tight smile. "Come in."

With luck, the addition of his sister-in-law should keep his father's tirade to a minimum. At least for now. Will had no illusions that he'd escape without hearing this same rhetoric again before the evening was over.

Stephen had no sooner seated his wife than Will heard his mother, Charisma, and Mrs. Papadopoulos approaching. Thank goodness. He'd survived the appetizer. Would he make it until dessert?

Charisma cast a concerned glance at Will as the women retired to the parlor, leaving the men to their after-dinner cigars in the library. He'd been quiet throughout the excellent meal, despite being the recipient of several pointed barbs from his father.

After tonight, Charisma doubted she needed any more lessons from Thalia. Several times she'd bitten her tongue to keep from blurting out the unkind thoughts in her mind. Now she understood why Will had not wanted to visit his home. If anything, the earlier tension had only grown worse.

Why was his father so angry with him? He showed obvious favoritism toward his elder son, yet Will was the better candidate. Couldn't Mr. Barclay see that?

Will cared about people. All people. After just a few hours in Stephen Barclay's company, Charisma already knew he favored the elitist position held by so many already serving in the senate. But who would stand up for the less fortunate? The miners? The servants? The working women? Will Barclay was the man she wanted to see in the senate.

"Would you care to walk with me in the gardens? They're quite lovely."

Charisma looked around as Abigail approached her. "That would be nice. Thank you." The woman had been even quieter than Will during the meal. Perhaps now Charisma would have a chance to get to know her.

As they emerged into the neatly trimmed gardens, fallen leaves crackled beneath their feet, the several trees in the yard a luxury in this growing prairie town. Still, Charisma enjoyed the crisp scent of approaching autumn. She inhaled deeply, clearing away her unease from dinner.

"Thank you for the invitation," Charisma said. "It's good to get outside."

"Yes. It can be tense during family gatherings." She smiled. "I do hope you will call me Abigail. I feel already that we will become good friends."

Charisma blinked. Evidently, this woman was much more personable than she'd displayed during the meal. "I would consider it an honor."

"Well, we will be related once you and William marry."

"Marry?" This was news to Charisma and her heart added an extra beat. "What makes you say that?" Did Will's family know something she didn't?

"Why the ease you and William have with each other, of course."

Charisma shook her head. "We're not getting married."

Abigail frowned. "But I thought . . . since William brought you here . . . I do beg your pardon."

"We are good friends," Charisma admitted, attempting to banish the lurking memory of that single overwhelming kiss that made her long for more. "But our arrangement is purely business-related. I have been introducing him to many of the influential leaders in Colorado Springs."

"I see." They walked in silence for some distance before Abigail spoke again. "But you do have influence over William."

"I wouldn't say that." As far as she knew, nothing she'd said had affected his outlook.

"I know this will sound strange, but would you be willing to speak to him for me?"

Speak to him? *What could Abigail want to ask Will that she can't ask herself?* Charisma held her tongue and smiled instead. "May I ask about what?"

Abigail stopped to face Charisma. "You must ask William to drop out of the senatorial race."

"I beg your pardon?" Surely she hadn't heard correctly.

"Stephen is the one who's been trained to take his father's place, not William."

Charisma's initial warmth for this woman faded quickly. "Perhaps they will both win."

Abigail shook her head. "His campaign is hurting Stephen's chances. Please, ask him to stop."

"I can't do that." *Ask Will to withdraw? Never.* "I *won't* do that. Will is an excellent candidate."

"You don't understand. He's only doing this as an act of revenge on his brother."

Revenge? That didn't sound like the man she knew. "I find that difficult to believe."

"Of course he'll deny it, but it's true. He's admitted as much to Stephen." Abigail dabbed her eyes with a scented handkerchief. "He wants to ruin Stephen."

Charisma hesitated. True, there was no love between the brothers, but Will was honorable. "I imagine Will just has opposite opinions from

Stephen, which makes him appear negative." Thalia should give her a commendation for that polite reply.

"Negative opinions? Have you heard his platform?" Abigail paced away, then back. "It's ridiculous. He wants to offer representation for servants, clerks, miners, and other riffraff." She wrung her hands. "It cannot be endured. He is making a laughingstock out of the Barclay name."

The initial cold chill along Charisma's back flared into passionate heat. She opened her mouth to respond, then stopped. She tried again and once more bit back the words. Finally, she gave up. There was no other way to respond to this.

"I am in complete support of Will's platform." Her voice was cold. "I find him more open-minded and accepting of others than most born to privilege."

Abigail's eyes widened. "You can't be serious. Surely you can see what this will do to people like us."

"Like you, perhaps." Charisma clenched the edge of her skirts. "There is something *you* don't understand, *Mrs. Barclay*. While my father is now very wealthy, not too long ago he was a miner himself. I spent most of my childhood in the mining camps of Leadville. I am proud to be a miner's daughter and proud of the men brave enough to do such dangerous work."

While Abigail gaped at her, Charisma continued, no longer caring what she said. "Having met your husband, I sincerely hope Will does win this competition, for he is by far the best candidate for the job. Now, if you will excuse me."

Not waiting for an answer, Charisma spun on her heel and stalked inside. Will was still imprisoned in the library with his father and brother. She knocked on the door. It was time they all escaped this place.

Mr. Barclay answered her knock and pinned her with his dark gaze. "May I help you?"

"I would like to leave now if Will can be spared." Charisma pulled the about-to-swoon routine she'd seen several other young women do, placing her hand against her forehead. "I'm not feeling well, I'm afraid."

Will's initial look of relief changed to concern as he crossed over to her. "We'll leave right away." He glanced back at Stephen and Mr. Barclay. "You may continue your conversation without me. You were doing fine on your own."

His father glared at him, but Will took Charisma's elbow and led her away. "Do you need to lie down?" he asked with sincere gentleness.

"No." She managed a wan smile. "I need to leave here." Blunt, perhaps, but true.

His answering smile was dry. "I concur completely. Let me get Mrs. Papadopoulos and we will be on our way."

As they prepared to leave, Charisma noticed Abigail speaking to Stephen at the rear of the room, no doubt telling him of Charisma's response. She would probably not be welcome in this house any longer.

Of course, right now, that didn't seem to be a bad thing.

Will watched Charisma closely as the train steamed toward Colorado Springs. Mrs. Papadopoulos had allowed Charisma to sit beside him while the older woman sat on the seat opposite, her gaze as concerned as his.

Though Charisma's flushed cheeks had faded, she'd been much quieter than usual since they'd left his parents' home. "Are you certain you're all right?"

"I'm fine." She touched his arm. "I just had to get out of there. I'm sorry for making you feel as if you had to go to that dinner."

His chest tightened. Though he felt as if he'd been beaten to a pulp by Stephen and his father's verbal attacks, none of it could be blamed on Charisma. Yet something had happened to her. "I made the decision to go." He touched her cheek, turning her gaze toward his, uncaring that Mrs. Papadopoulos sat across from them. "What's wrong?"

If his brother or father had said anything to her . . .

Charisma hesitated and he brushed his thumb over her smooth skin. "Tell me." He had to know.

"Your sister-in-law," she said with a grimace.

That surprised him. "Abigail?" True, she came from a wealthy family and had far more ambition than brains, but she'd always stayed in the background when around his family. Of course, neither Stephen nor Father placed any value in a woman's opinion, so why should she speak? "What is it?"

"She wanted me to ask you to drop out of the race." Charisma's eyes flashed. "I'm afraid I was rude when I answered. I told her I would never do that. You are by far the better choice."

Will felt as if the wind had been knocked out of him. Her adamant support almost unmanned him.

A surge of wild emotion followed, filled with the longing to pull her into his arms and kiss her senseless. For a moment, he tightened the hand on her cheek, but wisdom prevailed and he dropped his hand completely.

The train was sparsely populated at this late hour, but Mrs. Papadopoulos remained quite wide awake and far too near. He swallowed and finally managed to squeeze words from his throat. "I do not deserve such blind devotion."

"I'm not blind. I've listened to you and I agree with you." She met his gaze. "Even more, you care about these people you want to represent and that means everything to me. Even if you don't win, they'll at least know someone cared."

Damn if she didn't make his gut clench now. "I will win." He had to. To do otherwise was to let Charisma, and others, down.

Her smile warmed him. "I know you will." Turning away, she stifled a yawn. "I'm afraid my long day is catching up with me."

"Close your eyes and rest." Will needed time to think. "I won't let you miss our stop."

With only a little more encouragement, she complied, leaning her head back against the bench seat and closing her eyes. Will glanced across the aisle. Mrs. Papadopoulos appeared to be resting as well. At least, her eyes were closed.

Certain he was unobserved, Will took advantage of the moment to study Charisma. His gaze began at her riotous strawberry-blonde hair, which was starting to escape the pins that held it up. What would she look like with her hair down? What would it feel like if he could run his fingers through that hair? Kiss her?

He clenched his hands, his gaze dropping to her slightly parted lips. They begged to be tasted, devoured, cherished.

Recalling the sweetness of their all-too-brief kiss, he almost groaned. Heat flooded his veins and he shifted uncomfortably as he hardened with awareness.

But he couldn't look away from her. Instead, he eyed her gently rising chest, the curve of her bosom outlined by her travel suit. Her breast appeared just large enough to fill a man's hand. His hand.

The ache of desire hit him like a blow to the chest and he jerked his gaze away, turning his face to the window that revealed nothing but blackness outside. What was he thinking? To consider Charisma as anything other than a friend was begging for complications he didn't need. This campaign was everything. He didn't dare jeopardize it with such wayward thoughts.

Charisma was lovely, intelligent, and wealthy. She would make some man a wonderful wife. Just not him. A politician could not afford a wife who tended to blurt out her thoughts at inappropriate times.

Yet he could not imagine her with another man. Who would appreciate her intelligence, her sense of justice? Who would give her the respect she deserved? Who would see her for the unique woman she was instead of someone to bear sons and run a household?

Will grimaced as a physical pang stabbed his

chest. There had to be someone. The thought of anyone treating Charisma in the manner Stephen treated his wife—as a possession to be put on view at parties or to satisfy his urges, but never as a friend—added to the knot in Will's gut.

Feeling a weight on his shoulder, he turned to see Charisma had slid toward him in her sleep, her head resting against him. He glanced across to the facing bench seat to see that Mrs. Papadopoulos had succumbed to the rhythmic click-clack of the wheels as well, her head lolled to the side.

With new boldness, he caressed Charisma's cheek, then turned his attention to her soft, captivating hair. This brief touch only made him want more. He eyed her lips, aching to possess them. Did he dare?

With infinite care, he brushed his mouth over hers. A brief taste, a sampling, nothing more.

And not nearly enough.

He groaned low in his throat and kissed her again, reveling in the sweetness, the softness, the rightness of his action. More. He needed still more.

But Charisma shifted, a sigh escaping her, and he jerked back. What *was* he doing? Her eyes fluttered open but she remained on his shoulder for another minute before awareness dawned.

She sat upright with a gasp. "I . . . I'm sorry. I didn't . . ."

"I don't mind." He didn't mind at all. In fact, he missed her warmth and the gentle weight against his shoulder.

Blinking, she glanced around the car. "Are we home?"

Will firmly believed in fate when the conductor

chose that moment to enter. "Colorado Springs next stop."

"Almost." He smiled at Charisma, resisting the urge to touch her again. He had the sinking feeling that if he did, he would never let her go.

And he couldn't allow that to happen.

Nine

Charisma clutched the *Daily Gazette* in her hand as she hustled her sister to where Will was speaking today. Today, she'd find out where he stood on a woman's right to vote. He couldn't ignore her hints any longer. "Come on, Grace."

"Wait for me." Grace slowed to a stop and clutched Charisma's hand. "You know it's unladylike to run."

"I wasn't running." She was . . . hurrying. She hadn't seen Will since they'd returned from Denver, but she understood that he was busy campaigning throughout El Paso County. With only a month left until the election, every day counted.

If she hadn't read this small article in today's newspaper, she might have been content to leave Will alone while he campaigned, but this gave her a chance to finally get an answer from him.

Since she had met him, she'd been trying to discover where he stood on women's rights and he continually avoided giving her a direct answer. Well, he couldn't avoid the topic any longer. Surely a man of honor who championed rights for the less fortunate would also support equal rights for women. Weren't they among the less fortunate as well? Didn't they deserve to vote, to be treated as if their thoughts had merit?

Charisma sighed and began walking at a more stately pace, Grace by her side. Besides that, she missed him. Was he regretting that she'd met his family? Perhaps he was afraid they would all make the same assumption as Abigail—that he and Charisma were soon to be married.

When, of course, nothing could be further from the truth.

She spotted Will on a distant street corner and quickened her steps, nearly dragging Grace with her. He stood on two stacked crates with a small gathering of men around him. Everyone appeared to be listening intently. *Good.*

The crowd parted as she approached, creating a path to the front. *How thoughtful.* Charisma watched them eyeing Grace and smothered a smile. Or maybe they were being cautious around her clumsy sister.

Charisma beamed a warm smile at Will and felt the warmth spread through her veins when he returned it.

"Good morning, Miss Charisma." Will glanced beyond her. "Miss Grace. A pleasure to see you."

"Thank you." Charisma raised the newspaper she'd brought with her. "I have a question for you, Mr. Barclay. One I would particularly like answered."

Humor sparkled in his dark brown eyes. "Yes?"

"There's an article in today's paper about Aida Avery, a woman from Colorado. She was elected vice president of the National Women's Suffragette Association last week in Omaha, a clear sign that this movement is taking root across the country. Where do you stand on women's rights, Mr. Barclay?"

Will's good humor fled, his eyes darkening and

the line of his mouth tightening. "An interesting question."

"One that means a lot to me." Charisma shivered but didn't look away. At this moment, he much resembled his father.

Instead of answering her, Will addressed the crowd. "What do you think, gentlemen? Should women be allowed to vote?"

"Vote?" One man exploded with laughter. "Ha. My Millie can barely remember where she left her apron."

"A woman don't need to vote," another exclaimed. "They got us to do that for them."

Charisma whirled around, trying to see who had spoken. "But what if a woman would rather make up her own mind?"

"Women don't know their own minds." A miner shook his head. "Cain't hardly decide which geegaw to buy at the mercantile, let alone which man should be running our government."

So typical. "Women can make intelligent decisions," Charisma snapped.

"Ain't seen no evidence of that, miss."

Clenching her fists, Charisma turned back to face Will. "And that's your opinion, too?"

"Let's say it's an opinion I've heard more than once," he said slowly, his eyes blazing.

She'd heard enough. All this time she'd harbored the hope that Will was someone special, that he honestly cared about women having equal rights. She should have known better.

She spun around, startling Grace, who jumped backward, toppling one of the men. The man, in turn, crashed into the crates. They tumbled in a heap, tossing Will to the street.

"Oh, I'm sorry," Grace cried.

Charisma only hesitated a moment to ensure Will wasn't seriously hurt, then seized her sister's hand and fled.

"Have to be careful 'round them Sullivan girls," a man said, a chuckle in his voice.

"You don't have to tell me," Will answered.

Tears stung Charisma's eyes, but she blinked them away, letting anger overrule the sting of his words. Obviously, he didn't need her help any longer. She should have expected as much.

But she'd thought they were friends. And there was that kiss. A kiss that evidently meant far more to her than him.

Once they'd returned home, Charisma rushed up to her room, leaving Grace to make explanations to Belle. Charisma didn't want to talk to anyone. Not even her sisters.

She had hoped that Will . . . She flung herself across her bed. Foolish now that she thought of it. Why would any man want to give women the right to vote? It would be the first step toward equality, and they much preferred their women in the kitchen, the nursery, and the bedroom.

As much as Charisma hated to admit it, the madam at Missy's house of ill repute had been right. But that didn't mean Charisma was going to give up.

Mrs. Woodhull believed the sexes were equal. Susan B. Anthony and Elizabeth Cady Stanton were still fighting for women's right to vote. Charisma wasn't going to quit trying to make a difference just because Mr. William Barclay wasn't the man she'd thought he was.

"Charisma?" Belle peeked around the door.

"I don't want to talk," Charisma said, not bothering to look around.

"Mr. Barclay is downstairs. He wants to speak to you."

Charisma's pulse jumped. Will was here. He must have come straight from the street corner.

She rolled over, sat up, then stopped. Why should she run to listen to him? He'd given her his answer. Nothing he could say now could change what he'd already done.

"Tell him I'm indisposed," she said, finally.

Belle frowned. "Are you certain?"

"Very certain."

Her older sister sighed, then pulled the door closed behind her, as Charisma fought the urge to follow. What if Will did have a reasonable explanation for his behavior?

Yet what excuse could he have? He'd humiliated her and as much as admitted he agreed with the men who'd spoken. How could he explain that away?

He couldn't.

Yet when the door creaked several minutes later, Charisma allowed a surge of hope that Will had defied all convention and come to talk to her. When Belle stepped inside, her hope died. Of course, he wouldn't dare defy society's rules. He was too concerned with his image.

"Is he gone?" Charisma asked.

"He didn't believe you were indisposed, but he

left." Belle extended a folded piece of paper. "He asked me to give you this."

Charisma fought against her eagerness to take it. Instead, she turned away from Belle's outstretched hand. "I don't want it."

"Don't be silly." Belle waved the paper under Charisma's nose. "You know you're dying to read it."

Charisma refused to answer. She did want to read it, but she was afraid that she'd discover Will did have an excellent explanation for his treatment of her.

"If you won't read it, I will." Belle started to unfold the paper, spurring Charisma into action.

She snatched the paper, crumpling it in her fist. "It's mine. If anyone is going to read it, it'll be me."

Her sister sighed. "Then read it. Would it help if I said Mr. Barclay looked upset when he left?"

"Angry, no doubt. You didn't see how he treated me. Or hear what he said."

"Grace told me." Belle sat beside Charisma on the bed. "You like him, don't you?"

"I did." Now she wasn't so sure.

"No, I mean *really* like him." Belle wrapped one arm around Charisma's shoulders and squeezed.

Was she that obvious? Was that why Will no longer wanted anything to do with her? "I . . . we're friends. At least, I thought we were."

"I understand. I really do." For once, Belle sounded sympathetic rather than dictatorial. "I was confused, too, when I realized I was falling in love with Kit."

Charisma jerked her head up. "I'm not falling in love." Especially not with Will. She had far more important things to do.

Belle smiled. "Of course not. What could anyone love about Will Barclay? I mean, he is handsome . . . and charming . . . and well mannered."

"And intelligent and honorable and open to new ideas." Charisma couldn't stop her response, then twisted her lips in a wry grin. Leave it to Belle to wring an answer from her. "But that doesn't matter. I refuse to be treated as if my opinion has no importance."

"And so you should." Belle stood. "Just read the letter, dear. Maybe it will help." She slipped out of the room before Charisma could respond.

Maybe it would help. Maybe it wouldn't.

With trembling fingers, Charisma opened the missive and smoothed out the wrinkles.

Dear Charisma,

I wish to apologize for my response to your question this morning. However, I dare not address this subject during this election. There are too many opposing opinions which would cost me significant votes.

I will be busy visiting the populace for the remaining weeks until the election. While I appreciate your assistance in introducing me to the fine citizens of your city, I must ask that you refrain from visiting me any longer when I'm speaking.

Respectfully yours,
Will

Charisma stared at the note, reading it again. An unreleased sob caught in her throat. He'd made his position clear. *Fine.* She would leave him to his campaigning. He didn't need her. Well, she didn't need him either.

She'd been doing quite well with her tutoring of the women in Colorado City. She was making a difference all on her own.

Crumpling the letter, she tossed it across the room, then lifted her chin high. Who needed Mr. William Barclay?

Charisma stood on the front stoop of Mr. Gardner's home chatting with Missy. The young woman had blossomed in the past few weeks—her figure was fuller, eyes brighter, and smile genuine.

"I am very happy here," Missy said in response to Charisma's question. "I can't thank you enough for all you've done."

"And Mr. Gardner?" The few times Charisma had seen him, he appeared much improved as well. His demeanor was certainly much more amiable than in past months.

"He's a fine man to work for. Very fair." Missy grinned. "He treats me with such respect . . . like I was a lady instead of a servant."

"And why shouldn't he?" Charisma asked. "You're a lady as well as a servant. Mr. Gardner has always been an honorable man. I'm pleased to hear he remains so."

"Naomi is happy as well. Mr. Gardner regularly praises her cooking." Missy laughed. "She sings when she works now."

"Wonderful." Charisma hesitated. "Do you think Mr. Gardner has room for another maid? Emily has progressed so quickly she's ready to find a position."

"There's nothing available here. But the Williamses down the street are looking for a maid. Should I speak with their housekeeper?"

"Would you?" If Charisma could find a position for Emily, she'd only have four more women to worry about. "I'm going out there this afternoon and I'll speak to Emily about it."

Missy's smile faded. "You are being careful, aren't you? I don't like you going there."

"I leave before dark, before Mamie even wakes up. It's fine."

Missy's expression didn't change until she glanced past Charisma. At once, her face brightened.

"Good afternoon, Miss Charisma, Missy." Mr. Gardner climbed the steps two at a time and tossed his coat over the railing as he prepared to enter the house.

Missy cleared her throat. "Now, sir, haven't we discussed the coat on the railing?" The hint of discipline in her voice had Charisma blinking in surprise.

However, Mr. Gardner only grinned, a twinkle in his eye, and snatched up the coat. He then turned and deposited it in Missy's arms. "Better?"

Her answering smile was warm. "Thank you, sir."

"What's Naomi fixed for lunch? I am famished."

"You'll smell it as soon as you enter."

Mr. Gardner stepped inside and sniffed. "Ah, wonderful. Irish stew." He hurried toward the kitchen and Missy laughed.

"You're all in much better humor," Charisma said, amazed at the easy-going camaraderie between Missy and her employer.

"All he needed was someone to care about him." She stepped toward the hallway. "I must go now."

"Of course." Charisma waved her farewell and hurried down the street for the livery stable.

She'd made arrangements with the older gentleman who'd first taken her out to Colorado City to drive her each time she visited. Mr. Dunham always waited at the Blue House or showed up promptly by four to drive her home. Once she'd explained to him what she was doing, he'd become a very helpful assistant—almost as eager as Charisma to see some good come from these visits.

But she saw no sign of him today. A middle-aged man approached her, his gaze flicking to her dress, no doubt measuring the quality. "Kin I help you, Miss?"

"I'm looking for Mr. Dunham. We have an arrangement for him to transport me as necessary."

"Dunham's sick."

"Oh, dear." Charisma had promised to be there today. While the women would probably understand if she didn't arrive, she also wanted to give Emily the news of a possible position.

"I kin take ya, Miss."

Charisma hesitated. This man wasn't as grandfatherly as Mr. Dunham, but he was probably reliable. "I need to go to Colorado City for a few hours. I would need you to come back to pick me up at four o'clock. Is that agreeable?"

"Sounds good to me." The man turned away. "Let me get my rig."

This man, Mr. Albert, wasn't as much a conversationalist as Mr. Dunham, but he delivered Charisma to the door of the Blue House and promised to return at four o'clock. With a smile, Charisma rushed inside.

Several women waited for her in the main room
and they all offered warm greetings while she removed her shawl. The hot days of September had
given way to a cooler October with just a hint of
winter in the air. Soon Charisma would need to
drag out her heavy cloak, but for now, a warm shawl
kept her comfortable.

"We're going to work on serving tea today," she
said, motioning for Esther to bring in the tray.
They'd done this exercise before with mixed results. It amazed her how many of these young
women had never served or been served tea before.
"Emily, I'd like you to go first. Then Patsy, then
Rachel. Esther, you can sit with me."

They settled onto the divans and chairs in the
parlor as the other three women left the room.
Soon Emily returned, a pot of steaming tea and two
cups nestled on a battered tray.

Charisma watched her as she served, filling the
cups perfectly. Though younger than most of the
other women, Emily had been the fastest at catching on to the basics of being a serving maid. From
the little she'd said about her past, Charisma had
learned Emily's mother had been a servant at one
time. Perhaps Emily had seen enough then to understand what was needed.

"Thank you, Emily," she said as the girl finished.
Emily bobbed a curtsey, then grinned and gathered
the china back onto the tray before she returned to
the kitchen.

Patsy came in next, the tray wavering precari-
ously. She tried so hard to learn these skills, but
they continued to elude her. Perhaps today would
be better.

She asked the right questions and poured the first cup without a mistake, but as she approached Charisma, she smiled, somehow affecting her concentration enough that the cup wobbled once . . . twice, then tumbled onto Charisma.

"Oh, no." Charisma jumped to her feet at once, but not fast enough to avoid a good soaking from the now cooling tea. A large brown patch stained the front of her day dress. How could she explain this to her mother?

She'd say she'd had tea with Grace. *Of course.* It wouldn't be the first time someone had worn their beverage while dining with her younger sister.

"I'm so sorry." Patsy swiped at the stain, but only succeeded in making it worse. She gave up and buried her face in her hands. "I ain't never gonna get this right."

"You'll get it." Charisma squeezed Patsy's shoulder. "We haven't been working together for long. Learning takes time."

"Let me clean your dress." Esther took charge, motioning for Charisma to follow her upstairs. "You can wear one of my gowns while I wash yours."

Once Charisma donned the gown, she wondered if she'd made a mistake. Though the length and cut were fine and the blue color flattering, the bodice dipped so low she felt as if her breasts were likely to spill out—a result of having to send her chemise and corset for washing as well. Thank goodness no one other than these women would see her.

While Esther left to clean her dress, Charisma started tutoring again, leading Patsy once more through the steps of serving tea. The woman finally achieved success, and they moved on to the next topic—preparing a bedchamber.

Everyone laughed as Charisma displayed the proper way to tuck the sheet and comforter. "No need to fancy up a bed around here," Patsy said with a grin. "It's only gonna get messed up again."

Charisma grimaced. She tried to forget their sordid occupation while she was here, concentrating instead on her goal to train them all to be useful servants or clerks. To sell their bodies to men was unthinkable.

Though she had to admit, her body had tingled during Will's all too brief kiss in the gardens at General Palmer's. Still, that had been Will, not some stranger.

"Well, when you leave here, your employers will want neat and tidy beds." she said finally. "So, you need to learn."

Emily stepped forward, her eagerness a bright note in the otherwise slow afternoon. "Let me try."

As Emily worked, Charisma smiled. At least she'd be able to save another woman from this life. And perhaps more. Time would tell.

Thalia paced back and forth, her normally placid expression tight with worry. "What am I going to do? I can't find Mr. Barclay. He's gone out of town." She brought her hands to her head, her usual charm giving way to blunt speech. "Why now? He'll ruin everything. I need for him to rescue Charisma."

Aglaia shook her head. "I warned you about counting on mortals to behave as you expect."

"I must find him. If I don't . . ." Thalia trailed off as if saying the words was unthinkable.

"You can use your magic." Euphrosyne raised a graceful hand and a pot of tea appeared on the table before them.

"I don't dare." Thalia sank into a chair with a moan. "We agreed not to attract attention with what we're doing. If I used my magic and Zeus found out . . ." Again she faded away. "Oh, dear. Heracles and I will have to go save her, which will ruin everything."

"Now, Thalia . . ." Euphrosyne poured her sister a cup of tea.

"How can I help her find her true heart's desire if she and Mr. Barclay won't cooperate?"

Beautiful Aglaia patted her sister's shoulder. "Well, they are mortals. Perhaps it will work out on its own."

The look Thalia gave her said otherwise. "I must find Mr. Barclay. Before it's too late."

Charisma trooped downstairs with the young women, satisfied at last with their performance in preparing a bedchamber. She had never thought it was such a difficult skill to learn, but some of these women proved that to be a misconception.

She touched Emily's arm on the staircase and the girl stepped back beside Charisma. "You've learned very well and very quickly," Charisma told her. "I think you're ready to find a position."

Stark fear filled Emily's face and Charisma took her hands. "Only if you're ready for it," she added.

"I . . . I don't know." Emily gulped. "Who'd want me?"

"Missy knows of a family not far from where she's working that is looking for a maid. I know you will do a wonderful job."

"But won't they know?" Emily tightened her hold on Charisma's hands. "Won't they know what I am?"

Charisma gave her a reassuring squeeze. "What you *were*. I don't plan to tell them. They will only know if you tell them."

"But what if . . . what if one of these men sees me?"

"I doubt any men who visit you here will frequent the type of home you'd be working in, Emily." The image of the man who'd beaten Missy flashed into Charisma's mind, raising a few misgivings. He'd been well dressed, obviously a member of society.

Still, she hadn't seen him anywhere since.

Charisma dismissed that memory. That man had no doubt gone to another town. What mattered now was getting Emily, a girl of only sixteen, out of here. "Do you want me to make arrangements for you to interview with the Williamses?"

"I . . ." Emily swallowed again. "Yes."

"Good."

As Esther approached with Charisma's dress over her arm, her expression worried Charisma. "What's wrong?" Charisma asked.

"It's dark outside." Esther glanced over her shoulder toward the windows. "Shouldn't your hansom have come by now?"

Sudden terror clutched Charisma's heart, and she rushed to fling open the front door. Indeed, night had fallen. The traffic on the street had already increased with potential customers, but there was no sign of Mr. Albert and his buggy.

Had he come and left? Mr. Dunham always came to the door for her, often reminding her of the hour since she did sometimes lose track.

Charisma rushed to find the clock. Five-thirty. Her throat grew tight. She shouldn't be here at this hour. Her family would be looking for her by now.

She turned back to Esther. "Where can I find a carriage?"

"On Colorado Avenue. But you shouldn't go there alone." Esther set the dress over a chair. "In fact, you shouldn't be seen here at all. Let me get my cloak to hide you."

Charisma clenched her hands together. If her family discovered what she'd been doing . . . She could live with her sisters' censure and her mother's tirade, but her father's loss of trust would hurt the worst. Somehow she had to find a way home without alerting them.

But how?

"I'm here, ladies." A male voice rang out from the front lobby. "Who's going to get the pleasure of Carlton Parker tonight?"

Charisma turned, then gasped. It was *him*. The man who had beaten Missy.

And from the way his eyes widened as he spotted her, he recognized her, too.

A slow smile slid across his face, a smile that reeked of evil and Charisma took an involuntary step backward.

Oh, dear.

Ten

Will stepped out of his buggy in front of his hotel and stretched. What an unproductive day. His attempt to campaign throughout the smaller towns in El Paso County had met with little enthusiasm. The moment he mentioned he was running as a Democratic candidate, he lost most of his audience.

Well, what had he expected? This had been a fool's errand from the beginning. The only problem was now he honestly wanted to win.

He'd barely started to unhitch his horse when he heard someone shout his name. Turning, he saw Mrs. Papadopoulos rushing toward him. Where did she come from? He could have sworn no one was in sight only a moment ago.

"Mr. Barclay, I must speak with you."

The woman appeared more flustered than Will had ever seen her. She stopped beside him and clutched his arm, her breathing uneven.

"Are you all right?" he asked.

"I'm fine, but Charisma's not. You must save her."

"Charisma? What's she done now?" No doubt she'd spoken bluntly once again and ostracized herself. Will doubted she would ever learn to hold her tongue. Her question at their last meeting confirmed that. Surely she should have known better than to put him on the spot like that.

He was better off without her company.

But, damn, he missed her.

"Charisma can take care of herself," he added.

"I'm afraid this time she is in far over her head."

The concern on Mrs. Papadopoulos's face alarmed him. "What is it?" Will tried to imagine what trouble the young woman could be in now. Too many things came to mind.

"She's been going to a house of ill repute in Colorado City in an attempt to reform the young women there. She—"

"She *what?*" Will's alarm gave way to a blast of hot anger. Charisma couldn't be that foolish, could she? Did she want to completely destroy her reputation? "Who's with her?"

"No one, I'm afraid." Mrs. Papadopoulos hesitated and wrung her hands. "I just found out myself. She went out there today to the Blue House and hasn't returned. I'm so afraid for her. Can you—?"

Will didn't let her finish. He hitched the horse back in place and jumped into his buggy. As he snapped the reins, he called back to Mrs. Papadopoulos. "I'll find her."

Mrs. Papadopoulos's sense of urgency had transmitted itself to him. No matter how hard he pushed his already worn horse, he wasn't going fast enough. Night had fallen—the most treacherous time for a young woman in Colorado City, especially without a chaperone.

Leave it to Charisma to jump in without thinking. What was she trying to do? Surely she realized these women chose their lifestyle, no doubt enjoyed their intimate relationships with a multitude of men. They didn't *want* to be rehabilitated.

Of course, his knowledge of such women and their places of work was limited. His brother had taken him to a brothel at the tender age of twelve and paid to have him become a man. The experience had been unpleasant at best with Will losing control the moment he entered the sour-smelling, middle-aged woman. He'd made it a point to avoid such places after that.

And now he was on his way to a whorehouse.

He grimaced. *Leave it to Charisma.*

Charisma's blood turned to ice water as Carlton Parker stalked toward her, the fire in his eyes as much from lust as from the liquor that he must have bathed in. She struggled to keep from backing away again and forced herself to stand proudly instead.

"You are not wanted here, sir," she said in as stern a voice as she could manage. "I suggest you leave at once."

"Door was open." His oily smile made her want to retch. "And I have money. That's what all you fine young ladies want, isn't it?" He reached toward his crotch. "And this, of course."

Patsy stepped into his path, a forced smile on her face. "That's right." She fingered the collar on his shirt. "Why don't you come upstairs with me?"

He pushed her aside, his gaze never leaving Charisma. "I found the one I want."

"I am not . . ." Charisma could barely speak through her tight throat. "I am not a . . . a girl of the evening."

"Could have fooled me." He leered at her partially exposed bosom. "And if you're not, you will be before I'm done."

"She's only visiting." Esther extended her arm in front of him. "She's not available."

"I say she is." He backhanded Esther, knocking her across the room. As Charisma gasped and turned toward the other woman, he grabbed her shoulders with dagger-like fingers. "I expect you're going to make me one happy man."

"I expect you're in for disappointment." *Oh, Lord.* Where was her courage? Charisma struggled within his hold, then tried to stomp on his foot, but he avoided her attempt easily.

"I like a woman with a bit of fight in her." He drew her closer despite her struggles. "Makes it more fun to teach her who's boss."

He stank of liquor and sweat, a smell at odds with his fine silk shirt and tailored jacket. Charisma quit struggling. She wasn't gaining anything. There had to be a way out of this.

"Let me go," she ordered. Perhaps if he thought she wasn't afraid of him, he'd comply.

"Not likely, sweetheart." He clamped his mouth over hers and pulled her close to him.

He tasted foul, of evil and the desire to inflict pain. Charisma tried to twist her head away, whimpering as he pressed her lips roughly against her teeth.

Her protests only seemed to please him. He rubbed himself against her, the thickness in his pants obvious through the thin material on her dress. This couldn't be happening. She wouldn't allow it to happen.

Charisma turned just enough to sink her teeth into his lip. She tasted blood before he smacked her so hard she staggered backward, her vision whirling.

Not giving her sight time to clear, she tried to run. If she could blockade herself in a room, surely one of the girls would go for help. She knew better than to think she had the physical strength to defeat him.

Parker seized her, tearing the sleeve of her dress so that the bodice fell even lower, revealing her breasts completely now. Charisma gasped and tried to pull the dress back into place, but he dug his fingers into her shoulder as he swiped the back of his hand against his mouth to remove the trickle of blood.

"Like it rough, do you?" he asked with a sneer. "So do I."

Charisma clutched her dress together with one hand while she curled the fingers of her other hand into a fist. She'd never hit anyone before, wasn't even sure it would do any good, but she had to try. She would die before she allowed this man to take her.

She swung with all her might, surprised to hear him cry out before her fist connected with his jaw. Her swing had missed, but he had been thrown off balance nonetheless. Charisma looked up to see Patsy clinging to his back, her arms wrapped around his throat.

As he reached for Patsy, Charisma swung again. This time her blow connected, the pain of the impact reverberating up her arm. "Ow." She cradled her hand to her chest, pleased to see Parker stagger a little.

"Get off me, bitch," Parker yelled. "Or it'll go worse for you."

"Leave her alone." Patsy clung as long as she could until he wrestled her off and smashed her against the wall. She sank to the floor, a dazed expression on her painted face.

Charisma searched for a weapon and managed to seize the fireplace poker only moments before he grabbed her again. Her first swing connected with his shoulder, but he didn't release her. Instead, he snared the poker, fighting her for control.

"Give it to me, whore," he snarled. "Or I'll use it on you next."

"No." She tightened her grip despite the pain of her swelling knuckles. While she longed to use both hands, she didn't dare use the one hand holding her dress together. Yet if she lost her weapon . . .

"I suggest you release the lady now."

She knew that voice. Charisma twisted to see Will standing in the lobby, his eyes blazing with a fire she'd never seen before.

Parker looked at him as well, but didn't take his hand off Charisma's arm. "Who the hell are you?"

Will came closer, each step measured. "I told you to let her go." The cold menace in his voice sent a shiver up Charisma's spine. Surely this man could hear it.

Evidently, Parker was too drunk . . . or too stupid. "She's mine." He glared back at Will. "Go find your own."

"Do you realize what you're doing will most likely get you beaten to a pulp or thrown in jail for several years?" Will sounded deadly, unafraid as he took a step closer. Charisma's heart froze for several moments. "I prefer the beating part myself."

In one swift movement, he grabbed the poker

from their combined grip and tossed it away. He plowed his fist into Parker's stomach, then pulled Charisma behind him as the other man doubled over. "Stay back," he ordered.

She staggered backward, nearly falling, but managed to regain her balance, though she had to release her grip on her torn dress to do so. Amazed, she stared at Will. He fought with style, with a confidence and strength that surprised Charisma. He'd always appeared such a gentleman. Where had this talent for brawling come from?

Parker landed a solid hit that sent Will staggering backward. *No.* She couldn't let Will be hurt. Charisma snatched up a nearby lamp, ready to smash it on Parker's head.

Before she could, Will attacked with a ferocity that gave Parker no chance to fight back. Within moments, Parker collapsed unconscious on the floor, defeated. "Send for the law," Will said, his breathing ragged. "Have this creature locked up."

One of the staring girls hastened to obey as Will turned to Charisma. "What were you going to do with that?"

She still had the lamp in her hands. "I . . . ah . . ." She replaced the lamp, uneasy now beneath Will's searching gaze, and hurried to pull the edges of her dress over her exposed bosom.

"Are you all right?" He spoke gently now, crossing over to her.

"Mostly."

He touched her cheek and she winced at the sharp pain where Parker had hit her. Will's mouth tightened, his expression a mask. "I should have killed him."

He sounded as if he meant it.

"No, don't. Just take me home. Please."

"Of course." His gaze dropped to where she clutched her gown and his eyes widened. "What are you wearing?"

She felt the heat rise into her cheeks as she held the front of the dress together. "There was a spill . . . my dress . . . I . . ."

"Here, wear this." Esther placed her heavy black cloak around Charisma's shoulders, her eyes sparkling despite the darkening bruise on her face. Evidently, she'd enjoyed seeing Parker defeated. "It will cover you. I'll send your dress tomorrow."

"What's going on down there?" Mamie appeared on the staircase, her hands on her ample hips. "If anyone's breaking up my place, he's paying for it."

Before Charisma could speak, Will jerked a thumb to where Parker sprawled on the floor. "He's paying." He pulled the cloak's hood up to hide Charisma's face, his expression daring her to say another word, then spoke to Esther. "She won't be coming back."

"I know."

Will tightened his arm around Charisma's shoulders as he led her outside, his pulse still beating rapidly. To see that man with his hands on Charisma had triggered a rage he'd never before experienced. He'd actually wanted to kill him and that frightened him as badly as Charisma's appearance.

A fresh snowfall had more color than her face, which only highlighted the bruise appearing on her cheek, her wide eyes, and tumbling hair. Her lips were swollen and red, as if she'd been kissed harshly.

Will ground his teeth together, fighting the urge

to return and finish the man off. Any man who treated a woman in such a way deserved far worse than a simple beating.

To know that he'd seen far more of Charisma than any man but her husband deserved to see only irritated Will more. Her breasts were firm, enticing, all he'd ever imagined them to be. "God." Will groaned. He didn't need to be thinking of that now.

He glanced at her tucked inside the dark cloak. No one could tell who it was. *Excellent.* With luck, he'd manage to preserve her reputation.

"Well, well, well, if it isn't the illustrious Mr. Barclay."

Hearing the mocking tone, Will turned and bit back a groan. Just his luck—Benjamin Steele, the editor of the *Daily Gazette.* It was too late to avoid him now. "Good evening, Mr. Steele."

"What brings you here?" Mr. Steele asked, his gaze flicking to the Blue House and the cloaked Charisma, his lips quirked in a half smile. "Wouldn't think a man like you needed to buy his amusements."

"That, Mr. Steele, is none of your business." When the man tried to peek into the cloak, Will turned Charisma away and seated her in his buggy. He wasn't going to escape Mr. Steele's pen unscathed, but Charisma would if Will could help it.

He swung up beside her in the buggy and snapped the reins. *Time to get out of here. Past time.*

He drove his horse hard, the wild ride echoing his wild feelings. Though he and Stephen had wrestled and fought as they grew up, he'd never before knocked a man unconscious.

And what if Mrs. Papadopoulos hadn't found him?

What if he hadn't arrived when he did? Bile rose in his throat. If Charisma had been harmed . . . He tried to calm himself. But she wasn't, at least not as far as her virtue went.

Still, she could have been. Very easily. That she'd been coming out here on a recurring basis sent a chill through him. Had she no clue as to the danger of her actions?

Hearing his horse wheeze, Will eased back into a slow walk, then vented his anger on Charisma. "What the hell were you thinking coming out here?" Or had she thought? She spoke impulsively. She acted impulsively. The woman was a walking menace.

Her reply was a sniffle that dissipated his anger at once. God, what was he thinking? He eased the buggy to the side of the road and slid back Charisma's hood. Though she quickly looked away from him, he caught sight of the tears that stained her cheeks.

"I'm sorry," he said. She'd nearly been raped and he was shouting at her. A lot of good that did.

"I . . ." She had to swallow to continue. "I only wanted to help." Her voice broke on a sob and Will reached out to wrap his arms around her, his gut clenching.

She buried her face in his shirt, the sobs unrestrained now, shaking her entire body, and he could only hold her. He'd never seen her like this before. He wanted to fix it. But how?

Lord, he was a cad. What was he thinking yelling at her? She'd always appeared so self-confident, able to take care of herself. But now he knew better. She was far more vulnerable than either of them had wanted to believe. And that vulnerability created an ache in his chest he didn't want to acknowledge.

He ran his hand over her hair, absently plucking the remaining pins free to let it down completely. The silky strands were soft, sensuous, rebellious— so like the woman in his arms. The woman he cared about far more than he wanted to admit.

Bending to kiss the top of her head, he inhaled the unique scent that was Charisma, the scent that never failed to trigger an answering reaction within him.

What was it with this woman? She was outspoken, reckless, unheeding of society's dictates and far too intelligent for her own good—the worst possible kind of woman for him to associate with. Yet he worried about her, cared what happened to her. Worse, he wanted her with an ache that grew more each time he was near her.

Not now. Not now.

Her sobs eased until she only had an occasional hitch in her breathing yet she didn't draw away. She should. Will was far too aware of her breasts nestled against his chest, the sight of them still vivid in his mind.

"Charisma." He barely managed to choke out her name through his thick throat.

She glanced up at him, her damp eyes shimmering in the moonlight. "I'm sorry," she murmured. "Your shirt is all wet." She gave him a watery smile that pierced him from head to toe.

The worst possible woman.

Yet the only one to make him want like this.

"Oh, God." He bent slowly, giving her time to pull away, yet hoping she wouldn't. He needed to know she was all right. Gently, he touched her mouth, tasted her sweetness, swallowed her moan of pleasure. He needed to know she was safe.

He deepened the kiss, trying to go slow despite the hunger driving him. Her tentative response, the softening of her body within his arms, drove him on. He wanted . . . Dear Lord, he wanted.

He teased her lips until they parted and he delved inside to mate with her tongue, to dance in the heat of her mouth, to tease another moan from her throat. When she slid her tongue along the length of his, he groaned, his shaft hardening even more than he'd believed possible.

Entwining one hand in her hair, he held her fast, delighting in the taste and feel of her. She spread her hands over his shirt, brushing his taut nipples, smiling beneath his mouth when he moaned at the intense pleasure rippling through him.

She explored further, running her hands over his chest, tracing the bulge of his muscles until he ached to bury himself within her. Leaving her mouth, he blazed a trail of kisses along her throat, pausing to untie the cloak and push it back.

Her exposed bosom shone in the night, far more enticing than any mortal man could resist.

And he didn't.

He reached up to cup her naked breast, the softness of it filling his palm. At her gasp, he brushed his thumb over her rigid peak. She cried out, arching into his hand, issuing an unspoken invitation for more.

Eager to comply, he drew one peak into his mouth, teasing the nipple into an even tighter bud, while he caressed her other breast. Charisma's breath came in gasps, but she made no attempt to pull away. Instead, she clutched his head, holding him to her, allowing him to devour her sweetness.

Lord help him, he couldn't stop.

The sharp whinny of his horse pierced the night air, jerking Will out of his passion-induced fog. What was he doing? What *was* he doing?

He jerked away from Charisma as if he had been scalded. This was no way to treat a lady. He was no better than the man who'd attacked her. "I apologize. I have no right . . ."

Charisma didn't respond, but stared at him, her eyes wide and lips swollen. Unable to endure staring at her wonderful breasts, Will pulled her cloak around her and tied it with shaky hands. "I'm sorry," he repeated, needing her forgiveness for his abhorrent behavior. "I shouldn't take advantage of you."

"But I like it when it's you."

Charisma's frank response startled him as much as it pleased him. She was too innocent, too unaware of how such words could trigger a man's passion. As it was, he barely managed to keep from touching her again.

"I have no right to touch you in such a manner." He said the words to remind himself as much as her.

"It was wonderful." Charisma placed her palm against her cheek, her expression awed. "I never knew . . ."

Oh, Lord. She was making this even more difficult. "Only your husband has that right, Charisma, and that will not be me." As much as he wanted her, he could not afford the luxury of a wife at this time nor the liability of one as outspoken as she.

Her dazed smile faded and she looked away into the night. "Of course." She didn't speak for several moments, the silence thick in the darkness. "Please take me home."

Will snapped the reins and put the buggy in motion. Yes, the sooner he could deliver Charisma safely home, the better.

Charisma bit her lip to keep further sobs from escaping as the buggy made its way to Colorado Springs. Humiliation and despair warred with the fire burning in her veins—a fire Will had ignited, then tried to douse.

She'd never imagined anything could feel so wonderful. Will's kiss had been heavenly enough, but the sensation of his hands and mouth on her breasts had awakened desires inside her she hadn't known she possessed.

Then he'd tossed her away as if she were responsible for his actions, making it quite clear he had no intention of offering matrimony. She'd known that all along, but now that she knew the pleasures likely to come along with marriage, she no longer viewed it with total distaste.

However, if she ever did marry, she could see that it would not be to Will Barclay. There were many other men available. Only none of them held any appeal.

Jerking out of her reverie, she noticed Will slowing the buggy as they neared her home. She turned to him in surprise. "I can't go home like this." Not with her dress torn and bosom falling out.

He blinked as if that thought hadn't occurred to him. "Of course not."

"Take me to Thalia's, please." The older woman would know what to do.

Will drove the buggy to the rear of Thalia's home before he stopped. After descending, he extended his hand to help Charisma out, then dropped her hand the moment her feet touched the ground, his feelings completely clear.

Charisma straightened, holding her head tall. No matter how he treated her, she refused to be ashamed of her response to his actions. Not waiting for him to join her, she made her way to the rear door and knocked.

James answered so quickly, she wondered if he'd been waiting for her to appear. "Madam is in the parlor," he said, standing aside for her to enter.

"Thank you." Charisma hurried inside, the sound of footsteps behind her the only clue that Will had followed. He was so anxious to be rid of her that she'd half expected him to deposit her at the door and leave.

As Charisma entered the parlor, Thalia rushed forward to envelop her in a hug. "Are you all right?"

"I'm fine." It was easier to say that than to explain the wide range of her current emotions. "I just need a change of clothes."

"I still have the dress you let me use," Missy said.

Charisma smiled. She hadn't noticed Missy standing in the background until the young woman spoke. "That would be helpful."

"You're hurt." Missy came over, her gaze fixed on Charisma's cheek.

"I met Carlton Parker." Charisma held Missy's

gaze as the woman blanched. Yes, the girl had known his name all along.

"Oh, no." Missy touched Charisma's hand. "What happened?"

"He appeared, we fought." Charisma kept her words short, banishing the vivid images even that slight description created, including the unthinkable fate that had awaited her. "Will arrived and set him down." She glanced over her shoulder as Will entered behind her. "Did I remember to thank you for that?"

He acted as if he hadn't heard her, his gaze focused beyond her. On Missy. Charisma frowned. "Will?"

Missy paled even more, which Charisma wouldn't have thought possible. She dipped into a curtsey, then kept her head bowed. "Mr. Barclay."

"My God." Will sounded as if the breath had been stolen from his lungs. "Melissa."

Eleven

Charisma glanced from Will's startled expression to Missy's lowered gaze. "You know each other?"

"I . . ." Will blinked, then shook his head. "Yes. Melissa used to work for my family." He stepped past Charisma and gently touched Missy's shoulder. "I looked for you. You just disappeared."

She gave him a warm smile that had Charisma frowning. "I left Denver. I couldn't stay there."

"And you ended up here." Will abruptly turned on Charisma. "How do you know Melissa?"

"That man tonight? Carlton Parker?" Charisma waited for Will to nod. "He nearly beat her to death. Thalia and I took care of her for a few days."

"She also found me a position with the most wonderful employer," Missy added. "And tonight I have a chance to help in return."

She brushed past them. "I will return shortly with the dress."

"I told your family you were dining with me tonight so they wouldn't worry," Thalia said.

"How did you know where I was?" Charisma asked. She hadn't mentioned her tutoring to Thalia for she'd known the older woman would disapprove.

"I happened to look in on Mr. Dunham, who's ill with gout. He told me what you had been doing, my dear. And that you were scheduled to visit again today. I made a quick visit to the livery stable and discovered Mr. Albert had taken you to the Blue House but failed to pick you up. I was beyond myself with worry." Thalia's eyes glistened with moisture. "Thank goodness I was able to find Mr. Barclay."

She motioned Charisma toward a chair. "Sit, my dear. You appear ready to fall over."

Charisma sank down at once, her knees suddenly shaky. "I'm fine."

"I'm not so certain about that." Thalia beamed a smile at Will. "Thank you for your swift response, Mr. Barclay. I was terrified to think of what could happen to Charisma."

"What almost did happen." Will focused his dark gaze on Charisma. "I hope you learned something from this experience."

"I did." She'd never allow herself to be so vulnerable again. "Next time I'll take a pistol with me."

"There will be no next time." Will roared the words, then drew back, as if amazed at himself. "You are never to return to that place again."

"I'm helping them." Charisma couldn't desert those women.

"I forbid it. It's too dangerous."

Charisma stood slowly to meet Will's gaze, unable to believe what she was hearing. For once, she took the time to choose her words with care. "Forbid it? As I recall, you have no right to tell me what I can or cannot do, Mr. Barclay. You aren't my father . . . or my husband."

He flinched, then gave a curt nod. "Just so, Miss Charisma." He bowed to Thalia. "I will leave her in your capable hands. Good night."

His footsteps echoed down the hallway, followed by the sound of the door closing. Charisma collapsed into the chair, her bones gone to water.

"That was rather harsh, my dear," Thalia murmured.

"He deserved it." Charisma refused to regret her words. After all, Will had nearly seduced her, then tossed her aside. If he intended to behave in that manner, he had no right to control her actions.

But if he told her father . . .

Charisma buried her face in her hands, overcome by consuming weariness. Too much had happened. "I just want to go home."

"And so you shall." Thalia came to lift Charisma's chin. "Let me see what I can do to diminish that bruise. Missy will return soon and we will deliver you home to the safety of your own bed."

"Oh, yes." She longed for the safety of her bed, of her home and family, but where could she escape the turmoil of her emotions?

Charisma stirred, a rapping sound disturbing the uneasiness of her dreams. Drifting slowly to awareness, she squinted against the sunlight filling her room. The hour was much later than usual for her to awaken. Of course, she'd barely slept most of the night, her thoughts whirling and her body still tormented by the sensations Will had aroused.

"Are you still asleep?" Grace peeked inside her room, then bounded to the bed, Belle on her heels.

Charisma struggled to sit, not even bothering to save the pillows that tumbled to the floor from Grace's exuberant bounce. Her body ached from the physical effort of her battle the previous evening, but her heart ached even more.

Catching sight of the daunting expression on Belle's face, she reached out. "What is it, Belle? Has something happened to Mama, Papa, Kit?"

"No, no." Belle retrieved the pillows before approaching Charisma's bed.

"The wedding?"

"Not that either." Belle displayed a ghost of a smile. "We're still waiting for Kit's parents to arrive from England. No, this is about Mr. Barclay."

"Will?" Charisma's heart rose into her throat. Had Carlton Parker returned last night to extract his revenge on Will? "Is he all right?"

She tried to get out of bed, but Grace sat on her bedclothes, preventing her freedom. "Grace. Move."

"It's this, Charisma." Belle handed the *Daily Gazette* to Charisma, the newspaper folded back to reveal the glaring headline in large black print: SENATORIAL CANDIDATE SPOTTED LEAVING HOUSE OF ILL REPUTE WITH YOUNG WOMAN.

"Oh, no." Charisma skimmed the story, which was just as lurid as she expected from the headline. The editor cited Will by name and accused him of all manner of indecent behavior, demanding to know what he'd done with the young woman he'd spirited away. Charisma closed her eyes for a moment. "Oh, no."

This was all her fault.

Grace squeezed her hands. "He fooled us all, Charisma. I liked him, too."

"No, you don't understand." Charisma gasped as a new horror struck. "Has Papa seen this?"

"Not yet. He had to leave early this morning," Belle said.

"Good." She had a slight reprieve, but she had to do something. Go to the editor? Papa? She had to tell the truth before this ruined Will's career.

Pushing Grace aside, she jumped from the bed and rushed to her wardrobe. She would go to Thalia's. The older woman would know what to do.

"What is it, Charisma?" Belle followed her. "What are you not telling us?"

She hesitated, then nodded toward the paper lying on the bed. "The woman with Will. It was me."

"What?" Belle's voice rose to a new level of disbelief as Charisma disrobed.

"Charisma, your shoulder," Grace exclaimed. She approached slowly, her gaze fixed to the bruises created by Parker's fingers. "Are you all right?"

"I'm fine. Now." Charisma dressed as she spoke. "Will saved me."

Belle fastened her dress, then turned her around. "You're not leaving here without an explanation. Tell me everything, Charisma. Everything."

With a sigh, Charisma related the events of the previous evening, omitting the drive home with Will. Even sisters only needed to know so much. By the time she finished, Grace was staring wide-eyed and Belle shook her head with such force her curls bobbed.

"Why would you do such a foolish thing?" she demanded.

"I want to make a difference." Couldn't Belle understand that? "I was helping them."

"You could have been . . ." Belle trailed off and pulled Charisma into a tight hug. "Thank goodness no one knows that woman was you. I trust Mr. Barclay not to give away your secret."

"But I have to tell Mr. Steele the truth. This will ruin Will's political chances."

Belle drew back, her expression set. "Your reputation is far more important than Mr. Barclay's political career. He can always run in another election. You can never regain what you will lose."

"But this election is important to him."

"And your reputation is more important."

Charisma shook her head and wrapped her shawl around her shoulders. "I'm going to see Thalia. She'll know what to do."

"Then Grace and I are coming as well." When Charisma started to protest, Belle held up her hand. "I do not intend to let you out of my sight again."

Heaving a heavy sigh, Charisma grimaced. "Very well. I'm leaving now."

To her amazement, her sisters were ready to leave within minutes. She hadn't known Grace could move that quickly—at least, not without injuring someone.

Less than half an hour later, they arrived at Thalia's door. James led them to the parlor, then stood aside for them to enter the room. As Charisma passed, he gave her a smile and shook his head as if mildly amused.

She grimaced. Yes, she'd made a mess of everything, but she'd only been trying to do something good. She should have known better.

"Oh." She stopped abruptly when she spotted Will standing by the fireplace mantel. While not surprised to see him here, she'd hoped to speak to Thalia alone first.

His face was set in stony lines, his eyes dark, the line of his mouth grim. "You've seen the paper," she said. "I'm so sorry, Will."

He waved a hand in dismissal. "I expected as much when I saw Steele there. The question now is how do I handle it?"

"You tell the truth. You were only there to help me."

"Out of the question."

Charisma stiffened. "Then I'll talk to Mr. Steele myself."

Will snapped his head up. "No."

"I'm glad you agree with me." Belle sent Charisma a triumphant look. "She can't be allowed to ruin her reputation."

"But it's all right for Will's career to be destroyed?" Charisma paced across the room. "I believe there is far too much weight put on a woman's reputation. Anyone who knows me will believe me."

"You'll never get a husband," Belle said.

Charisma turned to frown at her sister. Becoming engaged had made Belle nearly as bad as Mama. "I don't want a husband." She shot Will a quick glance, then faced Thalia. "There must be something we can do."

"I have no ideas right now." Thalia sipped her tea, the only calm presence in a room filled with tension. "I hadn't expected this."

"I think the only solution is obvious." Charisma clenched her fists. "We should invite Mr. Steele here and talk to him. I'm sure he'll understand. He has a wife, a daughter."

"He will *not* understand." Will crossed the room to her. "He is a reporter and cares only about the story. Revealing that the woman was you would guarantee even more sales. The man would betray his own mother for a headline like this."

"And what is so horrible about the truth?" Charisma looked askance at Will. "I was helping some women. You came to take me home when my hired buggy didn't show up."

Belle sank into a chair. "Charisma, you were at a . . . a house of ill repute."

"I was helping those women find a better life." Charisma focused her glare first on Belle, then on Will. "I wasn't . . . I wasn't joining them."

"The fact that you were there implies you were." Will lowered his voice and touched her cheek with one finger. "You had honorable intentions, but no one will care about that."

"But—"

He placed his finger over her lips. "Not only would your reputation be ruined, but you could ruin that of your sisters as well. Are you willing to throw away Grace's chances for a good marriage, Belle's engagement?"

Charisma stared at him, her chest tight. She hadn't thought of it that way. If she harmed her sisters in any way, she'd never forgive herself. "I—"

Lowering his voice, he leaned closer. "Why are you so concerned about protecting me, Charisma?"

"Because I—" She stopped herself before her impulsive words leapt free. Because she loved him. Charisma drew in a deep breath to calm the sudden leap of her heart before she continued. "Because it's my fault."

"This will work out." Will gave her a reassuring smile. "Many of the senators currently in office have been caught in far more compromising positions than this. There is still enough time before the election for this incident to fade from people's minds. The trick is to present it in the right way." He glanced back at Thalia. "I'm hoping you can help with that."

Thalia tapped her finger on her chin. "Perhaps we could say you were passing by and heard the sounds of a fight, then intervened to help. A woman was injured and you took her to the doctor. That is close enough to the truth."

"But won't people wonder why he was on Cucharras in the first place?" Charisma asked. Cucharras Street was lined almost solely with houses used for the purpose of male entertainment.

"Maybe he became lost while returning from giving a speech," Belle added.

Thalia nodded. "You *were* out campaigning yesterday, Mr. Barclay."

"True enough." Will returned to his position by the fireplace. "There is enough truth in the statement to be verified."

Grace stumbled over a stool as she jumped up. "But won't people still be angry because you went inside a . . . a . . ." She dropped to a whisper. "That place?"

"I imagine there will be significant talk for several days, but if I proceed in my campaigning as before, I may be able to overcome it."

"However, you must not avoid questions about this subject if they are put to you," Thalia said. "Be calm, forthright. Show that you have nothing to hide."

Will nodded, his expression brightening for the first time. "That could work."

"It is vitally important that you be seen with Charisma as well. If she does not condemn you for your actions, the people of this town will be inclined to follow her lead."

Spend more time with Will? Charisma linked her hands together in an attempt to appear neutral. As much as she would love to spend every moment with Will, to do so would only make the inevitable parting that much harder to endure.

Will fastened his gaze on her, as if trying to read her deepest thoughts. Charisma managed a small smile. If her support was necessary for Will to win the election, then he would have it. After all, this mess was all her fault.

"Are you willing to be seen with me?" he asked, an odd note lingering in his deep voice.

"Of course." She kept her response brisk, afraid her emotions might leak into it. "You are still the best candidate for the senate, Will. You deserve to win."

Dark lights glimmered in his eyes until he closed them and looked away. "Then that is what we'll do."

"Excuse me." James appeared in the doorway to the parlor. "Miss . . . er . . ." He glanced behind him, listened, then continued. "Miss Melissa Houser." Standing aside, he allowed Missy to enter the room.

Heightened color dotted her cheeks and her eyes were bright. Seeing the seriousness of her expression, Charisma reached out to her. "Are you all right?"

"I have solved Mr. Barclay's problem," she announced.

"What?" Charisma darted a glance at Will, but he shrugged, evidently as puzzled as she.

"Mr. Gardner was discussing the article about Mr.

Barclay with me this morning. I knew at once I could make things right."

"Come, my dear. Sit and tell us what you mean." Thalia waved Missy to the divan. "What have you done?"

"I went to Mr. Steele and told him I was the woman Mr. Barclay took out of the Blue House last night."

Will echoed Charisma's obvious question. "Why?"

What *had* Missy done? Charisma sank beside her on the divan, momentarily speechless.

"Mr. Barclay had said he'd been searching for me." Missy cast him a worried look. "I explained to Mr. Steele that after he located me, Mr. Barclay removed me at once from my place of employment in an effort to rescue me."

"But what about your position with Mr. Gardner?" Charisma couldn't keep the dismay from her voice. Even this one small achievement would be ruined, along with Missy's life.

"I explained my past to him. I told him everything, Miss Charisma, and asked for his permission to talk to Mr. Steele. He not only gave his permission, but he assured me I was in no danger of losing my position." Missy released a sad smile. "He is truly a wonderful man."

Will came over and sat in the chair opposite Missy. "And what did Mr. Steele say when you told him this story?"

Her gaze met his briefly, then dropped to her lap. "I told him everything, Mr. Barclay. Why I left your parents' home and why you felt you needed to find me."

"Oh, God." The bleakness returned to Will's face.

What was the problem? Charisma tied together the pieces of information she knew. Missy had been tossed out of her place of employment without references, which resulted in her earning a living the only way she could. Will had been searching for her since she'd left his parents' employ.

"Will's parents are the ones who released you without references?" she asked. While she could believe the elder Mr. Barclay capable of such an act, it seemed out of character for Mrs. Barclay. Of course, that was assuming Mr. Barclay allowed her any input to his decision.

Missy nodded, not looking up. "There were reasons."

Charisma aimed a frown at Will. "I would like to hear them. Your family did this?"

"It's complicated." He leaned back, tipping his face to the ceiling. "This will ruin Stephen's career."

"Stephen?" Charisma wouldn't care if his brother's career was ruined, but what did that have to do with this?

With a sigh, Will straightened again. "I . . . my family . . . we've tried to keep this quiet, but now . . ." He ran his fingers through his hair. "Up until a year ago, Melissa worked for my parents as an upstairs maid. She was young, quiet, and an excellent servant. My parents had no fault with her."

"Then why—?"

He held up his hand. "Let me finish. Melissa is also very pretty. Stephen noticed. Though I was unaware of it for many months, Stephen forced Melissa to . . . to submit to him."

This was one time Charisma didn't hesitate to be blunt. "You mean he raped her."

Grace gasped when Will nodded. "I caught him in the act." A muscle jerked in his jaw. "We fought over it, which brought the situation to Father's attention. After I had left in total disgust, Father summarily dismissed Melissa without references and threatened her with prison if she spoke to anyone about what had happened."

"He . . . he said no one would believe me anyhow. That I was nothing." Missy spoke so quietly Charisma could barely hear her. "That I was only trying to snare a rich husband."

Charisma jumped to her feet, her heart pounding, unable to stand still with such fury pulsating within her. "That's ridiculous. That's not who Missy is. Stephen was already married. The man should be held responsible for his actions." She faced Will, her fists on her hips. "And you let this happen?"

A brief flare of anger appeared in his eyes. "When I found out Melissa had been dismissed, I started looking for her. I've kept looking but I could find no sign of her once she left Denver." He stood as well, indignation clear in every line of his stance. "Do you believe I condoned this? That if I'd known about any of this I wouldn't have stopped it?"

"No." If he'd done that, Will wouldn't be the man she knew, the man she loved. She touched his arm. "I'm sorry."

"When I couldn't locate Melissa, I entered the senatorial race, leaving my home and lifelong political party in order to thwart my brother." Will took her hand in his, his gaze locked with hers. "I could not allow Stephen in the senate without being able to watch over him, to stop him from further harming others."

"Why not just reveal what he'd done?" Charisma asked.

"As I mentioned to you, other people can be affected by doing the right thing." He squeezed her hand before dropping it, and turned away. "This will devastate my mother. She knows nothing of it."

"Oh." Charisma could feel his pain. He loved his mother, had attempted to protect her. Just as he'd been willing to risk ruin to protect Charisma's reputation. Her eyes filled with tears. "I'm so sorry, Will."

"If I may make a suggestion." Thalia held up her hand to get their attention. Charisma had almost forgotten she was even there.

"Please do," Will said.

"My advice would be to go visit your mother. Today. And explain this to her. It will be far easier to take coming from you than to read it in the cold print of the newspaper or hear about it through gossip."

"You're right." Will started for the door. "I will leave at once."

"I didn't mean to do you harm, Mr. Barclay," Missy said, glancing up. "I thought I was helping."

Will paused and knelt down before her. "You have done no harm, Melissa. You told a truth that should have been revealed before now. I have no sympathy for Stephen. Only for my mother . . . and you. You're certain your position is secure?"

"Mr. Gardner has said he does not intend to let me go." Missy twisted her lips. "Of course, the people in this town may have something different to say about that. I may be forced to leave."

"I won't allow that to happen." Now that Missy finally had a better life, Charisma wouldn't let small-minded people take it away from her. "I'll tell them—"

Will caught her arm as he stood. "While I admire your defense of Melissa, think for a moment, Charisma. Think about what you might say and how it could affect others. Others besides Melissa and Mr. Gardner."

Hearing the angry words in her head, Charisma winced. If such a defense was possible, she'd have to be much more circumspect. Could she be? All too often her emotions spoke for her. "I don't want them to ruin her life again."

"Neither do I." Will gave Missy a smile. "We'll do our best to ensure that doesn't happen."

Belle shook her head. "How do you get into these situations, Charisma?"

Will chuckled. "I can answer that. Strong convictions, a desire to make a difference, and a boldness that far surpasses any other woman of my acquaintance."

None of those sounded like particularly good qualities for a lady to possess. Of course, that was her problem. Had always been her problem.

Charisma pulled her arm from Will's grasp and walked away. "I have been trying to do better."

"And you've made remarkable progress, my dear." Thalia said with a bright smile. "A person cannot change who she is overnight."

"It's been weeks." Charisma sighed. "I'm never going to be charming."

"You can be," Will said quietly. "I've seen it."

"You've also seen far too much of the opposite." No wonder he had no intention of marrying her. She would ruin his political career.

Before Will could respond, James appeared once more in the doorway. "Mr. Gardner," he announced.

Mr. Gardner? Surprise filled everyone's face as the man entered. Missy jumped to her feet, her hand clenched in front of her chest.

"How kind of you to visit." Thalia came forward to meet him and draw him further inside. "Please do take a seat. I believe Mr. Barclay was just preparing to leave."

"I can't stay." Mr. Gardner gave them a wry smile. "And neither can Mr. Barclay, I'm afraid. We've been summoned."

"Summoned?" Will echoed. "For what?"

"For explanations, I believe. We are to proceed at once to the courthouse for a meeting with Mr. Steele and the constable."

"The constable?" Charisma's heart dropped to her stomach.

"Did they say why?" Will asked.

Mr. Gardner glanced at Missy, then turned to Will. "I believe it's about your brother. And Missy's story."

Will groaned. "Oh, Lord."

Twelve

Will experienced a sharp stab of dread when he entered the meeting room at the courthouse, the town's main gathering area, and found not only Mr. Steele and Constable Simmons but the entire city council and General Palmer in attendance. Was he to be tarred and feathered for his assumed indiscretion? Unlikely, yet he suddenly wished he hadn't allowed Charisma to accompany him.

Of course, knowing her as he did, she probably would have followed whether he'd granted her permission or not. At least Mrs. Papadopoulos had insisted on coming as chaperone. Maybe she would be able to stop Charisma from speaking out.

Charisma still insisted this entire misunderstanding was her fault. If he expected to keep her reputation intact, he needed to have her nearby to counter whatever she might feel compelled to say.

Not only that, but he had to admit a certain amount of guilt. If he'd put even a fraction of the interest Charisma invested in his campaign into learning more about her and her aspirations, he might have been able to forestall her actions before they'd led to this indiscretion.

Of course, he'd only been protecting himself.

With an attraction to her that was already far more compelling than he desired, he'd been unwilling to risk knowing her any better for fear such knowledge would lead to a place of no return. He could not afford any involvement with Charisma Sullivan, especially if he had any hopes of a future political career.

Knowing that, however, didn't make her appear any less lovely. With her chin held high and eyes flashing a brilliant green, Charisma drew the admiring gaze of every man present in the large meeting room. With luck, her appearance by his side would provide the affirmation Mrs. Papadopoulos had predicted.

Constable Simmons greeted them with a short nod. "Gentlemen, Mrs. Papadopoulos, Miss Charisma." He waved his hand toward some empty seats. "If you gentlemen will have a seat. I'm afraid I must ask you ladies to leave. These discussions are not fit for a woman's ear."

"I intend to stay, Constable." Charisma didn't show the slightest sign of backing down. "You forget I grew up in a mining camp. There is nothing you can say that I am not prepared to deal with." Not allowing him a chance to answer, she slid onto a seat beside Will.

He cast her a quick grin. "Does anyone ever win an argument with you?"

"Only my father," she admitted, a twinkle in her eye.

Mrs. Papadopoulos finally spoke. "I will wait outside." She left the room, leaving Will to manage the wayward Charisma on his own.

Belle had made him and Mr. Gardner swear

upon their lives to keep Charisma out of trouble—a feat easier promised than upheld. Especially now.

"Miss Charisma," General Palmer spoke now, "I must ask you to reconsider."

"While I appreciate your concern, sir, I am staying. Having become a friend to Mr. Barclay and Miss Houser, I find I have a vested interest in these proceedings." She beamed a warm smile that nearly every man returned before they caught themselves and resumed their stern expressions.

Will swallowed a grin. As a beautiful, intelligent woman, Charisma made a formidable ally. If only she could better control her wayward speech.

"Very well." Mr. Steele took control now and stood to face the gathering. "Mr. Gardner, Mr. Barclay, I have asked you here to confirm the story given to me by Miss Houser. Shall I assume you are familiar with it?"

"Very familiar," Will muttered while Mr. Gardner nodded.

"Mr. Barclay, Miss Houser accuses your brother Stephen of violating her." Mr. Steele paused to glance at Charisma, who somehow managed to keep all expression off her face, before continuing. "Several times. Do you have knowledge of this?"

"I do." A cold lump sat in Will's stomach. He could already tell where this was leading.

Constable Simmons took over now. "Can you tell us why this was not reported to the police?"

There was no evading this. "Both my father and Stephen are political officers, gentlemen. To bring such a revelation to light would ruin their careers." Of course, now his career was probably over as well.

"Besides . . ." Charisma jumped to her feet. "Who

do you think the justice system is going to protect—
a wealthy, well-known political candidate or a poor
servant girl?"

A ripple of unease ran through the men.
Charisma had struck a chord, but it was one they
did not want to face. Will tugged her down into her
seat. "Be quiet," he said, softly yet sternly.

"If I may, Constable." Mr. Harrison, the Democratic leader for El Paso County, raised his hand for
attention. Once the Constable nodded at him, he
continued. "I do believe Mr. Stephen Barclay is one
of those candidates supported by Mr. Chaffee."

"Ah." A new ripple crossed the room now—a ripple of understanding. Mr. Chaffee, known as "Boss"
Chaffee was facing severe criticism during this political campaign for choosing and backing his own slate
of candidates. Rumor had it he was not opposed to
using unethical means to achieve his purpose.

Nodding, Mr. Steele focused again on Will. "Do
you approve of your brother's actions, Mr. Barclay?"

"Of course not." *What a ridiculous question.* "Why
do you think I am running in opposition to him?"

The men nodded and spoke in low voices to each
other. The animosity between the Barclay brothers
was no secret. Stephen's last visit had even merited
a brief mention in the society column of the *Daily
Gazette*—a mention that included the "tension" between the brothers.

"Let me see if I have this correctly then." Mr.
Steele glanced at his notepad. "After searching for
Miss Houser over the past year, you located her at
the Blue House on Cucharras Street in Colorado
City and took her away from there."

Will hesitated only a second. Though not the

exact events, he would have done so if he'd known she was there. "Yes."

"Still—"

Will cut him off, weary of this exchange. "I did what I did and I would do it again, gentlemen, because I believed it was right. Miss Houser was dismissed from my parents' employ through no fault of her own. I wanted a chance to help her." He shifted his gaze across the assembly, daring them to doubt him. "Take that as you will."

Mr. Steele shifted uneasily, then nodded. "Very commendable of you, Mr. Barclay, to do all this for a young woman who is nothing more than a former servant." A hint of impropriety clung to his tone.

"Very commendable of Mr. Barclay," Charisma said angrily. "But that is because he is a true gentleman who genuinely cares about people. Have any of you taken the time to listen to his platform? If so, you'd know this already."

Mr. Steele blinked in obvious surprise while Will bit back a groan. Charisma was going to help him get booted out of town at this rate.

To Will's amazement, General Palmer spoke up, instantly gaining everyone's attention. "I have taken the time to listen to this young man's campaign speech and what Miss Charisma says is true. He espouses rights for all individuals—servants and miners as well as those of means."

The general leaned back in his chair. "I tend to believe this story. It is very much in Mr. Barclay's character. But, of course, the question is, gentlemen, do you?"

The fist clenched around Will's chest eased as one by one each man nodded in agreement, leaving

Mr. Steele to shoot Will a searching gaze, then add his affirmation as well. Will's campaign might not be over after all.

With Will cleared, Mr. Steele turned his attention to Mr. Gardner. "Yet you, Mr. Gardner, have had Miss Houser employed as your housekeeper for the past few weeks. Were you not aware she had other employment as well?"

Feeling Charisma tense, Will squeezed her arm to keep her from speaking again. This was tricky, a question he should have foreseen, but he had confidence in Mr. Gardner's wit and calm demeanor.

"Miss Houser has worked solely for me since I hired her," Mr. Gardner said. "Last night she asked for permission to go visit friends. It was fate that Mr. Barclay found her at the Blue House."

"So you had no idea she was a fallen woman?" Mr. Steele demanded.

Charisma jerked against Will's hold. "I—"

Mr. Gardner raised his voice. "While I was not aware of Miss Houser's past when I hired her, she has since made it known to me."

"And you have dismissed her, of course."

"I have not."

Will's admiration for the man rose, but the reaction of many of the others was far less admiring. "Is that because she warms your bed now, sir?" Mr. Steele asked.

The expression on Charisma's face matched the anger surging within Will. That was doing it much too brown.

Mr. Gardner stood slowly, still unruffled. He met Mr. Steele's gaze and held it. "No, she does not warm my bed. Miss Houser is a capable and reliable housekeeper. Her past profession was forced on her through no fault of her own. I have no inclination to return her to such dire straits. Now, if you will excuse me, gentlemen. I believe you have heard far more than you have a right to know."

To Will's amazement, Mr. Gardner turned and left, ignoring Mr. Steele's cries to return. *Good for him.*

"I will ruin him," Mr. Steele muttered. With the newspaper at his disposal, he could do it, too.

"I think not, Mr. Steele." Charisma pulled free of Will's hold and jumped up again. "If you try, I will make it known that you are a man of prejudice and small thoughts. After all, you were on Cucharras Street last night as well."

Mr. Steele could only stare at her, aghast. Will tugged at her skirt. "Enough, Charisma."

She moved away from him, the fire in her eyes blazing. She was beautiful, formidable, and possibly ruining her life.

"Missy never wanted to become a prostitute. I doubt that many women do, yet they are the ones held to blame when forced to use their bodies to survive. It is men like you who frequent them, then belittle them." Her voice quivered. "Missy hated what she had to do. *Hated it.* That Mr. Gardner offered her gainful employment is a crime? I wish every man in this town was so willing to break the law, then perhaps most of those women could finally be free from submitting to men's base needs."

A tear rolled down her cheek. "Missy was fired without references because a man raped her. Was this her fault? Yet would you have given her a job?" She jabbed her finger against Mr. Steele's chest, then aimed her gaze at the city council. "Would you? Unlikely. Men make the rules, but they are far from being the right rules. Men visit the prostitutes, but keep them from tainting the pretty lives they live. Well, who tainted them, gentlemen?"

Charisma's words caught on sobs now. Will no longer tried to stop her. All he could do was listen in awe.

"Just think, if no one ever visited places like the Blue House, then all those women wouldn't have to be there. They'd be able to find employment as seamstresses, cooks, maids, housekeepers, but you don't want that, do you? You don't want them around here because they remind you of who you really are."

She swiped at the tears coating her cheeks and sent Will an apologetic glance. "I'm sorry." Without another word, she ran from the room.

Will stared after her. Dear Lord, *she* should run for the senate.

"Knew we shouldn't have allowed her to stay," Mr. Steele muttered.

A chill traveled over Will's skin and he rose slowly, not realizing he meant to speak until the words emerged. "I believe Miss Charisma has a point."

All gazes turned to him, many of them unfriendly, but Will continued. Politics or not, this had to be said. "Miss Houser is a young woman who ended up in unfortunate circumstances. I do not see where she is a danger to me, to you, or to the women and children of Colorado Springs. Now that she has a chance to better herself, would you deny her that chance? If so, then ask yourself why?

Fear? Guilt?" Will saw several men lower their gazes. "Or merely ignorance?"

"Mr. Barclay, your political career has been tenuous from the beginning," Mr. Steele said, icily. "Would you prefer to have it nonexistent?"

"Excuse me, gentlemen." General Palmer stood again, his eyes sharp beneath bushy eyebrows. "As you all know, I am a Christian man."

Everyone nodded. Christian enough to keep Colorado Springs a dry town, which resulted in so many men going to Colorado City where the liquor was plentiful.

"Yet if there are women cast into this profession unwillingly, who are we to judge them? I believe tolerance is called for here." The general swept the room with his gaze. "On everyone's part."

"Thank you, sir," Will murmured. The general's opinion outweighed the other ten in the room. Few ever disagreed with him . . . at least, not openly. "If this . . . meeting is concluded, may I be excused?"

Mr. Steele gave him a grudging nod. Will didn't hesitate, but fled the courthouse. Somehow he'd managed to escape that relatively unscathed. Well, until tomorrow's newspaper appeared.

But for now his main concern was Charisma. Where had she gone after bolting from the courtroom? Home? He had to find her, reassure her that Mr. Gardner would not be ruined. No doubt she blamed herself for that as well.

Mrs. Papadopoulos had left the courthouse so he stopped by her home first. She assured him all the Sullivan girls had returned home, including Charisma. He should look for her there, then.

To his surprise, Belle answered his knock instead

of the Sullivan's butler. The depth of sorrow in her eyes didn't bode well.

"Is Charisma here?" Will asked, the urgency to see her even more demanding. "Is she all right?"

"She's here, but I'm sure she doesn't want to see anyone right now." Belle started to close the door. "Perhaps in the morning."

"I need to talk to her. She was upset when she left the meeting." And Belle's actions stirred his fears even more.

"She is *very* upset." Belle met his gaze with a sad smile. "She won't even talk to me. Go home, Will. I'm sure she'll be more herself in the morning."

Unwilling to give up, but more unwilling to force his way inside, Will nodded. "If she asks to see me . . ."

"I'll send word at once." Belle shut the door with a soft click, leaving Will standing on the step staring at it.

What now? He glanced at the upstairs windows, hoping for some sign that she was watching for him, but none of the curtains moved. Knowing that she hurt added to the ache within him. He *had* to talk to her.

"Mr. Barclay."

He paused in midstep, certain he'd heard his name whispered nearby. Glancing back at the house, the door remained firmly closed.

"Mr. Barclay."

Turning, he spotted Grace motioning to him from the side of the house. With a frown, he joined her. "Miss Grace, is—?"

"This way." Not giving him a chance to respond, she led the way to the large garden at the rear of the house, oblivious to the branches that smacked him in the face after she passed. "Charisma's in here." She paused by a narrow walkway and pointed into the depths of the dying foliage. "She's been crying since she came home."

Grace caught his sleeve, her heart in her eyes. "Please, make her stop crying."

"I will," he vowed, squeezing her hand briefly. "I promise."

She gave him a slight smile, then headed back for the house, knocking over one of the garden statues en route.

Will ventured along the path, not seeing anything for several steps. He heard Charisma before he finally saw her, the sound of her sobs causing his heart to drop. Rounding a large bush, he found her seated on a marble bench, her face buried in her hands.

"Charisma."

Charisma jerked her head up. She'd come to the garden to be alone, but she recognized the voice long before she spotted Will standing a short distance away. Wiping at her tears, she struggled to clear her throat. "I don't want to talk to you right now."

"It's all right," Will murmured.

"No, it's not." She'd managed to ruin several lives through her foolish attempt to make a difference. What made her think she was anyone special? That she could possibly make a difference?

"I was proud of you today."

She blinked. Had she heard him right? "Proud?" After the way he'd tried to shush her at the courthouse, she'd been convinced he wouldn't want anything more to do with her.

"You spoke from the heart. Those men may not have wanted to hear it, but you told them what they needed to hear." Will drew closer, one step at a time. "And they heard."

What did that mean? "What about Mr. Gardner?"

"I very much doubt that Mr. Steele will be doing anything to ruin Mr. Gardner."

She wanted to believe that. "Are you certain?"

Will sat beside her. "After you left, General Palmer declared his agreement with you."

Her eyes widened. "General Palmer?" She'd forgotten that he was there. "And he agreed with me?" The general was a man with many years of military training. If anything, she would have expected his views to be completely different from hers.

"He agreed with you." Will smiled and brushed the dampness from her cheeks with his thumb. "So, no more tears. I believe Melissa and Mr. Gardner will be fine."

This was too good to be true. "What about you?" Had she hurt his career even more with her outburst?

At Will's hesitation, she caught her breath. He shook his head. "Don't worry. I am just uncertain of the slant Mr. Steele will put on his article tomorrow. I don't think he will be too harsh with me."

"And your brother?" Mr. Steele was unlikely to omit that piece of news, which would affect Will one way or another.

Will grimaced. "I need to go home today, to talk to my mother. I don't know how she will react."

Charisma didn't envy Will this task. "If I can help in any way . . ."

"Come with me." Will paused after speaking as

if he hadn't intended to say the words, then he smiled and cupped her face between his hands. "Come with me," he repeated. "I think it will help if you are there."

An all-too-familiar longing began to seep through Charisma's veins at his touch. "But your mother barely knows me."

"I think having another woman there—a woman who can explain things." He grinned. "A woman who isn't afraid to explain things can only help. I doubt if Abigail will suffice."

Stephen's wife? Unlikely. "I would be honored," Charisma whispered, her thoughts clouding as Will's gaze dropped to her lips.

"Good." His voice sounded deeper as he drew closer, his hold tightening slightly. "I'll ask Mrs. Papadopoulos to accompany us. We'll probably remain for the night. I don't want to leave Mother after I give her this news."

He brushed his mouth over hers in a caress so simple and sweet that a knot twisted deep in Charisma's stomach. Closing his eyes, he leaned his forehead briefly against hers, then straightened. "I'll go ask Mrs. Papadopoulos now."

Charisma stared after him. For once, he hadn't apologized for kissing her. Could that mean he didn't regret it? Or was she trying to fool herself with romantic dreams?

Now that she knew she loved him, his every move, every word, took on more meaning. He probably still saw her as a friend, a helper. Nothing more.

Except that he had kissed her.

More than once.

Her sorrow forgotten, Charisma ran inside to

prepare for travel. They could catch the midafternoon train to Denver and Will had said they'd remain overnight.

Her heart jumped. Would that provide her an opportunity to be alone with Will again? Would he touch her? Kiss her? Her breasts swelled, remembering his caress, the heat of his mouth.

Charisma fanned her suddenly warm cheeks with her hand. "Oh, my." To ensure that no one had seen her blush, she dashed up the staircase to her room.

She had finally decided which dress to wear when she was called downstairs again. Belle and Grace stood in the entry with Will. Why had he returned so soon?

"Will, what is it?"

"I'm sorry." His first words had her brief elation fading. "Mrs. Papadopoulos is unable to accompany us to Denver. She has another engagement."

"Denver? What's this?" Mama appeared, honing in on Will at once.

He presented her with a slight bow. "I had intended to ask your permission to have Miss Charisma escort me to Denver tonight to visit my mother, but I find Mrs. Papadopoulos is unable to act as our chaperone." He turned to Charisma. "I am sorry."

"To meet your mother?" Mama's eyes lit up, no doubt imagining another prestigious marriage in the family.

"It's about the election," Charisma added. It wouldn't do for Mama to get unrealistic expectations. Something Charisma needed to remember as well.

"Couldn't Belle accompany you? She's quite reliable and suitably engaged."

Charisma glanced at her sister. Belle would most likely be a firmer chaperone than Mrs. Papadopoulos. "Would you, Belle?"

"I would love to help," Belle said. "But I have promised to attend the annual ball with Kit tonight."

The anual ball? Charisma had forgotten all about it with the events of the past few days. "Of course, you must go." Knowing now how Belle must feel about Kit made Charisma far more sympathetic to her older sister.

"Could I act as chaperone?" Grace asked, quietly.

Everyone looked at her in shocked silence. Grace? A chaperone? She was a year younger than Charisma.

"I don't see why not," Mama said as if determined to overlook that fact. "If you are agreeable, of course, Mr. Barclay."

Will hesitated, his gaze meeting Charisma's. His lips quirked in a half smile. "That would be perfectly agreeable, Mrs. Sullivan."

"Excellent." Mama's beaming smile filled her face. "Since you are leaving so late in the day, will you be remaining at your parents' home overnight?"

"That is very likely," Will said. "I feel certain my mother will insist we stay with her."

"Then Charisma and Grace need to pack immediately." She shooed them toward the stairs. "They will be ready to leave within the hour, sir."

Will nodded. "I will return at that time."

Once he'd left, Grace spun in a circle, her arms outstretched. "I'm going to Denver," she cried.

Charisma hurried to protect the table of figurines her mother prized as Grace whirled close by.

She adored her sister, but Grace brought disaster with every step.

"Oh, no." Charisma gasped with sudden realization at the new complication of Grace acting as chaperone.

How was she going to keep her sister from destroying Mrs. Barclay's exquisite home?

Thirteen

Charisma hesitated beside Will outside his parents' home. They'd made it that far without mishap, unless she counted Grace's little episode of tumbling over a stack of luggage at the train depot. Which Charisma didn't.

"Will your father be home?" she asked Will as he held open the gate for them.

"Not at this hour. With luck, I'll be able to speak to Mother without his interference." Will grimaced. "I hate to do this. She's going to be devastated."

"Better she hear it from you than read about it in the newspaper." Charisma caught Grace's arm as her sister tripped over an uneven stone in the walkway and was able to keep her upright. "I'll help however I can."

Will gave her a dry smile. "I'm counting on that." He rapped on the door, which was answered by the same sour-faced butler. "Good afternoon, Henry." Will stepped inside without waiting to be invited. "Is Mother at home?"

"Is Mrs. Barclay expecting you?" Henry asked, his tone so stuffy Charisma exchanged a broad grin with her sister.

"I'm her son." Will kept walking. "I didn't think I needed an appointment."

A quick look of affront crossed Henry's face, but he managed to smooth his expression before he replied. "I believe she is in the parlor."

"Excellent. Thank you." Will motioned for Charisma and Grace to precede him.

The parlor door was open and Will stepped inside. "Hello, Mother."

Mrs. Barclay looked up and broke into a radiant smile. "William. This is a wonderful surprise." She rose to hug him. "And Miss Charisma. A pleasure indeed."

Will quickly introduced Grace to his mother, then led her back inside the room. Charisma kept her hand on Grace's arm as she guided her sister to a chair. There were far too many breakables in here for her peace of mind.

Once Grace was safely settled, Charisma took the chair beside her.

"What brings you here?" Mrs. Barclay asked as she sat on the divan.

Will crossed to close the door. "I'm afraid I have some unpleasant news for you."

"Unpleasant?" Her eyebrows shot up and she glanced at Charisma. "And I was hoping it might be good news."

Charisma glanced down at her hands. Perhaps she shouldn't have come if even Will's mother was imagining a union between the two of them. Not that Charisma was totally opposed to the idea, but Will had made his stance very clear.

"No." Will didn't look in Charisma's direction. "This is about Stephen."

"Stephen?" Mrs. Barclay's face clouded. "Is he all right?"

"Physically, yes." Will sat beside his mother, then hesitated. "There is going to be an article in the Colorado Springs newspaper tomorrow that makes a disturbing revelation about him."

"Disturbing revelation?" Mrs. Barclay looked from Will to Charisma, her tone anxious. "What kind of revelation?"

Again, Will paused, only this silence became lengthy. Unable to wait any longer, Charisma tried to prompt him. "About a year ago . . ."

He shot her a dark look, then returned his attention to his mother. "Do you remember the upstairs maid, Melissa?"

"Of course I do. She was a very sweet girl and an excellent worker. I was very unhappy when she left us so abruptly." Mrs. Barclay frowned. "What does she have to do with this?"

"She didn't actually leave us of her own accord." Will swallowed. "Father dismissed her."

"Why would he do that? I had no complaint with her."

"The fault was not hers. She was let go because of what happened to her."

Charisma resisted the urge to roll her eyes. At this rate, it would be tomorrow before Will finished with his explanation. She bit her tongue to hold back the forthcoming words that would bring the truth to light.

Mrs. Barclay was only becoming more and more confused. "I'm afraid I don't understand, William. What are you trying to say?"

Inhaling deeply, Will took his mother's hands, then spoke quickly, the words tumbling over one another. "Stephen was violating Melissa on a regular

basis. When I learned of it, we fought, which brought
the situation to Father's attention. He dismissed
Melissa at once with no references and threatened
her with jail if she mentioned it to anyone."

The color left Mrs. Barclay's face in a rush.
Charisma leaned forward, ready to assist if the
woman fainted. She shot Will a scathing look. And
he said she was blunt. This had to be a terrible
shock for his mother.

"I . . ." Mrs. Barclay cleared her throat and started
again. "What happened to Melissa? Was there a
child?"

"No child, thank God." Will squeezed her hands.
"But after Father dismissed her, she had to turn to
prostitution to survive. I . . ." He hesitated and
glanced back at Charisma. They'd agreed he
should tell the story that the newspaper would
carry. "I found her in Colorado City and brought
her out, but a newspaper reporter saw me, which
resulted in the entire story coming out. I'm sorry."

He bowed his head while Charisma held her
breath. How would the woman react?

Mrs. Barclay slid her hands free and stood, then
crossed the room to face the fireplace. "Stephen,
Charles." She paused. "And you knew about this as
well?"

"Yes," Will whispered.

"How dare you!" She whirled around, her cheeks
flushed pink, her eyes snapping. "How dare you
keep this from me."

Will jerked back, obviously startled. "I . . . I didn't
want to hurt you."

Charisma blinked in surprise. She hadn't expected this reaction either.

"I am not the fragile flower you must think I am."
She advanced on him. "I could have helped Melissa
if I'd known, found another position for her."

"I had been looking for her."

Mrs. Barclay shook her head. "Too little. Too
late. That poor girl." Her gaze bored into Will while
Charisma stared in amazement. She'd obviously
judged the woman incorrectly, but it gave her some
comfort to realize he had as well. "I can understand
your brother and father keeping secrets from me,
but I had more faith in you than that, William."

He looked so confused, Charisma felt a stirring
of pity for him.

"I thought—" Will began.

"No, you didn't think." Mrs. Barclay leaned
closer. "Tell me, if this article wasn't appearing tomorrow, would you have ever told me?"

When Will hesitated, she released a sharp curse
that had Charisma flinching. Grace jerked back,
her mouth a large O, nearly toppling the fine Dres-
den figurine on the nearby table, but Charisma
managed to snag it before it fell. The last thing they
needed right now was to break anything.

"I'm sure Will did what he thought was right,"
Charisma said to fill the tense silence.

"But it wasn't right." Mrs. Barclay sighed and
sank back onto the divan. "I thought William knew
me better than that."

"I do," he protested.

"Not enough to tell me the truth." She waved at
him in dismissal. "Leave us now."

"But . . ."

"Now, William. I'm too disappointed and angry
to want to look at you right now."

He did as she commanded, pausing by the door to glance over his shoulder. "Charisma?"

"I prefer Charisma and her sister remain. Go." Once he left, Mrs. Barclay fixed her gaze on Charisma. "Is he telling me the truth?"

Charisma winced. She'd never been good at lying. "Most of it."

"What is he leaving out? Was there a child?"

"Oh, no." Charisma was sure Missy would have mentioned that. "It's mostly omissions to protect me."

Mrs. Barclay only cocked her head, an unspoken question in her eyes.

Charisma hesitated. Judging from the woman's response to this latest news, Charisma thought she could trust her. "I was the one who found Missy. I removed her from the Blue House to a respectable job in town."

"Why would William not tell me that?"

"It's my fault that this ended up in the newspaper." Charisma caught a sympathetic look from Grace, which gave her the courage to continue. "I was going to the Blue House to teach the other women there some skills so they could obtain respectable positions as well. One night my driver didn't return and Will rescued me." Charisma drew in a deep breath, her heart hammering so loudly she felt certain the older woman could hear it. "I was the woman he was seen taking out of there. Missy told Mr. Steele it was her to protect me and this all came out. I'm very sorry."

Now Mrs. Barclay would ask Charisma to leave and Charisma couldn't blame her. After all, she'd managed to bring scandal to both of the woman's sons.

To Charisma's surprise, Mrs. Barclay wore a slight smile. "My dear Miss Charisma, you are not the woman I thought you were."

Charisma bowed her head, her chest tight. That wasn't a surprise.

"And I am very grateful for it," Mrs. Barclay continued.

Jerking up in surprise, Charisma met the woman's gaze. "I beg your pardon?"

"I had assumed you were only a nice girl from a wealthy family. I am pleased to discover you are so much more than that." Mrs. Barclay leaned forward. "You actually went there? By yourself?"

"All by herself," Grace piped in. "She didn't even tell me."

"You would have tried to stop me," Charisma told her sister. "And I had to try to help. Mrs. Woodhull believes all women deserved equal rights and opportunities and I do, too."

"Mrs. Woodhull?" Mrs. Barclay asked. "Mrs. Victoria Woodhull?"

"Yes, do you know her?" Charisma couldn't keep the excitement out of her voice. She'd never met anyone who actually knew Mrs. Woodhull.

"I had the pleasure of meeting her briefly, once long ago. A very dynamic woman unafraid to express what she believes is fair and right."

"She is someone I greatly admire," Charisma said. And to think that Mrs. Barclay had actually met Mrs. Woodhull.

Mrs. Barclay studied Charisma. "Has my son asked you to marry him yet?"

Charisma nearly choked at the abrupt question.

"Will and I are just friends. He . . . he says he's never going to marry."

"Did he? I find that difficult to believe." Mrs. Barclay smiled and stood. "In that case, let us forget men for a while. I have an engagement this evening at my friend's house. I would be pleased if you and your sister would accompany me."

"What about Will?"

"William needs time to think." The woman threw open the parlor doors. "Will you stay the night? Did you bring an overnight case with you?" Charisma nodded. "Excellent. Let me show you to your room. You can both freshen up before we leave."

"I don't want to impose," Charisma said, though she had to admit her curiosity was aroused. Will's mother was turning out to be far more intriguing than she had first assumed.

"Elizabeth will be thrilled to have you." Mrs. Barclay led them up the staircase. "This is very informal. Just some friends getting together." She paused to glance at Charisma, a twinkle in her eyes. "I feel certain you will enjoy it."

"Then we would be pleased to accept." Charisma kept her hold on Grace's elbow—less danger to the surroundings that way. "Thank you."

Just over an hour later, they were welcomed by a small, slender woman into a stately mansion. Elizabeth Harvard, the wife of a prominent statesman, drew Charisma and Grace into her sitting room and introduced them to the two other women already seated

"Mrs. Alcorn and Mrs. Montgomery, may I present Miss Charisma and Miss Grace Sullivan from Colorado Springs. They are friends of Susan's

William." Mrs. Harvard guided them to chairs. "Would you care for a sherry?"

"Yes, please," Charisma murmured, automatically. These women were all so open and warm—very different from many of the city council wives in Colorado Springs.

Accepting the cut-crystal, stemmed glass, she sipped at the deep red drink. It had a slightly nutty flavor that tantalized her palate. "Very good."

Grace took a large swallow. "I like it."

Mrs. Harvard settled onto a divan beside Mrs. Barclay and sipped at her drink as well. "What is the latest *on-dit?*" she asked with a grin.

"Mr. Spencer Preston has offered for my Melanie," Mrs. Montgomery said with a broad smile.

"Excellent," Mrs. Barclay responded, raising her glass. "A very good match for them both."

"He is a good choice." Mrs. Montgomery eyed Charisma before addressing Mrs. Barclay. "Though she would much have preferred your William."

"As you know, William is very particular." Mrs. Barclay laughed. "Miss Charisma tells me he says he will never marry."

All the women laughed, leaving Charisma and Grace to exchange puzzled glances. Charisma believed Will when he said that. Didn't they?

"Wait until he falls in love," Mrs. Alcorn added. "He'll change his tune quickly enough."

"He says he doesn't have time for a wife," Charisma said.

"What a man says and what a man does aren't necessarily the same thing." Mrs. Harvard rose and refilled all the half-empty glasses. "It's just a matter of knowing how to handle him."

"Handle him?" Men were impossible to understand, let alone know how to control. "I don't believe that's possible."

Mrs. Barclay chuckled. "Oh, it's possible. You're young still. Believe me when I say men are often persuaded to think and do what we want them to think and do."

"But men only consider women possessions."

"Not all of them, and most men grow very quickly accustomed to a smooth-running home and regular meals. When that schedule is altered, they become very easy to manipulate." Mrs. Alcorn waved her hand in the air. "My Duncan thought the new decorating in the house was his idea simply because I was unable to function due to the state of the place. One cold supper was all it took for him to see the need for a change in the decorating scheme."

"And Thomas believes he is the one pushing for a woman's right to vote." Mrs. Harvard set her glass on the table beside her. "He doesn't even remember how adamantly opposed to it he was when the subject was first raised."

Charisma frowned. "You mean, you can really make them think what you want them to?" This concept was new. She'd always assumed women needed equal rights to be taken seriously, especially after seeing how so many husbands treated their wives. Even her own father was often dismissive of Mama at times.

Mrs. Barclay nodded. "I know it appears as if Charles is the one controlling every situation in our household, but he has many times supported a motion because of subtle hints in our conversations."

"Isn't that manipulative?"

All the women laughed. "Would you prefer to be a quiet possession?" Mrs. Barclay asked.

"Never." Charisma wanted equal rights in her marriage, which more than likely meant she would never have one. Then again, perhaps she was approaching it all wrong.

"This is quite good," Grace murmured. She extended her empty glass for a refill and it dropped from her fingers to bounce on the thick Persian carpeting. "Oops."

Charisma glanced at her sister. Grace's cheeks were becoming quite pink. "Perhaps you shouldn't have any more," she suggested.

"Nonsense." Mrs. Montgomery immediately refilled their glasses. "This is *our* evening."

"I must admit I have some news to confess," Mrs. Barclay said once her glass was topped. She lowered her voice to a conspiratorial whisper. "We are to have a scandal in my family."

The older women leaned forward. "Do tell," Mrs. Montgomery said.

"Stephen has been caught in an act of indiscretion," Mrs. Barclay said with a wry twist of her lips. She sounded far calmer than Charisma would have expected. Of course, Charisma wouldn't have expected her to tell the tale at all. These must be very good friends.

"A bit of muslin caught his eye?" Mrs. Harvard asked.

"My maid Melissa. Charles dismissed her when he learned of it."

Mrs. Harvard frowned. "But I thought she left some time ago?"

"She did." Mrs. Barclay sighed. "I only just learned of this today. Apparently, it will come out in the Colorado Springs newspaper tomorrow."

"Stephen will most likely lose the election," Mrs. Alcorn said.

"I'm afraid so."

"However, I can no doubt convince Duncan to offer him support." Mrs. Alcorn glanced at Mrs. Montgomery. "And you, Marie?"

"George will support him as well." Mrs. Montgomery shook her head. "Foolish Stephen. Doesn't he realize his wife's anger will be far worse than anything the press will do to him?"

Mrs. Harvard lifted her glass. "I imagine it will be a thirty days' wonder. Stephen will lose the election, but not his career."

"That's unfair," Charisma said, unable to stop the words. "He deserves to be punished for what he did."

The looks the women gave her were more pitying than angry. "As you've realized, it is a man's world," Mrs. Barclay said. "Men are very forgiving of one another's indiscretions. However, Abigail will make sure Stephen suffers for quite some time."

"She didn't appear the type to do so," Charisma admitted.

Mrs. Barclay smiled. "Not in public. Though Stephen would be loathe to admit it, Abigail is very important to him in his career. He won't want to jeopardize that."

Sipping her sherry, Charisma settled back in her chair, trying to adjust to this new way of thinking. Evidently women did have some power of their own. The trick appeared to be handling it discreetly— something that had always been difficult for her.

She smiled. *Another reason to be charming. Interesting.* She continued to listen to the conversation, her thoughts slowing as the evening progressed.

When Mrs. Barclay stood and announced it was time to return home, Charisma glanced up to find her glass empty and the room swaying. *My goodness, was she that tired?*

Grace jumped up. "Let me help," she announced. Though her eyes were far brighter than normal, she gathered all the empty glasses with care, her movements much slower than usual, while Charisma winced, already imagining the crash of broken crystal.

To her amazement, Grace set the glasses on the tray without dropping even one. "Lud," Charisma exclaimed, her tongue far looser than normal. "Grace is graceful."

"Of course she is," Mrs. Barclay said with a smile. "Come, dear. It's late. We must return home."

Charisma stood, finding it difficult to maintain her balance. It took all her concentration to make her way to the waiting carriage. Once seated, she closed her eyes to block out the melding of colors. "I feel strange," she murmured.

"I'm afraid you're a trifle disguised, my dear," Mrs. Barclay said. "Are you and your sister not accustomed to sherry?"

Grace hiccuped in reply. "We've never had it before."

"A good night's rest will help."

Rest? At the moment Charisma would settle for having her surroundings in focus again. All these thoughts of women actually having power over their husbands assured that she'd never be able to sleep.

* * *

Will paced the front hallway in his parents' home, pausing en route to glance once again at the nearby grandfather clock. Where was everyone?

He had remembered it was his father's night for a meeting with his cronies, but that didn't explain his mother's disappearance. Especially since Charisma and Grace were with her. Where had they gone? All Henry would tell him was that they had gone out. That didn't help.

After a cold supper thrown together by the kitchen staff, who hadn't expected to serve anyone tonight, Will was finding his mood growing fouler as the night worn on. First, his mother had taken him to task for not telling her of Stephen's indiscretion earlier, which had been the last reaction he'd expected. Then she'd disappeared, taking the Sullivan sisters with her. Where? For how long? He needed answers.

Will made another circuit of the entry. Worse yet, if asked, he couldn't honestly say whom he was more concerned about—his mother or Charisma. *Damn.* He didn't want to be concerned about Charisma. She already occupied far more of his thoughts than he found to his liking.

Hearing a carriage stop before the house, he threw open the front door and glared into the night as his mother, Charisma, and Grace descended. They approached the house with slow, unsteady steps, Charisma in-between the other two. Were they supporting her? Apparently so.

The moment she greeted him, he knew why. The strong scent of sherry clung to the three women.

"You've been drinking." He hadn't been aware that his mother drank spirits, let alone Charisma.

"Only sherry," his mother said. "Can you help get Charisma upstairs, dear? She's a little more foxed than I thought."

"I'll get the doors." Grace led the way, negotiating her way past the tables with ease. Nothing fell. Nothing broke. Incredible.

Will did a brief double-take, then returned his attention to Charisma. "I'll take her."

He wrapped one arm around Charisma's waist and she melted against him, her smile and eyes overly bright. "Thank you, Will."

Halfway up the staircase, his mother paused. "I hear your father arriving home. I'll see to him. Take Miss Charisma to the spring bedroom. Miss Grace is there as well."

Will nodded, struggling to control his body's reaction to Charisma's closeness. Reaching the bedroom, he sighed with relief, then groaned.

Grace had fallen face-first across the bed. Quiet snores drifted from her direction. So much for her presence as a chaperone.

Removing his arm from Charisma, he pointed her toward the bed. He had no intention of going into that room. "You'll have to see to yourself."

Charisma swayed slightly, then turned to face him. "Aren't you going to kiss me good night?"

The urge to do just that rose quickly. "Most certainly not," he replied more adamantly than he'd intended.

"But I like your kisses." She linked her arms around his neck, pressing her soft curves against him. "They make me feel all quivery inside."

Which was a mild reaction compared to how her kisses affected him. All the more reason to get away from here. Quickly.

"Good night, Charisma." He extricated himself from her arms and tried to push her away from him, part of him protesting the entire time.

To his surprise, she rose up on her tiptoes and pressed her lips against his. His shock at her forwardness gave way to an intense surge of desire as she flicked her tongue over his lips.

With a groan, he released her arms and pulled her closer, allowing her to continue her tentative exploration. When she nipped his bottom lip, he lost what little control he had and answered in kind, hungry for her sweetness and passion.

Her response was equally fierce, adding to his growing ache. Lord help him, he wanted her.

He cupped her breast while drinking her quiet moan of pleasure, then traced the outline of her lips. Reason faded fast.

Only the sound of his father's deep voice below snapped Will back to reality. In horror, he held Charisma away from him. What was he doing? Ravishing her in his parents' home? That made him no better than Stephen.

He pointed her toward the bed and gave her a gentle push. "Good night, Charisma."

She staggered forward and collapsed onto the mattress fully dressed, then remained unmoving. She would be uncomfortable if she slept in her clothing all night, but Will was not about to assist in that arena.

Backing away, he clenched his fists. He'd send a

maid to help her and Grace disrobe. Anyone but him.

Touching Charisma held far more danger than a loaded pistol and he had too much to lose.

Fourteen

An all-too-cheery whistling pierced the fog wrapped around Charisma and she cracked her eyes open. The sunlight stung them and she squeezed them shut again, but her head continued to throb.

"Are you finally awake?" Grace's cheerful voice sounded far too loud to Charisma's ears.

"Sssh." Charisma squinted against the bright light and saw Grace fixing her hair. "Doesn't your head ache?"

"No." Grace smiled. "I feel fine." She drew closer and frowned. "You don't look well."

"My head has miners working in it." The pounding grew worse when she sat up and she placed her hands over her ears. "I cannot possibly go downstairs. Please give Mrs. Barclay my apologies."

"The *Daily Gazette* will be out this morning."

Grace could not have said anything with more meaning. Charisma had to be there to defend Missy, and to help Will. As she thought of him, she experienced a brief flash of memory, of his lips on hers. *Ah, our ride back from Colorado City . . . my only pleasant thought thus far this morning.*

With Grace's help, Charisma dressed. She'd slept in her chemise—unusual, especially since she didn't recall getting undressed. To be truthful, she didn't remember much after leaving Mrs. Harvard's home.

Finally, she and Grace ventured downstairs, every step a lesson in agony, every noise reverberating in her head. They entered the dining room to find Will and Mrs. Barclay already seated at the table.

"I'm sorry to be late," Charisma murmured. "It has been a difficult morning."

She caught the hint of a smile on Will's lips as she took her seat with exaggerated care. "Are you laughing at me?"

"There are consequences when one imbibes too much." He kept his gaze on his plate, but she could see his grin.

"I had never had sherry before."

"Tea, Charisma?" Grace attempted to pour Charisma a cup of tea, but as usual, ended up pouring most of it on the tabletop.

As the maid hurried in to clean up the mess, Charisma frowned, another fuzzy memory intruding. *Grace being graceful? No, it has to be an illusion brought on by the drink.*

Before Charisma could sip what remained of her tea, another maid set a glass before her filled with a sickly red-colored beverage. "What is this?"

"Drink it, my dear," Mrs. Barclay said with a warm smile. "It will help."

Fortunately, the drink tasted slightly better than it looked and Charisma managed to gulp down better than half the glass. To her surprise, her headache eased within minutes. In fact, the food no longer looked repulsive but inviting.

She sent Mrs. Barclay a grateful smile. "Thank you."

"It is the least I can do."

"Mother says she took you to visit her friend, Mrs. Harvard, last night," Will said.

"Yes, it was a very enlightening evening." Charisma exchanged a glance with his mother. At least she remembered most of the night's discussions and the lessons she intended to take to heart.

"Enlightening?" Will raised his eyebrows. "How?"

Charisma only smiled and filled her plate.

Before Will could question her further, Mr. Barclay entered and went directly to the seat at the head of the table. He was served at once and drained an entire cup of tea before he spoke. He didn't display any signs of the distress that had afflicted Charisma this morning so he was evidently not suffering the effects of drink. Perhaps he was just not a social person in the morning. Her mother was that way.

"Cold this morning." He directed his words to Mrs. Barclay as if the rest of them were not even present.

Charisma grimaced. Or it could be he was just rude. She glanced at Mrs. Barclay. Had the woman spoken to her husband last night about the upcoming newspaper article?

Mrs. Barclay returned a brief smile, but the sparkle in her eyes indicated Mr. Barclay's bad mood hadn't come from anything she'd told him. Apparently she preferred he face the news when it arrived. Charisma smothered a grin. *Good.*

"I expect it will snow soon," Mr. Barclay said finally.

"Quite possible." Mrs. Barclay turned her gaze on Will. "Has it been cold in Colorado Springs?"

"Cooler than last month." Will shook his head slightly as he glanced at his father, then returned his attention to his meal.

"I like the snow," Grace announced. "It covers all the dead brown grass on the prairie and makes it so much prettier."

"Hrrumph." Mr. Barclay picked up the newspaper lying beside his plate and Charisma held her breath until she realized it was the Denver paper.

Evidently, Will had the same fear as she for he placed his fork on his plate and turned to his father. "There is something you should know, Father."

"You're withdrawing from the race?" Mr. Barclay asked without looking up.

"No."

"Then you have nothing to say."

"I do think you should listen to this, dear," Mrs. Barclay added. "It's about Stephen."

Now Mr. Barclay set his paper aside. "Stephen? What about Stephen?"

Before Will could reply, his brother burst into the room, a newspaper crushed in his hand. Charisma shot Will a comforting glance, knowing all too well what would follow.

"I'm ruined," Stephen declared. He tossed the newspaper onto the table before his father. "That trollop has talked."

Charisma pushed back her chair, enjoying the screech it made on the wood floor, then stood. "I beg your pardon?"

Stephen started as if just realizing others were present. "Miss Charisma, I . . ." He broke off as he spotted Will. "You. You knew about this."

"If you read the entire article, you would have noticed I was quoted." Will placed a carefully folded copy of the *Daily Gazette* beside his plate. "Very succinct, don't you think?"

"You set out to ruin me." Stephen's face flushed so red Charisma feared for his health.

"The revelation of your misdeed wasn't planned." Will rose to his feet. "But I can't say I'm dismayed it has come to light."

Mr. Barclay looked up from the newspaper. "It says here you were seen bringing a woman out of a brothel. How can you be so foolish?"

"Foolish? To rescue a young woman who was sullied and tossed out without references, with nowhere to go?" Will remained amazingly calm while Charisma's stomach twisted into knots. "I believe it was the only honorable thing to do."

"She is a wanton." Mr. Barclay thrust the paper aside. "Her present career is evidence of that. You risked our family name and your brother's reputation for that . . . that . . ."

Charisma could remain silent no longer. "Her name is Melissa. Don't you remember?"

Mr. Barclay aimed a glare in her direction, but she met it without flinching. He would not intimidate her. Knowing what he'd done to Missy gave her strength.

"You've even told your light-skirt about this?" Stephen snapped.

Will's expression hardened. "You will apologize at once for that remark. Miss Charisma is a lady."

Stephen sneered. "And if I refuse?" The look he gave Charisma filled her with disgust.

"Stephen, you will apologize. Now," Mrs. Barclay said, her voice firm.

Though he grimaced, he complied with a mocking nod. "My apologies, Miss Charisma. But none for you, dear brother." He removed his coat and rolled up his sleeves. "I prefer to settle this with you in a different manner."

Will shook his head. "I've done that already. As you recall, you were the one on the floor last time we fought."

"You're going to pay for this," Stephen muttered.

Charisma sucked in her breath. Seeing Will fight at the Blue House had been unnerving enough. "Don't," she murmured.

"Not to worry. I won't." He gave her a quick smile that faded the instant Stephen planted a facer on him, knocking him against the wall.

"That's unfair," Charisma protested. She crossed over to Will and dabbed at the cut on his lip with her napkin. Angry fire blazed in his eyes.

"Don't fight," Grace cried as she rushed forward. She stumbled over Charisma's foot and staggered forward, her arms outstretched. Tumbling into Stephen, she knocked him backward so that he tripped over a chair and crashed to the floor. "Oh, dear."

Grace hurried to help him up. "I am so sorry." She flung her arms wide as she spoke, connecting with a heavily laden tray carried by a servant. A tray whose messy contents cascaded over Stephen, the teapot bouncing off his head before it crashed to the floor. "Oh my."

A slice of toast sat on Stephen's head, butter side down, while a smear of jam coated his shirt. The spilled tea puddled in his lap and heavy cream dripped from the end of his nose. Charisma glanced at Will and found him smothering a smile. For once, she was grateful for Grace's clumsiness.

When Grace went once again to assist Stephen,

he held up his hands to ward her off. "Stay away from me," he ordered.

"But I am so sorry." Grace's sincerity kept Charisma from laughing. She crossed to her sister and wrapped her arm around Grace's shoulders.

"I believe it is time for us to leave," Charisma announced.

"Past time," Mr. Barclay added.

Charisma's lips twitched again. They made their farewells quickly and were barely outside before she and Will burst into laughter while Grace stared at them, confused.

Will grinned when Grace nearly toppled the conductor who was taking their tickets on the train ride back to Colorado Springs. As long as she was around, he wouldn't have to worry about fighting Stephen.

His smile faded. He didn't want to fight Stephen. After all, his brother had brought on his current troubles himself. He would undoubtedly lose this election, but far worse would be explaining the situation to Mr. Chaffee.

"Mr. Steele made you sound like a hero." Charisma folded the newspaper after reading the notorious article. "And Mr. Gardner as well."

"You don't have to sound so surprised." Though Will had to admit he hadn't expected the article to be so complimentary either. "I told you it would be all right."

"So you did."

The smile she gave him held such warmth that his gut knotted as he recalled her kiss from the previous evening. Obviously, she remembered nothing of it. Just as well. He preferred not to recall how ungentlemanly he had behaved.

"Now there is nothing to worry about," he said.

"Except for you winning the election." Her eyes sparkled. "I know you can do it. And after meeting Mrs. Harvard and her friends last night, I have an idea of how I can help."

"You've done enough." Through her assistance, he'd gained access to most of the prominent citizens in the city. He was making strides slowly. "And I do appreciate it."

"You might as well let her help," Grace said with unusual outspokenness. "She's not happy unless she's doing something."

"Isn't she?" Will grinned, but studied Charisma. Who was this woman that attracted and infuriated him? He had thought he knew all that was necessary about her. She came from a wealthy family and had the contacts he'd needed.

But there was far more to Charisma Sullivan than that. Already he found himself caring about her, admiring her when he knew he shouldn't.

"When we lived in Leadville, she was always helping people. She watched over many of the children and kept them safe," Grace added.

A becoming blush colored Charisma's cheeks. "Enough, Grace," she murmured.

But her sister only shook her head. "And she would visit the families of injured miners to find out what they needed. Mama never could understand why our oil and food kept disappearing. She always blamed the boys in our camp."

"Papa knew what I was doing." Charisma waved her hand in a dismissive gesture. "He cared about

the men who worked for him and he knew Mama
wouldn't give them all the things they needed."

"So the Blue House is not your first attempt at
saving people?" Will asked. He wasn't surprised.
The fire and passion in her hinted at great things.

"It was my first attempt at something that daring."

"And last," he added. He couldn't handle another
rescue.

Charisma bowed her head and he stretched across
the seats to lift her chin. "And last?" he prompted.

"I can't promise that. So many of the women are
so close to finding a way to escaping that way of
life." Her gaze pleaded with him. "I can't just desert
them."

He sighed. She cared about people—all people.
Was that a result of her upbringing in the mining
camps or was it just Charisma? "Then we'll find another way to do it." As soon as the words left his
mouth, he regretted them.

But her face lit up. "You'll help me?"

"There must be some kind of program in place
to do this type of thing." He preferred to remove
her completely from possible harm.

"If there isn't, we'll create one," she said firmly.

If anyone could do that, it would be Charisma.
Not for the first time, he recognized that if she'd
been a man, she'd be ideal for the senate herself.
"What do you gain from this?"

No one did anything without expecting something
in return—power, wealth, prestige. What drove
Charisma to endanger herself and her reputation?

She looked away from him. "You'll think it's silly."

"Not at all." He considered her many things, but
never silly.

She fixed her gaze on his. "I want to make a difference. I want to know I have a reason for being here."

Her earnestness tugged at Will. "And you can't
find a safer way to do this?"

"My safety isn't important. Mrs. Woodhull says—"

Grace groaned. "Not Mrs. Woodhull again." She
looked at Will. "Don't let her get started. Please."

Will grinned. He was very familiar with Mrs.
Woodhull's far-fetched ideas as she was a favorite of
his mother's as well. "I know all about Mrs. Woodhull. Please spare me."

With a grimace, Charisma crossed her arms and
settled back on her seat. "Very well."

"Instead of reciting Mrs. Woodhull's philoso-
phies, why don't you tell me what *you* care about?"
Will touched her hand. "Tell me, Charisma."

"You won't like it." Her expression remained
stubborn.

"I'd still like to know." *Very much so, in fact.*

"I care about women's rights." Defiance danced
in her eyes. "We should have the right to vote, the
right to be treated fairly and not as second-class citizens, the right to offer our opinions without
condemnation. Not all women have difficulty de-
ciding which geegaw to purchase."

No, not all by any means. Charisma would always
know her mind. He squeezed her hand. "Women
could not have a better representative for their
cause."

The light dimmed in her eyes. "You're not going
to admit where you stand, are you?"

He knew what she meant. "I cannot take a position on this, Charisma." To do so would be political
suicide.

"Of course not." She tugged her hand free and turned to stare out the train window.

The loss of her smile hurt. More so than the censorious look Grace shot at him. Will struggled to find a safer topic of discussion.

"Have you heard about the Halloween ball coming up in two weeks?" he asked. All women liked discussing dances.

"It's an annual tradition." Charisma continued to gaze out the window. "And it's invitation only."

"I happen to have received an invitation." An invitation he'd told himself to throw away, but he hadn't. Now he knew why. "Will you attend with me?"

She glanced at him from the corner of her eye. "Won't you be busy campaigning? That's only days before the election."

"The best place to campaign is at the ball." Which was true, but not the sole reason he wanted to attend. "And I would like to dance with you." To hold her in the only way he could without compromising her.

She turned back to face him. "You would?"

Presenting his best smile, he nodded. "I would."

"I would like that as well." She responded with an equally warm smile. "Thank you."

The conversation drifted to other topics, but Will couldn't escape the desire to hold Charisma once more. He'd have to wait until the dance. Still dangerous, at best, but they would be in a public place. What could be safer?

Until then, though, he'd have to be careful. Already he found her intriguing beyond just her beauty—outspokenness and all.

And that terrified him.

* * *

Charisma had no difficulty in arranging a ladies' gathering at Mrs. Papadopoulos's house several days later. No doubt, many of the influential wives had agreed to attend in order to hear details of Will's rescue of Melissa, a story that had stirred the city's interest in the dark horse candidate.

Well, she intended to talk about Will, but not quite in the way they imagined. If women were as influential as Mrs. Barclay had insisted, then who better to persuade that Will was the best man for the senate?

She'd coerced her sisters into ensuring Mama stayed away, which was no simple task. But she trusted Belle and Grace to keep Mama occupied and unaware of this gathering. Her mother just wouldn't understand the purpose of this meeting.

Miss Kingsley was the last to arrive and Charisma seated her next to Miss Mattingly. Perhaps Miss Kingsley would be a good influence on the notorious gossip, who had already asked Charisma several impertinent questions.

"Does anyone wish more tea?" Charisma asked. Receiving a negative reply, she stood before the expectant gathering, her palms moist. Every word counted now. Could she do this without blurting out something she shouldn't?

"Thank you for coming," she continued. "I want to talk to you about Will Barclay as a candidate for the Colorado senate."

"I would like to know more about Mr. Barclay's

relationship with that lady-bird he rescued," Miss Mattingly said with a titter.

Charisma managed to keep a smile on her face. "Mr. Barclay felt Miss Houser was ill-treated by his family and endeavored to set things right. This is an excellent example of why he is someone we want in our government. He cares about people."

Mrs. Bell waved a dismissive hand. "I leave all the political decisions to Dr. Bell."

Several other women nodded in agreement. Charisma bit back her frustration.

"But how do you know he is making the best choice for you? As women, we are often left out of important decisions. Have you agreed with all the choices your husbands or fathers have made on your behalf?"

That caught their interest. "I absolutely detest the new stablehand Matthew has hired," Mrs. Carroll added. "The man is rude and uncouth, but Matthew says he is excellent with horses and that's enough for him."

"And I dislike the house Mr. Adams purchased for us. He merely brought me to town and told me to live in it. It's dark and far too small for our needs, but he refuses to see that." Mrs. Adams punctuated her words with a sharp nod.

The discussion disintegrated into a list of grievances against the men in their lives, which Charisma allowed to continue for several minutes. Finally, she interrupted.

"Mr. Barclay is willing to fight for rights for the lower class and haven't we as women been relegated to the lower class for long enough?" Charisma had no qualms at twisting Will's stance to fit her ideal. Not if it brought him votes.

Besides, he did support those without a voice and that included women, whether he admitted it or not.

She continued to outline his platform, adding her own interpretation for the benefit of the women. Before long, many were nodding in agreement with her.

"We don't have the right to vote," she concluded. "Men feel we are unable to make such a momentous decision, but that doesn't mean we can't let the men, who do vote, know how we feel. Only through them do we have a say in our lives."

She smiled. "I've heard that women can actually persuade men to their views by using cold suppers, cold baths—"

"Or cold sheets," Mrs. Morgan added.

Several women tittered while heat rose in Charisma's cheeks. She continued anyway. "I wonder how much of that is true?"

As she finished issuing the indirect challenge, she saw Thalia beaming at her. Mrs. Adams stood, her eyes gleaming. "Mr. Adams will never know that he didn't change his own mind."

The other women joined in, each vowing to influence her spouse or parent. Even Miss Mattingly smiled and assured Charisma that her father could be brought around to whatever she wanted. Somehow, Charisma didn't doubt that.

"I do have one more question," Miss Mattingly said.

"Yes?"

"When will you and Mr. Barclay be announcing

your engagement?" Miss Mattingly exchanged looks with the other women present. "We all know it is just a matter of time."

Charisma struggled to control her blush and racing heartbeat. "Mr. Barclay and I are not engaged nor do I expect that we will be. We are simply friends."

"I find that difficult to believe after the way he looked at you at the Bee Line dance." A knowing smile slid across Miss Mattingly's face. "He practically ignored every other woman there."

"Strange." Charisma kept her voice even. "I saw him dance with several others that night."

Miss Kingsley nodded. "That's true."

Charisma smiled and sought to change the subject. "I thank you all again for coming. Do bundle up warmly for your return home. It has grown quite chilly outside."

With Thalia's assistance, the gathering dispersed within minutes and Charisma released a sigh of relief. That had gone well.

"Do you think it will make a difference?" she asked Thalia.

The woman embraced her. "You were magnificent, my dear. I would say you have learned to be quite charming."

"But is it enough? Will it help Will?"

"Time will tell."

And it did. Within a week, the polls conducted by the newspaper showed a rise in Will's support. Charisma resisted the urge to share the results of her success with Will. He had stayed away from her since their return, but she knew he was busy campaigning as well.

She would see him soon enough at the Halloween ball next week. For now, she would continue to discuss Will with the women of Colorado Springs. They might not have rights, but they would be heard.

Fifteen

The day of the Halloween ball dawned with cold and overcast skies, hiding the recent snowfall on the nearby mountains, but Charisma refused to let her spirits be dampened. Tonight she would be with Will—be held in his arms.

It was pitifully little, but she would savor it.

Her sisters were attending the ball as well. Kit was taking Belle, of course, and one of Kit's friends was squiring Grace. Her youngest sister was so excited she'd already broken two vases and torn the hem of her dress. The question now was would they all survive until time to depart?

Mama fluttered over them all, angry over Papa's refusal to take her to the ball, eager for her daughters to make a good showing, tutoring them in manners and behavior, instruction they'd heard a thousand times before. By noon, Papa jammed his hat on his head and left, announcing his intention to visit his mine for a few days.

Charisma wasn't fooled by his escape, but neither could she blame him. Even she was experiencing jitters as she dressed for this special event.

The Halloween ball drew only the most elite from the town and provided gossip enough for several days afterward. New gowns were discussed.

Behaviors were examined as well as the various relationships formed during the dance. Grace's new
escort would provide some fodder for that.

Standing before her mirror, Charisma examined
her appearance. She hadn't used any cosmetics.
Belle's horrible experience months ago, when
cosmetics had turned her face gray, had quickly
convinced Charisma to avoid them.

The dark jade silk of her gown dipped low, revealing her shoulders and the beginning swells of
her breasts. The waist was long and narrow and a
large train flowed over her bustle. With her hair
caught on top of her head and a single curl at either side of her face, she appeared quite the lady.

Would Will think so?

The color of the dress highlighted her eyes and
they sparkled now as she anticipated seeing Will
again. It had been nearly two weeks since they'd
spent any time together. Had he missed her even
half as much as she longed for him?

Probably not. He'd been busy campaigning. Just
because she'd fallen in love with him didn't mean
he returned those feelings. In fact, he'd made it
clear they had no future together.

But at least they would have tonight.

Belle and Grace departed early with Kit to fetch
Grace's escort. Charisma would follow with Will
since the carriage couldn't hold all the sisters and
the men.

Will arrived shortly after the sisters' departure
and Charisma descended the stairs slowly, her
mouth dry. Why should she be nervous at seeing him again? They were just friends, weren't
they?

His eyes lit up as he spotted her and his slow smile started butterflies fluttering in her stomach. He crossed to the bottom of the staircase to take her hand and raise it to his lips. "You are too lovely for words," he murmured.

"Thank you." Charisma tried to ignore the heat in her cheeks. "You cut a fine figure yourself."

He wore a black tailcoat with a white waistcoat and tie, which emphasized his dark hair and eyes. She had always thought him handsome, but tonight he put all other men to shame.

"You make a very attractive couple," Mama added from her position by the door. "I feel certain everyone who sees you tonight will say it is so."

Charisma hid a smile, but caught the twinkle of merriment in Will's eyes before he tucked her hand through his elbow and led her to the door.

"Don't forget your cloak," Mama said. "It is already starting to snow and from the way my finger aches, I feel certain we will see much of it soon."

"Yes, Mama." Charisma turned to allow Will to place her cloak around her shoulders, savoring the brief but lingering touch of his fingers.

"Shall we?" he asked. He bowed toward Mama, then donned his top hat. "I don't want Mrs. Papadopoulos to freeze waiting for us."

Thalia assured them she was quite warm as Will assisted Charisma into the carriage, and Charisma found herself grateful for the enclosed conveyance tonight. As it was, the icy wind managed to whistle through even the tiniest of cracks so that she also found herself grateful for the roaring fires at the Manitou House.

A heavy crowd was already present, though the

dancing had yet to begin. They exchanged greetings as Will led Charisma and Thalia inside.

"Ah, there is Mrs. Adams. I do believe I will sit with her for the evening." Thalia gave Will and Charisma a warm smile. "However, I expect to see you engage in several dances."

"I believe we can accommodate you," Will answered. Once Thalia departed, he took Charisma's elbow. "Would you like something to eat or drink first?"

"No, thank you." Her stomach was far too nervous for dining.

He shot her a teasing glance. "Don't tell me you're one of those women who wears her corset so tight she can't eat?"

That he would say something so familiar eased Charisma's tension, enabling her to smile. "No." Her corset was snug, but not overly restrictive. "I will probably eat later. For now, I'm too excited just being here."

"Ah, Mr. Barclay." Mr. Harrison paused beside them to pump Will's hand with enthusiasm. "I must congratulate you. The latest polls have you neck-and-neck with Mr. Howbert. That is quite an achievement."

"Thank you." Will beamed at the praise. "I'm pleased myself. The polls have risen steadily over the past couple of weeks."

"How did you do it? I had no hope that you'd overcome the Republican stranglehold on this county."

Charisma bit her lip and glanced down at her hands to keep from blurting out the answer. Neither man would be pleased to hear that women were influencing the election.

"I've talked to nearly every person in the county," Will said. "I guess it helped."

Mr. Harrison shook his hand once more. "Keep up the good work. I'll be looking for you at the polls."

He left and Will grinned at Charisma. "Do you believe it? I've actually caught up to Howbert."

"I'm not surprised." *Not at all.*

The band began a lively polka and Charisma looked around. Her sisters and their escorts were already on the floor dancing. Belle appeared totally enraptured with Kit while Grace looked less happy. Her partner didn't appear very enthusiastic either. Was she stepping on his toes?

"Do you want to dance?" Will asked.

"Why don't we meet everyone first?" she suggested. This was a perfect opportunity for him to make one last push. The dancing would continue for several hours yet. She'd waited this long. She would survive a little longer.

As gratitude filled Will's face, she pointed across the large ballroom. "Look, there's General Palmer. I must tell him how grateful I am for his support."

In less than two hours, they had managed to spend some time conversing with nearly every man in attendance. Charisma forced herself to remain mostly silent, but exchanged significant glances with the women she'd spoken previously to about Will. Their answering smiles told her all she needed to know. If the women in Colorado Springs had anything to do with it, Will Barclay would be the next El Paso County senator.

When the notes of a slow waltz began, Will removed the punch glass from Charisma's hand and set it beside his own on the table. "I believe now is our chance to dance."

Not giving her a chance to refuse—as if she would—he led her onto the dance floor. Warmth darkened his eyes as they danced, his steps sure and easy to follow.

The heat of his body—close and yet not close enough—generated an answering fire within Charisma. Was she wanton for desiring his touch, his kiss? For a brief moment, she considered finding Belle and asking her older sister for advice, but she quickly discarded that idea. At this moment, she wanted to believe she was the only one to ever feel this way.

She met his gaze, trying to understand the depth of his feelings. He liked her. She felt certain of that. But he'd also made it clear he had no intention of settling down with any woman, especially her.

Did all men bestow kisses and caresses that meant nothing? Perhaps. They visited places like the Blue House, didn't they?

Well, the way Will looked at her now, a fire burning deep in his eyes, made her feel as if he were touching her. Her insides twisted and grew warm, her skin tingled, her breasts swelled within the confines of her dress. Just his lingering gaze made her long for something she didn't completely understand.

He drew her closer until his body brushed hers as they danced. Even that brief contact fanned the fire low in her belly.

Her throat tightened and her mouth grew dry. When she moistened her lips with the tip of her tongue, his gaze followed the movement with such intensity she could almost feel his lips on hers.

"Charisma, I don't know how to thank you for all your assistance." His voice sounded thick, rough, which sent a shiver dancing down her spine.

A kiss would do, but even she wasn't so bold as to ask for one here in the middle of a crowded ballroom. "It will be enough if you win the election."

His slow smile caressed her. "For the first time, I feel as if that is a possibility." He tightened his hand on her waist. "And I know you had something to do with it."

"Me?" She'd been proud of the way she'd held her tongue tonight.

"There is a sparkle of satisfaction in your eyes that I'm learning to recognize."

"Oh." That was more difficult to control than her tongue. She gave him a careless smile. "That is nothing but your imagination."

He spun her around as a blast of cold air blew into the room. "I—"

"You should see it snowing outside." The man who rushed in proclaimed his news with excitement. "Looks like a big one."

Several dancers rushed to peek outside, but Will didn't even miss a step of the dance. "It can wait," he murmured.

"Yes." Charisma wanted to enjoy every moment she could be close to him, for however long it lasted.

Which probably wouldn't be long. Though she dreaded hearing the answer, Charisma finally asked the question that had been nagging her for days. "Will, what are your plans after the election?"

He hesitated and glanced over her head, avoiding her gaze. "If I win, I'll go to Denver and join the senate."

"And if you don't?" Would he stay here? Spend more time with her?

"I'll probably return to my law practice in Denver." His voice revealed nothing of his emotions.

"Oh." She couldn't hide her disappointment. Then this was the last opportunity she'd have to be with him. Ever. With the election only days away, he wouldn't have time for her after this wonderful evening.

If only it could last forever.

The orchestra seemed to read Charisma's mind, for the next few tunes were waltzes, each melody tightening the fist around her heart and deepening the ache inside her. They danced to every one of them, Will's gaze holding hers, so potent that the room faded away until she saw only him. Words became unnecessary. The intensity of his presence was enough.

When the orchestra finally paused, Charisma glanced around, surprised to discover that the room was more than half empty. Where had everyone gone? Even Belle and Grace had departed. Why hadn't they said something?

Thalia approached them as they left the dance floor. "May I suggest we start home? Miss Sullivan and Miss Grace left some time ago. They asked me to offer their farewells as you were otherwise engaged." She smiled, then gestured toward the door. "The latest reports have the storm getting worse and I am eager to get on our way. At my age, I want the comforts of my own home."

Though disappointed, Charisma nodded. She never wanted this evening to end, but it appeared the weather had made that decision for her.

Will led them to where they had left their cloaks. "I'll bring the carriage to the door."

The moment he stepped outside, Will realized he'd treated the reports of this storm too lightly. The wind had picked up considerably, wailing through the night, driving a thick wall of snow ahead of it. Already, several inches coated the ground, which would make the ride home slow and treacherous.

Should they remain here until it passed? Perhaps not. At the moment, he could still see for some distance—enough to guide the carriage home. And Mrs. Papadopoulos preferred her own bed.

Will grimaced as he hitched his horse to the carriage. To be honest, he didn't dare spend any more time here with Charisma. Every moment he held her made him dread the moment he'd have to let her go. She made him ache with a longing that drove out all reason, all his plans for the future. To remain could be dangerous. Far better to brave the storm.

At the entrance, he assisted the women into the carriage, shivering despite his heavy wool coat. "Take me home first," Mrs. Papadopoulos said as he helped her inside. "It will make less time that you have to be out in this."

He agreed with that. Once assured they were safely tucked inside, he directed the horse toward the city. The wind bit at his nose and ears, pelting him with dagger-like snow. By the time the first signs of the city appeared, he could barely feel his hands and the snow had increased, decreasing his range of vision to only a few feet.

Hoping that he had the correct house on the right street, he pulled his horse to a stop. He went to open the carriage door, his cold fingers fumbling with the latch until it finally opened.

Mrs. Papadopoulos leaned forward. "You poor man. You're frozen half to death. You and Charisma must come inside to warm up."

"It's not that much further." Though in this storm, even a few blocks felt like miles.

"I insist. Charisma's lips are blue as well. Pull the buggy to the back. I'll have James put the horse in the carriage house for now."

Will didn't bother to protest any longer. The cold penetrated into his bones and he nodded, teeth chattering. The few minutes it took to lead the horse to the carriage house felt like an eternity.

Grateful, he left the horse with James and hurried to assist Mrs. Papadopoulos and Charisma. They ran into the house, the fierce wind howling at their heels and icy snow slashing at their faces.

Once inside, Will took the time to glance at the ladies. Charisma's lips were blue and she shivered from head to toe. Without thinking, he wrapped his arms around her and pulled her close.

"You need to warm up," he murmured.

"There's a fire in the parlor." Mrs. Papadopoulos led them into the room. "Go, stand before the fire and thaw out. Both of you. I'll get some tea."

Will needed no second invitation. Facing Charisma, he ran his hands over her arms in an attempt to stop her shivering. "You're like an ice statue."

She gave him a wan smile. "This dress was designed for appearance, not warmth."

Though she still wore her cloak, he had no difficulty in recalling the cut of her gown, her creamy flesh revealed by the low neckline, her curves accentuated by the tiny waist and flowing train. No, not designed for warmth but to make the wearer appeal to a man. It worked.

"And you're coated with snow." Charisma fumbled with the buttons on his ice-encrusted coat and helped him out of it, the simple act oddly seductive. "Your hands are frozen. Here."

She turned him to face the flames, then removed his gloves and massaged his numb hands between hers. Will began to warm up again. Far warmer than necessary, in fact.

When James came to take his coat, Charisma gave up her cloak as well. Will found his gaze dropping to the swell of her breasts—the urge to kiss her, to touch her, almost overpowering.

The return of Mrs. Papadopoulos with a steaming teapot saved him. "Here's some tea to warm us." She smiled at them. "Are you better now?"

Will swallowed and drew his hands away from Charisma, thankful for the interruption. "Much, thank you." He'd be even better once he delivered Charisma safely home and retreated to his own small hotel room . . . far removed from temptation.

"Thank you, Thalia." Charisma accepted the tea with a smile and cupped her hands around it as she sat. "I had no idea the storm was so bad."

"I'll admit I was so engaged in conversation with Mrs. Adams that I paid the announcements no mind," Mrs. Papadopoulos said. "And I did hate to disturb the two of you during your dance."

Charisma's already pink cheeks flushed even

more, adding to the streak of longing that filled Will as he recalled how it felt to hold her close, to inhale the freshness of her scent. He gulped at his tea, then nearly spat it out as it scalded his tongue.

Mischief danced in Mrs. Papadopoulos's eyes. "Be careful. It is hot, my dear."

"Yes." He was careful to sip after that. Once he drained his cup, he stood. "We should be going before it gets too late."

"Already too late." James filled the parlor doorway. "I bedded down your horse."

"I beg your pardon?" They had to go. Will had to see Charisma home.

"It's too bad out there for man or beast."

Will rushed forward. "No." He *had* to get Charisma home.

James shrugged and led him to the front door. "See for yourself."

The frigid wind stole Will's breath away as he opened the door. Snow blew so intensely now that he couldn't see beyond the front steps. No sane person would venture out in this.

"Oh my."

He heard Charisma's quiet exclamation behind him and turned to meet her gaze. The same spark of awareness lingered in her eyes that he'd seen earlier. To remain near each other much longer was too dangerous.

Glancing back outside, he sighed. He had no choice. He closed the door and turned to face her. "We don't dare go out in that."

Several emotions crossed her face so quickly he couldn't name them all—apprehension, happiness, awareness. Much like the tensions warring within himself.

Charisma returned to the parlor to face Mrs. Papadopoulos. "What about my family? Won't they worry?"

"Your sisters left before you did. I'm certain your family will assume you stayed at the hotel until the storm passed." Mrs. Papadopoulos smiled as she stood. "Come, I'll show you both to rooms for the night."

To Will's relief, he was given a room at the opposite end of the hallway from Charisma's. The room was clean, the bed soft and the fire blazing. He needed nothing more.

At least, nothing he could have.

Will woke with a jerk, startled by his unfamiliar surroundings until the night's events returned in a rush of memory. *Oh, yes, the storm.*

The wind continued to howl outside, rattling the glass window. Will shivered. Sitting up, he noticed the fire had nearly burnt itself out. With a grimace, he slid from the bed to supply it with fresh wood.

"Damn." There was no wood beside the fireplace.

Will hesitated only a moment, then pulled on his pants. He'd have to restock or the room would be frigid by morning. He'd noticed a large stack of wood in the back hallway earlier. That would do.

The temperature in the hallway was even colder than in his room and Will moved briskly, telling himself how good the newly fed fire would feel once he returned. The firewood was where he remembered and he grabbed a large stack in his arms, regretting the lack of a shirt. The rough edges scratched his chest. Too late now. At least this amount should last until morning.

He hurried for the staircase, then stopped abruptly, the wood spilling to the floor as he collided with Charisma. She gasped and landed in a heap on the bottom step, a quilt clutched around her, held closed by her fist.

"I'm sorry." He hesitated before reaching out to help her to her feet. "I didn't see you."

The quilt parted slightly as she took his hand, providing a tantalizing glimpse of silk and skin. A fiery shot of desire sizzled through him and he dropped her hand as soon as she regained her footing.

Turning, he concentrated on picking up the wood. Anything to avoid the sight of her before him.

"My fire went out." Her voice sounded shaky. "I . . . I came for more wood."

He stood and dared to meet her gaze. "Me, too." He motioned for her to go ahead of him. "I'll take some to your room. Go on."

She preceded him up the stairs, her shape thankfully hidden by the voluminous quilt. Not that his imagination didn't provide the unseen contours. Once he delivered some wood to her room, he would retreat to his room as soon as possible. He half expected someone to greet them, awakened by the noise of the falling wood, but the hallway remained quiet and empty. He wasn't certain whether to be grateful or not.

Stepping aside inside her room, she allowed him to squat beside the fireplace and deposit his load of wood. Her fire was down to embers. The room had grown so cold, Will could see his own breath.

Using the fresh wood, he stirred the embers until new flames blazed to life. The difference in heat was noticeable immediately. "That should do for the rest of the night," he told her as he stood.

She'd come to stand before him and her eyes were wide through the dim light, her gaze focused on his bare chest. Shaking her head as if to clear it, she gave him a shaky smile. "Thank you."

They both moved at once. She turned to give him room to pass and he stepped forward to leave. His foot came down on the edge of her quilt and her motion caused it to fall to the floor, revealing her enticing figure.

Will gulped, unable to look away. The sheer material of her chemise hid nothing. In fact, the light from the flames illuminated her rose-tipped breasts and the dark strawberry-blonde hair between her legs. His shaft hardened at once, all the night's frustration making him ache with a wild ferocity.

Charisma stared back at him, but made no move to cover herself. Instead she stepped toward him, hesitant but unrelenting.

As she grew closer, he could see her nipples had tightened into hard buds. He clenched his fists, longing to touch her, knowing he shouldn't. But he didn't move away when she paused before him.

"I know how you can thank me," she said, her voice trembling.

Thank her? He barely recalled their earlier conversation. Oh, for her assistance with his campaign. Will sucked in his breath, dreading her next words. "How?"

"Make love to me."

Sixteen

Charisma saw the fire flare in Will's eyes, but he remained still as if frozen in place. She placed her palms against his bare chest, then bent to place kisses over it. All her life she'd been told she was too bold, too impulsive. She'd always thought it the only way to get what she wanted.

Well, she wanted Will.

She would never love anyone else. After tonight, she'd never see him again. He was the only one who could ever make her feel this way, burning with a longing she couldn't describe. If she was ever to experience the joys of lovemaking, she wanted him to be the one she shared it with. It wasn't as if she'd even consider a life with anyone else after he left.

His skin trembled beneath her lips and she glanced up to see a muscle jerk in his jaw. In any other circumstance, she might admire his restraint, but not now. She'd managed to dash thoughts of propriety, of tomorrow, from her mind. Couldn't he do the same?

"Kiss me, Will," she whispered, trailing kisses along his collarbone and throat. "Touch me."

"Charisma, I—" He choked off his words and she softly pressed her mouth to his.

Would he turn away from her once again?

He tensed, his hands wrapping around her arms. For a moment, she feared he would push her away. Then he pulled her close, her body flush against his, as he devoured her lips with a passion that ignited the longing simmering inside her.

Yes, this was what she wanted.

She responded with equal passion, meeting his tongue and lips with a ferocity of her own, her breathing ragged and her heart hammering. When he cupped her breast and ran his thumb over her sensitive peak, she moaned from the intense ripple of pleasure that seared through her.

He dropped his hand and left her mouth. "Charisma." The agony of his inner battle sounded in her name.

This was one time she did not want him to be a gentleman. Charisma stepped back, then slid her chemise from her shoulders and let it pool to the floor. She faced him then, her knees trembling only slightly. Would he still refuse her?

His gaze lingered on her, the intensity of it warming her skin. "You are so beautiful," he murmured.

He scooped her into his arms and she gasped, the feel of her skin against his creating an even tighter ache inside her. Her breasts tingled, longing for his touch. Her breath came in short bursts from her tight throat. She couldn't doubt, wouldn't doubt this. She loved him.

Carrying her to the bed, Will placed her upon it. Though he sat beside her, he kept his hands clenched in fists, his eyes blazing. He tried to speak once again, his voice barely audible. "I . . . you . . . we . . . "

"Please, Will." She held his gaze as she took his hand and placed it on her breast, amazed by her own boldness. But she wanted this, wanted him.

He remained still, closing his eyes, then slowly curved his palm around her flesh. "Charisma, I . . ." She didn't dare let him doubt this. Nothing that felt so right could be wrong.

"Please." She arched against his hand, then inhaled sharply when he brushed his thumb over the tip of her breast. The heat flared higher within her. "Oh, Will, please."

"God, Charisma. I can't deny you." Bending down, he whispered against her lips. "It will be wonderful. I promise."

Relief mingled with the ache in her. Charisma smiled. "That's one campaign promise I hope you keep." Her voice only wavered a little.

He smiled in return, then kissed her with such tenderness she wanted to weep. The wildness was still there but restrained as he seduced her mouth, awakening incredible new sensations throughout her. His tongue and lips made more promises—promises she wanted fulfilled.

Leaving her mouth, he trailed kisses to the swell of her breasts, caressing them everywhere but where she wanted his mouth. She twisted beneath him and he chuckled. "I always knew you'd be demanding."

He brushed the palm of his hand over her nipple, increasing the ache between her legs. Finally, he drew her breast into his mouth, his magical tongue busy fulfilling his promises.

Charisma found her hips moving through no thought of her own, rocking, wanting . . . something.

Sliding his hand lower over her abdomen, Will

touched her at the center of her heat and Charisma
gasped. He hesitated, then stroked her until she
could no longer control the rhythm of her hips.
The ache inside her wound tighter until she feared
she would explode.

When he slid one finger inside her, the ache
burst into a thousand tiny stars, stealing her breath
and flooding her veins with pleasure. She had
never dreamed anything like this existed . . . could
exist.

"You . . . you know how to manage a magnificent
campaign," she said, gasping.

Will chuckled and stood up to shed his pants.
"This campaign is just beginning."

As he dropped his drawers, Charisma stared at
the male part of him jutting forward. She had
heard whispers of how men and women came together, but her imagination hadn't come close to
this.

She stretched forth a tentative hand to touch
him, surprised that he was soft and warm, yet firm
beneath her fingers, pulsing with life. Cautiously
she stroked her fingers along the long, solid length.

Will groaned and jerked away, grabbed her hand.
"While I might appreciate that at another time, that
time is not now." He sat beside her again.

"Does that . . . ?" Charisma paused to swallow.
Surely the stories she'd heard couldn't be true.
"Does that go inside me?"

Humor danced in Will's eyes. "It does."

She stared at him. "It won't fit."

"Oh, it will. Trust me, Charisma." He kissed her
slowly. "This is going to be a mutually satisfying
campaign."

The tremors of her body had subsided to a gentle shudder, but Will's kisses and caresses soon had her writhing again, her inner ache swelling. Now that she knew the pleasure that awaited she eagerly raised her hips toward his hand and moaned as his fingers once more filled her.

Before the pleasure could peak, he withdrew. She frowned, then inhaled sharply as he knelt over her. Will kissed her. "Trust me."

She did. She trusted him completely, but she couldn't toss away her apprehension. "Will it . . . will it hurt?"

"Only for a moment." He drew a long kiss from her lips, then nuzzled her breast and her thoughts became cloudy.

He entered her in one sudden movement. A brief flash of pain was followed by the sensation of being filled in a most marvelous way.

"Oh my," she whispered. No one had ever mentioned this. How could they? It was wonderful beyond words.

"Are you all right?" Will froze above her, his expression concerned.

Smiling, she touched his face. "Yes."

Keeping his gaze locked on hers, he moved against her, his strokes at first slow, then gaining intensity when Charisma threw back her head, her breathing ragged, her fingers digging into Will's shoulders. Holding him? Helping him? She didn't know.

All she knew was the building pressure, the wonder of the new sensations, and the final explosion of joy that rippled through her shortly before Will groaned. It was even better than before. She wouldn't have believed it possible.

As Will propped himself on his elbows, his breath coming in gasps, Charisma brushed the hair from his eyes. "I like the way you keep your campaign promises," she said quietly. "You have my vote."

Raising his head, Will laughed. "And you most definitely have mine." He kissed her softly. "All right?"

"Oh, yes. I never knew. I . . ." Words failed her. Nothing could describe all the new feelings she'd experienced. If she hadn't been in love with Will before this, she certainly was now. "Thank you."

A strange look crossed Will's face and he rolled over, then drew her into his arms. "I'm sorry, Charisma."

She sat up abruptly and pushed him away. "Don't you dare apologize." He was going to ruin everything. Couldn't he have wanted her, loved her as much as she did him?

Rising up on one elbow, he reached for her. "But I shouldn't have—"

"I asked you to make love to me. There's nothing to apologize for." Couldn't he understand that she wanted him? That she knew what she'd asked him to do?

He sat up. "But this changes things."

As he touched her shoulder, she slid off the bed and pulled the quilt around her again, blinking rapidly to keep the threatening tears away. She didn't want his guilt. "Nothing has to change."

"But I've compromised you. I—"

"No one knows that but me and you." She whirled around to face him, her heart clenching. "I knew what I was doing, Will. I expect nothing from you."

"But—"

"Nothing," she snapped. He was taking the most wonderful experience of her life and making her feel tawdry. "You said often enough that you have no intention of marrying. I don't expect you to offer marriage. I don't *want* you to offer marriage." For all his sweet, soft-spoken words, he'd never once mentioned that he loved her.

Will looked stunned. With slow deliberate movements he stood and pulled on his pants. "What are you going to do now?"

Why did he need to ask that? "I imagine the same as I always have." Was she suddenly now branded as a harlot? "Or maybe I'll go work at the Blue House."

Will seized her shoulders, his eyes ablaze. "Don't talk like that."

"What would you have me say?" she demanded. "You're making me feel dirty."

His anger disappeared. "Charisma, I—"

She pushed him away from her. "Get out of here." When he hesitated, she crossed over and opened the door. "Go."

He joined her, then paused. "What if there's a child?"

Her heart skipped a beat. Sadness followed a brief surge of joy. *A child. His child.* But it was not to be. The women at the Blue House had told her many of the tricks they used to prevent pregnancy. "There won't be."

The silence stretched for several long moments. Finally, Will stepped through the doorway. "We'll talk later."

"There's nothing left for us to talk about." She shut the door after him, the sharp click of the latch loud in the night, then turned and climbed into bed. The bed that only minutes before had been a place of wonder.

Charisma pulled the quilt tighter around her and buried her face against her upraised knees. When the wind wailed outside, she wailed along with it.

The storm had eased by morning, but Will couldn't decide if he was relieved or chagrined. Charisma refused to speak with him and he found himself no closer to a solution than last night.

The honorable thing to do was to speak to Charisma's father and ask for her hand in marriage. True, he had no desire to marry now, especially with his future still uncertain, but he'd be lying if he didn't admit to wanting to hold Charisma again, to explore the curves he'd barely discovered.

She'd said she wouldn't marry him, but that had been her anger talking. She would change her mind once he presented his proposal properly. He was not penniless by any means and his family name did have some weight. Even if he lost the election, he had his position as a barrister.

Will nodded as he drove the carriage to the front of the house, the wheels plowing through the thick snow. If he had to marry, Charisma was not an entirely unwelcome choice. He found her attractive and her family was wealthy enough to please even Father. Of course, they were not old money, but his mother liked Charisma and that mattered more to Will.

It would be a beneficial arrangement for both

families. Yes, he would present it to Mr. Sullivan in just that way.

At the front of the house, he jumped from the carriage and went to the door for Charisma. She refused to meet his inquiring glance, but turned to give Mrs. Papadopoulos a hug. "Thank you for your hospitality."

"It was my pleasure." Mrs. Papadopoulos looked from Charisma to Will. "I do trust all is well?"

The older woman was observant, though even an idiot would have noticed Charisma's abrupt responses to his questions this morning. "It will be," he told her.

He was prepared to carry Charisma through the deep snow to the carriage, but she brushed past him, nearly slipping in her eagerness to reach the conveyance. Will sighed. As always, she was stubborn, outspoken, and too willing to face the world alone. Why had he expected anything different?

Seeing her secured inside, he drove carefully to her home, the horse and buggy barely making it through some of the towering drifts. Fortunately, the overcast skies were breaking up and already the sun poked through tiny holes in the clouds. He was sure it would make short work of the heavy snowfall.

When he reached her house, Will jumped down to assist her from the carriage. When she reached for his hand, he scooped her into his arms and turned for the house.

"I can walk," she said, her voice as cold as the surrounding air.

"You'll ruin your gown."

"It's already ruined."

He glanced at her, but she looked away, refusing to meet his gaze. "Charisma?"

She ignored him. When he set her on her feet on the door stoop, she tried to hurry inside, but he caught her hand. "Charisma." If she didn't want to talk now, so be it. There would be other opportunities. "There is going to be a reception for all the candidates on Saturday night at the courthouse. Will you accompany me?"

Her surprise almost made him laugh. Then she narrowed her eyes. "Are you certain you want to be seen with me?"

He ignored her baiting sarcasm. "Yes, very much so." After all, she was going to be his wife.

Her anger gave way to puzzlement. "Very well."

He brushed her cheek with his hand. "May I come inside for a short while?" What better time to speak to Mr. Sullivan?

"It would not be wise right now. Papa has gone to the mine for a few days and Mama . . . well, you know Mama."

He did, indeed. Hiding his frustration, Will nodded and opened the door for her. "Then I will see you on Saturday night." *Perhaps by then Mr. Sullivan will have returned.*

"Until then." She shot him a confused look, then vanished inside.

Will tromped through the snow back to his carriage, unable to fathom his disappointment. After all, now he had a reprieve from taking his first steps to becoming leg-shackled.

Still, the end result was inevitable. He was a Barclay and this Barclay, at least, did the honorable thing.

* * *

Charisma couldn't believe how quickly the snow melted over the next few days. By Saturday, she couldn't even tell there had been three feet of snow right outside her house. Only the shaded spots toward the north still held evidence of the sudden snowstorm. If she didn't know better, she would think it had never happened.

But it had happened.

She had stayed the night at Thalia's and she had made love with Will—a wonderful, thrilling sharing of bodies that still made her tingle. Seated in her window seat, she drew her fingertips over her throat, recalling Will's passionate kisses.

This thought was followed by the memory of how fast he'd turned cool, to discussions of doing the right thing, of honor. The devil take his honor. She wanted his love and if she couldn't have that, then she wanted none of him.

She'd seen too many loveless marriages. Even her own parents, who had started out very much in love, were disintegrating into the type of existence in which they barely acknowledged each other's presence. She would never agree to that. Never.

"Charisma?" A quiet rap on her door was followed by Belle peeking inside. "Can I come in?"

She motioned her sister inside and Belle came to curl up on the opposite side of the window seat. "Are you all right?" Belle asked.

"Of course." Charisma forced a bright smile. "Why wouldn't I be?"

"I don't know." Belle cocked her head. "You seem . . . different somehow. You've been much quieter than usual lately. Ever since you spent the night at Mrs. Papadopoulos's house."

Belle hesitated, then reached out to touch Charisma's hand. "Did something happen there? With you and Mr. Barclay?"

Startled by her sister's accurate guess, Charisma gazed out the window. As much as she wanted to share her heartbreak with Belle, she couldn't . . . wouldn't discuss what she'd shared so intimately with Will.

"I love him," she said finally.

"Of course you do."

Charisma looked at Belle in surprise and her sister laughed. "I saw that coming a long time ago. I know what it's like to be in love, remember?"

"But at least Kit loves you."

Belle's smile faded. "And Mr. Barclay?"

"He doesn't love me. He's made that clear. In fact, he has often declared his intention of never marrying."

"Many a man has said that and later recanted. In fact, I saw him leaving here just yesterday. Maybe he talked to Mama. Or asked about Papa."

Charisma shook her head. Will was a man with plans—plans that didn't include her. He would go on to the senate and forget he'd ever known her. "I don't want him if he doesn't love me. I won't marry him any other way."

Her vehemence made her voice shake, and Belle studied her with too-observant eyes. When Charisma looked away, Belle squeezed her hands. "I understand, Charisma. I do. If you ever want to talk to someone, I'm here."

She stood, then hugged Charisma, triggering the ever-close tears. "Remember that," she added.

"I will." Charisma wiped at her eyes and rose to her feet. "Enough feeling maudlin. I want to see Missy this afternoon before I prepare for the reception tonight."

"Reception?"

"Will is taking me to a reception for the candidates." She still didn't understand his sudden invitation. She'd been convinced he never wanted to be around her again.

"Isn't that a good thing?" Belle asked.

"I don't know." Charisma grimaced. "Maybe." The gleam in Will's eyes when he'd issued his invitation hinted at a mysterious secret. What could that be?

She shook her head to clear away thoughts of Will. She would see him soon enough. "Come with me to Mr. Gardner's?" she asked.

Though Belle sighed, she smiled in reply. "I would enjoy a brisk walk."

And it was brisk. Though the sun shone brightly, the air was cool. By the time they reached Mr. Gardner's house, Charisma's nose was cold and Belle's cheeks were pink.

Charisma rapped on the door and was gratified to hear approaching footsteps. Missy answered, then cried out in glee. "Miss Charisma, how did you know?"

"Know?" Charisma stared at her without comprehension. "I came to see how you were doing now that all the furor from the newspaper article has passed."

"I am wonderful." *True enough.* Missy glowed with happiness. "More than wonderful." She caught Charisma's hand in hers. "Do come inside.

Thomas . . . Mr. Gardner . . . is here. He will want to thank you as well."

Still confused, Charisma glanced back at Belle, then followed Missy inside. "Thank me?" If anything, she had assumed Mr. Gardner would never want to look upon her again. She had brought nothing but chaos into his life.

As they entered the parlor, Mr. Gardner rose to his feet, a broad smile on his face and a sparkle in his eyes. He appeared in far better health than when Charisma had first seen him. Almost joyful, in fact. "Miss Charisma. Miss Sullivan. What a wonderful coincidence. You should be the first ones to hear our most excellent news."

Excellent news? Charisma looked from Missy's beaming face to Mr. Gardner. "What is that, sir?"

"I have asked Miss Houser to do me the honor of becoming my wife and she has accepted. I am most fortunate to have fallen in love when I thought I would never know that state again."

Charisma stared for several long moments. How had this happened?

Belle spoke first, extending her felicitations to Mr. Gardner and Missy, and Charisma shook off her stupor. "That is truly wonderful news." She hugged Missy with enthusiasm. This was far better than she ever had hoped for the young woman. "I am so happy for you both. I am just . . . stunned."

Mr. Gardner laughed. "It was not planned by myself or Miss Houser, I assure you. I must thank you for bringing her to me."

"Even after . . . ?"

He nodded. "I saw her merely as an excellent housekeeper. At least I thought I did. The situation with both Mr. Barclays made me realize I did not want to lose her . . . as a woman more so than as a housekeeper. I began to realize how much I appreciate her company when I dined and how she anticipated my needs so that my life as well as my household ran smoothly." He reached out to pull Missy to his side. "And I fell in love."

Charisma hesitated before asking her next question, but the issue needed to be addressed. "And her past?"

"Her past is in the past as is mine." He gave a wry smile. "You well know that I have not always been the most temperate of men. We are both starting anew."

When Charisma started to speak again, he held up his hand. "Yes, I know there will be gossip, but I refuse to let it stop me. Love is too rare a thing to throw away."

A lump formed in Charisma's throat. "Too rare indeed." She couldn't say any more.

Belle spoke for her. "Everyone will be very happy for you both."

Missy shook her head. "There will be some who say I set out to ensnare Thomas, that I used my . . . my wiles on him."

Mr. Gardner chuckled. "And nothing could be further from the truth. She has not even allowed me to kiss her yet."

Whereas Charisma had shared far more than kisses with Will. "When is the wedding?" she asked.

"As soon as possible," Mr. Gardner said. "I see no point in waiting." He clasped Charisma's hand. "I am counting on you for support, Miss Charisma. You've been such a good friend to Missy. That means a lot to both of us."

"You always have my support." If the town gossips tried to ruin Missy's happiness, Charisma would gladly set them straight.

"Excellent." Mr. Gardner beamed at Missy; a man obviously besotted with love.

Charisma tried to ignore the twinge of pain in her chest. If only Will would look at *her* like that. "Now we must be going. I am sure you have much to do."

"So many things." Missy stepped forward. "Let me show you out."

In the hallway, she hugged Charisma once more. "I don't know how to thank you. I am so happy. I fell in love with Thomas almost immediately after I arrived here. He was so sad, so lonely. I never dreamed he would notice me. When he spoke of his feelings, I . . . I became the happiest woman on earth."

"I am thrilled you found each other." Charisma truly was happy for the couple.

She remained silent on the walk home, giving Belle a slight smile when her sister squeezed her hand. "Can people truly fall in love again? I can't imagine loving anyone but Will, no matter how long I live."

"I feel the same way about Kit. If he had not returned my feelings, then I would have gone to my grave an old maid."

"But Kit does love you." And Mr. Gardner loved Missy. While Will felt only a sense of duty and honor.

And that would never be enough.

Seventeen

As Will led Charisma and Mrs. Papadopoulos into the courthouse meeting room, Charisma studied the other attendees. All of the El Paso County candidates were represented, along with most of the more prestigious families, yet the group was not overly large.

The men far outnumbered the women but Charisma noted several wives in attendance. Thank goodness. She had been afraid she and Mrs. Papadopoulos would be the only females. "What is the reason for this gathering?" she asked Will.

He shrugged. "To commiserate, perhaps, or celebrate that the elections are almost over." His gaze followed Irving Howbert, his Republican opponent, as the man approached General Palmer. "Or to get in one last push," Will added.

"Mr. Howbert is a formidable opponent," Charisma admitted. After all, Mr. Howbert had been instrumental in the creation of Colorado Springs and had just given the opera house to the city last year. "But you will beat him."

"We will see." Will smiled as he placed his hand on her waist, his gesture almost proprietary. He'd been his normal self since he'd picked her up, but something was different about him, something in his attitude. "My numbers are good, but it is the turnout at the polls that will determine the outcome."

They had barely crossed the room when Mr. Harrison approached them, his smile so wide it stretched from ear to ear. "I just heard this morning that you are actually surpassing Mr. Howbert in the polls," he told Will. "I asked twice to ensure I wasn't confusing things." He shook Will's hand with enthusiasm. "This is excellent. Excellent. For once the Democrats may win in this county."

Will returned the man's grin. "I would be glad to be that winner."

"We will have quite the celebration, I assure you." Mr. Harrison turned abruptly and raised a hand in greeting. "Excuse me, please."

Charisma giggled as he rushed away. "I have never seen him like that. I fear that if you win, Will, he may have an attack and die."

"I should hope not," Thalia added, a twinkle in her eyes. "He is far too young for that." Her eyes widened. "Look there, Mr. Howbert is approaching."

To Charisma's surprise, the older man did come to greet them with a formal bow for the ladies and a handshake for Will. A resident of Colorado Springs since its inception in the early 1870s, Mr. Howbert was in his early forties, his receding hair already graying. In fact, the large bushy mustache that covered his entire upper lip had gone completely white.

But now he smiled, his piercing eyes warm. "Mr. Barclay, I must congratulate you. You have made me work for every vote in this election and taught me a lesson." He winked. "I will never take anything for granted again."

"It has been a pleasure to run against such a worthy opponent," Will replied. "I wish you the best of luck."

"And you, young man." Mr. Howbert turned to depart, then paused and bowed over Charisma's hand. "And I must congratulate your young lady for her campaign strategies. I have never thought of appealing to the women, but I may have to reexamine that approach in the future. You are a credit to Mr. Barclay, Miss Charisma."

His remarks startled her so badly that she almost forgot to respond. "I . . . thank you, sir."

He left them, and Will pinned Charisma with his gaze. "What did he mean by that—appealing to the women?"

"It's nothing." She was certain that Will wouldn't approve of her scheme. "Are those refreshments over there, Thalia? I am parched."

Will caught her elbow before she could follow Thalia toward the far wall. "You're not going anywhere until I get an explanation. What have you done now?"

At the disparaging tone of his voice, Charisma lifted her chin in defiance and met his gaze. "I campaigned to the women in this city and persuaded them that you were the best candidate. They, in turn, persuaded their fathers and husbands." Let him be disparaging now. "Women do have power, you know."

"I have always known that." A slow smile crossed his face and he shook his head. "I can see that life with you will never be boring, Charisma."

She frowned. *What does that mean?* He made it

sound as if they had a future when she knew better. "If you will excuse me, I am thirsty."

"Of course." He released her and she hurried to join Thalia beside the long table laden with food and drink.

"What did Mr. Barclay think of your plan?" Thalia asked, handing Charisma a cup of hot cider.

"He wasn't angry." *In fact, he'd almost seemed approving.* Perhaps Charisma didn't know him after all.

"I never thought he would be." Thalia patted Charisma's shoulder. "Mr. Barclay appreciates honesty and intelligence, my dear, and you have ample quantities of both."

Oh, yes, honesty and intelligence. Charisma knew better. She rarely heard those terms used in connection with a woman. Beautiful, perhaps, or a good homemaker or a good mother, but she had yet to hear a man praise a woman's intelligence.

"Well, this intelligent woman intends to find out more on the scandal I read about in the paper today with Boss Chaffee in Denver." She spotted the *Daily Gazette*'s editor nearby. "Mr. Steele will know all the details, I'm sure."

And he did. Apparently, Mr. Chaffee had bribed two men to break into the Democratic headquarters in Denver to steal their books and destroy them. The men had been captured before the books could be destroyed, thank goodness, but now Mr. Chaffee, a very powerful man, was under suspicion.

Charisma kept her face solemn as she listened to Mr. Steele's lengthy explanation while inside she wanted to cheer. This could only be good news for the Democrats, which included Will.

"Have they arrested Mr. Chaffee?" she asked.

"Not yet, but it's coming." Mr. Steele sighed. "This is going to hurt all of Chaffee's candidates."

Charisma managed to keep from saying what she thought about that. Perhaps Stephen was fortunate that he'd been ruined as a candidate before this. Else he would be tarred with the same brush of duplicity as his sponsor, Mr. Chaffee.

Leaving Mr. Steele, she learned precious little from anyone else. In fact, Mr. Kerr was more inclined to elaborate on the speech the previous night by the secretary of the interior, the Honorable Terry M. Teller. His talk at the opera house had drawn a huge crowd and incited the city's Republicans to vote.

This was not what Charisma wanted to hear.

Searching for Will, she found him deep in discussion with Dr. Bell and a group of men. Better she didn't bother him now. Thalia had located Mrs. Adams and they sat in a corner conversing. That was not what Charisma wished to do either.

Instead, she walked to the side door where she could get some fresh air. She'd barely cracked the door and drawn in one deep breath when she heard her name spoken behind her.

As she turned, her eyes widened. "Abigail? What are you doing here?" Too blunt yet again. Charisma tried to soften her greeting. "I mean, I did not expect to see you here."

"I came to speak to William. I'm certain he can help me."

"Will?" She'd come to Will for help? Charisma would have expected the woman to be angry with Will and herself for their parts in Stephen's ruin. "He's here somewhere." Charisma peeked past Will's sister-in-law, not completely able to believe she'd come all this way on her own. "Is Stephen with you?"

"Stephen." Abigail spat his name with disgust, obviously far more angry with her husband than with Charisma and Will. "After what that man has done to me?"

"I am sorry." While Charisma was glad to see Stephen punished, she knew Abigail would bear some of the dishonor as well.

Abigail waved her hands in the air. "The men are congratulating him in private. Congratulating him! For dallying with a maid? While I am humiliated and pitied by my friends."

"None of this was your fault." Charisma placed a comforting hand on Abigail's shoulder. "Surely your friends can see that?"

"It is just too much to bear." Tears welled in her eyes. "I am expected to act as if nothing happened, to support my husband no matter what."

No doubt political wives were expected to behave in that manner, but Charisma knew she never could. "You can leave him," she suggested.

"I can't do that." Abigail looked horrified. "I'm his wife. It would be a terrible scandal."

She would rather endure the scandal of Stephen's rape of Missy than the talk if she left her philandering husband? "Have you thought this through?" Charisma asked, pleased that she hadn't voiced the first words to pop into her mind—*are you crazy?*

"I have no money of my own. When I married Stephen it became his. My family won't take me in because of the scandal." She sighed. "Besides, there are benefits to remaining. Stephen is wealthy and well-respected, despite this latest nonsense. And the Barclay men are such wonderful lovers."

"Yes, but—" Charisma cut herself off as she saw Abigail's eyes light up. Oh, no, her tongue had gone ahead without her brain yet again. "I . . . I mean, I . . . I've heard they are."

Abigail dropped her voice to a whisper. "Have you and Will . . . ?"

"Oh, no." Charisma denied it at once, but she couldn't control the rush of color to her cheeks. A slow smile of triumph crossed Abigail's face.

"And he has not asked you to marry him?"

"I am not marrying Will." *Not out of a sense of duty.*

"I wouldn't be too sure about that." A sly grin in place, Abigail left Charisma standing there, numb. Charisma stared after her. She'd been duped. Abigail *was* angry with her and Will.

Lud, she'd done it now. She hadn't admitted to anything, but judging from Abigail's demeanor, just the hint of slander was enough. And she had no doubt Abigail would do something damaging with it. She had to inform Will.

As she went in search of him, she spotted Abigail at the far end of the room talking in a conspiratorial fashion to Stephen. He *was* here. Together they turned to look at her, the evil smile on Stephen's face speaking volumes. He intended to ruin his brother.

Oh, no.

She found Will speaking with Mr. Weller and waited impatiently for him to finish, then touched his arm. "Will, I need to talk to you."

"Just a moment," he murmured before he even had glanced at her. Once he did, the smile left his face. Apparently her expression held some of the horror she felt. He nodded toward Mr. Weller. "If you will excuse us, please."

Charisma dragged him to a deserted corner, then caught her lip between her teeth. How to begin?

"What is it?" he asked. "What's wrong?"

"Abigail is here."

"Which means Stephen probably is, too. I can handle him."

Charisma shook her head, her heart thudding in her chest. "It's worse than that. She found me and we were talking. She was going on about how awful this scandal with Stephen was for her. I felt sorry for her."

His eyes narrowing, Will grasped her arm. "Then what?"

"She . . . I . . ." Charisma swallowed the lump in her throat. "I think she suspects we made love."

The color drained from Will's face and his fingers tightened painfully around her arm. "Why would she suspect that?"

"She . . . she said something about Barclay men being great lovers and I agreed without thinking." Charisma glanced down, unable to watch the horror slide across his features.

"That has always been the problem, hasn't it, Charisma?" Though Will kept his voice pitched low, his anger came through easily enough. "You don't think before you talk."

He released her and paced away from her. "What have I been thinking? You'll never change."

"I . . . I tried to cover up my slip. I didn't admit anything." If possible, he was able to make her feel worse than she already did.

"Abigail has enough for innuendo. That's all she needs." Will turned back to face her, despair clouding his features. "You'll be ruined, Charisma."

"No, I won't. All we have to do is deny it." Surely they would be believed over his estranged brother.

"It won't matter. The damage will be done." Will's gaze skirted the room. "From the looks coming our way, it appears the rumors have already begun." He groaned. "In fact, Mr. Harrison is hurrying this way."

Will managed to have a smile on his face by the time Mr. Harrison reached them. "Mr. Barclay, I have just heard the worst rumor. It says that you and Miss Charisma . . ." He lowered his voice and glanced from Will to Charisma and back. "That you have anticipated your wedding vows."

Before Will could respond, Charisma shot Mr. Harrison a shocked look. "And you believed it?"

The man appeared startled. "Of course not, but we must do something about this."

"I believe we have already overcome this problem." Will spoke so smoothly that Charisma blinked to cover her surprise. "Miss Charisma has just agreed to become my wife."

While relief covered Mr. Harrison's face, Charisma stood straighter, her chin jutting forward. How dare Will announce something like that so casually, just so he could save his career.

She took a step backward. "I did not. I have refused him."

Both men gaped at her in total shock. "Charisma—" Will began.

She didn't try to keep the quiver of anger from her voice. "I will never marry a man just to put some unfounded rumor to rest. Excuse me." Not giving Will a chance to respond, she fled to find Thalia. The sooner she could leave this place, the better.

Will watched Charisma flee, his future vanishing with her. She'd refused him. She'd actually refused him. In all the scenarios he'd played in his mind, her adamant refusal had never been a possibility. "She'll change her mind," he muttered.

Once she could be made to see that marriage was the only solution, she would agree. How else could he save her reputation? His campaign?

"I do hope so, Mr. Barclay. For your sake as well as hers." Mr. Harrison clapped Will once on the shoulder, then abandoned him as well.

For several long moments, Will remained there, unable to take a step in any direction. What now? He'd already been considering marriage as the only honorable thing to do, but now it had become a necessity. If he could announce their engagement, the rumor would die out before it fully began.

Why didn't Charisma see that?

Determined to make her understand, he crossed the room to where she stood by Mrs. Papadopoulos and gripped her elbow in a firm hold. She was not going to flee from him again.

She sent him a look of pure defiance. "I wish to go home now."

"Very well." He noticed the concern on Mrs. Papadopoulos's face. "Are you ready?"

"Yes, of course." Mrs. Papadopoulos preceded them to the door, pausing to collect her cloak. When Will helped her into it, Charisma used the opportunity to stalk to the middle of the courtroom.

Oh, Lord. What now? He took two steps toward her, then froze when she began to speak.

"If you believe this rumor, then you are all fools." The room silenced as soon as she spoke and Will cringed. "You would be better served to ask who started this rumor and why. Why now with the election only days away? Why not ask who is vindictive enough to do this to his brother?"

Will rushed forward to take her arm. "That's enough." He hustled her outside, wrapping her cloak around her as he walked. The busy sound of conversation followed them until the door finally closed.

He dropped Charisma's arm. "What did you hope to accomplish with that . . . that display?"

"I want them to see they're being manipulated." Anger flared in her eyes. "This is ridiculous."

"We can stop it all now, Charisma." Will struggled to keep his tone gentle. "Marry me."

"No." A brief flash of emotion dashed over her face before she looked away.

His anger rose. Why was she being so unreasonable? "We must. It's the only way to save face."

"I don't care about saving face," she retorted. "That's not a reason to marry."

"In this case it is." Grateful that Mrs. Papadopoulos was remaining quiet, Will faced Charisma. "Your reputation is being smeared as well. No other man is likely to have you after this."

"Then I will have no other man." He thought he heard a slight tremor in her voice. "That doesn't seem such a big loss to me."

Will sighed. Was she deliberately being stubborn? "Once your father hears about this, he will insist on our marriage, Charisma. I've been trying to contact him all week. And I will try to speak to him as soon as we reach your home."

"He's still in Leadville. The storm dropped much more snow there and it doesn't melt nearly as quickly. I doubt if he'll be home for several more days." Her eyes sparked in the night. "Besides, he won't force me to marry."

Taking her hands, Will tried to recall the warm passionate woman in his arms only days earlier. "Charisma, we are well suited. You can't deny there is a certain attraction between us."

"That's not enough," she murmured, refusing to meet his gaze.

"What more do you want? I come from a good family. I have enough money to support us well. It would be a good match."

The words had sounded good earlier, but now they fell from his lips like empty promises. Charisma looked up, sadness etched on her face, her eyes glistening.

"Just take me home. Please." She drew her hands away and turned toward Mrs. Papadopoulos. "Please."

Will stared after her. What was he doing wrong? Any other woman would leap at this proposal.

"Not quite working out the way you expected, eh, brother?" Stephen stepped out of the darkness, a gloating smile on his face. "Life so rarely does."

Curling his hands into fists, Will stepped toward his brother. "You and Abigail came all this way just to ruin me?"

"It's the least I could do after you so efficiently destroyed my chances for election."

"But the crime you committed was real." Will hadn't raped anyone. "You're both hurting Charisma as well as me with this rumor you've started."

Stephen shrugged. "Abbie seems to think it's true. And if not, oh well. I imagine the chit could warm your bed easily enough."

Will reacted without thinking, plowing his fist into Stephen's face. His brother staggered backward, then threw himself at Will with a growl.

"Will, don't." Will heard Charisma cry out, but no longer cared. Fury filled him, drove him to pummel his brother. Though Stephen returned the blows, Will felt nothing. Nothing but a wild rage.

All these months of campaigning and work would be for nothing. His political career would be over before it ever started. And Charisma's reputation would be shattered. All because Stephen wanted revenge.

"Will, stop." Charisma tugged at his arm, pulling him back, and Will finally realized that Stephen lay sprawled on the ground, no longer moving. "You're going to kill him if you don't stop."

Abigail rushed to Stephen's side, then glared at Will. "Now you know how it feels to have your life ruined."

The fight left him in a rush and he bowed his head. He normally prided himself on holding his temper. Was he losing control along with everything else?

"A very spectacular display, Mr. Barclay."

Glancing up, he spotted Mr. Steele and several others standing by the doorway. Will didn't bother to respond. He waved a dismissive hand in their direction, then staggered to the buggy, allowing Charisma to guide him.

He refused, however, to let Charisma drive. He seated the women, then swung up to the front and snapped the reins. Ignoring the crowd spilling outside, he headed away from the courthouse.

What did it matter? His political career was over.

Eighteen

Despite Charisma's compelling speech of bravado at the courthouse, the rumor took root and spread. She was immensely grateful that her father wasn't home—an impending threat her mother threw at her daily. Would Papa force her to marry Will? She couldn't endure it. No marriage was preferable to one without love.

Belle and Grace had been so understanding she wanted to scream. Not that she didn't appreciate their sympathy, but she needed to do something. Monday's newspaper showed Will slipping in the polls. Not as drastically as Stephen probably would have liked, but enough so that he was falling behind Mr. Howbert.

Of course, Mr. Steele's short article on the fight between Stephen and Will hadn't helped either, though he had mentioned that "the current innuendo surrounding Mr. William Barclay was no doubt started at the instigation of Mr. Stephen Barclay."

She hadn't seen Will since he'd brought her home Saturday night. Belle said he came daily asking to talk to Papa, then left when he learned her father was still not home. Charisma could only hope the snow kept Papa confined for a long time yet, for she was far from ready to face him.

Mama's punishment had been swift. Charisma was confined to the house—to protect her from the unsavory gossip in town, according to Mama. More likely to stave off more humiliation to her mother.

Charisma paced her room, restless. If Will lost this election, it would be her fault. All because she could never be charming, could never learn to control her wayward tongue. What man would want a woman like that?

Certainly not Will. If not for his integrity, he would have abandoned her long ago. That he still insisted she marry him only added to Charisma's heartbreak. He honestly didn't see that his name and his money weren't enough.

She wanted his love.

And that was far from likely.

Still, she had to do something. She needed to find a way to make this right, aside from marrying Will. The election was tomorrow, which meant if she was to do anything, it would have to be today.

But what?

The only way for him to win the election now was for Mr. Howbert to drop out and she didn't see that happening. Charisma paused in her pacing. But could Mr. Howbert be persuaded to withdraw? Could she make him understand that Will was the best man for the senate?

No, Charisma couldn't do it. At this point, she doubted she could convince even her *sisters* to do anything. Her lack of charm was a distinct disadvantage when it came to persuasion.

But Thalia had charm in abundance. If she would do it . . .

Charisma didn't hesitate. Ensuring that her family

was otherwise occupied, she slipped from the house and ran the entire way to Thalia's house. James admitted her at once, his expression concerned instead of his usual amused expression.

"This is a fine kettle of frogs," he said as he led her to the parlor.

Charisma had to smile. "Fish, James." When he looked at her in confusion, she clarified. "A fine kettle of fish."

He shrugged. "Frogs. Fish. It is a fine kettle."

"That it is." Charisma entered the parlor and allowed Thalia's warm hug to comfort her. "I have an idea," she said as soon as she was seated.

Thalia hesitated. "I fear the time for ideas is past, my dear."

"No, this can work. If Mr. Howbert can be persuaded that Will is the best man for the senate, perhaps he'll withdraw."

"And why would Mr. Howbert be willing to do that?"

Charisma leaned forward. "He's a reasonable man. He wants what's best for Colorado and that's Will."

"I would assume Mr. Howbert believes he is the best candidate."

"But you could persuade him otherwise." Charisma twisted her hands together. "I know you could."

Thalia shook her head. "Not I, I'm afraid."

"But you're the only one who can."

"I don't have the same passion for Mr. Barclay's campaign as you and he do. While I believe Mr. Barclay would be an excellent senator, I also find admirable qualities in Mr. Howbert as well."

"But—"

"I am not the one to do this. You are the one who believes so strongly in Mr. Barclay. You should talk to Mr. Howbert."

Charisma scowled and sat back in her chair. "I am the last choice for such a task. I have no charm. I am blunt to a fault and useless in political matters." Hadn't this current state of affairs proven that?

"I don't believe that." Thalia stretched her hand out to cover Charisma's. "And you don't either. You were quite eloquent when defending Miss Houser and campaigning to the women. I expect you can find the words to defend Mr. Barclay as well."

Unable to picture herself with any type of eloquence, Charisma shook her head. "I would only make it worse."

"My dear, how could it be worse?"

That question held far more truth than Charisma wanted to hear. "I've ruined everything."

"Then it is up to you to make it better." Thalia squeezed her hand. "Believe in yourself, Charisma. You can make a difference."

"I'll consider it." Charisma excused herself. She could at least try. Mr. Howbert lived several blocks away. If she hurried, she could reach his home before the day grew late. She hesitated only a moment. With the present state of her reputation, what difference would a chaperone make now?

Mr. Howbert answered her knock himself, startling her from her carefully prepared speech. "I . . . er . . . I . . ." She drew in a deep breath. "I would like a few moments of your time, sir. If you have it to spare."

"Of course. Come in." He held open the door for her to enter, then waved his hand at the rosy cheeked woman standing in the hallway. "You know Mrs. Howbert, I believe."

"Yes. Good afternoon, ma'am."

"How good to see you, Miss Charisma. You're growing up so fast." Mrs. Howbert spoke with honest warmth. "I swear it was just yesterday you were attending your first dance. Now look at you."

Uncertain of how to respond, Charisma nodded. "Thank you."

"Miss Charisma has a matter of great importance to discuss with me." Mr. Howbert met Mrs. Howbert's gaze as he stopped beside her. "Please join us in the study."

"Of course."

When Mrs. Howbert accompanied them, Charisma briefly considered telling Mr. Howbert she didn't need to speak with him after all. It was obvious he didn't trust her. She discarded that idea at once. No, she had come this far. She would see it through.

Once inside Mr. Howbert's study, he showed first his wife, then Charisma to high-backed chairs before taking his own seat behind a heavy oak desk. "How can I help you, Miss Charisma?"

"I would like you to withdraw your candidacy." Charisma knew the statement was blunt, but how else could she begin?

He raised his eyebrows. "I beg your pardon?"

"This . . . this malicious rumor about me and Mr. Barclay is hurting his chances for election. If you withdraw, then he will win by default."

"So he would, but why would I do that?" Mr.

Howbert spoke in such reasonable tones that Charisma felt compelled to continue.

"Will should be in the senate. He's the best candidate."

Mr. Howbert's mustache quirked as he smiled. "Knowing of your friendship with Mr. Barclay, I will not allow that to hurt my feelings."

Oh, dear. She was ruining things already. "I apologize, sir, but I do believe in Will."

"I can see that." Mr. Howbert studied her for several long, agonizing moments. "However, I believe I am the best man to represent this county in the senate. I've held four terms as county clerk. I've assisted with significant improvements to this city. I have plans for even greater things once I'm in the senate. Tell me, Miss Charisma, why Mr. Barclay is the better candidate."

"Because he cares." The words tumbled from her, almost emerging on their own. "He cares about everyone from the lowest servant to the wealthiest man in Denver and he would represent each of them fairly. He would not allow those in a position of wealth to dictate the rules for their benefit and ignore those with less wealth. He would work hard to make things better for everyone. He's honest and trustworthy and dedicated. People *need* someone like Will in the senate."

"I am almost persuaded, Miss Charisma, however I do believe I have the better qualifications at this point in time. While an admirable candidate, Mr. Barclay has no experience in politics despite his family's connections. In a few years, perhaps, he'll be ready. But not now."

"Won't you please reconsider?" Her hopes sank. If he refused her, she had nothing left to try.

"I'm sorry." Mr. Howbert stood, then surprised her with a blunt question of his own. "Why have you refused to marry Mr. Barclay when you are so obviously in love with him?"

A blush heated her cheeks, but his question deserved an honest answer. "I will not marry a man simply to satisfy a rumor. I . . . I don't consider it a good foundation for an enduring marriage."

"Marriages have been made on far less."

Not her marriage. "If I marry it will be for love and nothing less." Despite her breaking heart. Charisma stood and turned away. Evidently, everything she attempted was destined for disaster. "Thank you for your time, sir."

"The pleasure is mine." Mr. Howbert escorted her to the door, his manner still amiable.

Charisma walked slowly toward home, fighting back tears. So much for being persuasive and charming.

Will stood at the entrance to the courthouse, the voting station for all residences north of Pikes Peak Avenue, and attempted to shake the hand of every man who entered. As he took the hand of an obviously well-to-do gentleman, he spoke his standard phrase. "I'm William Barclay and I would appreciate your vote."

The man stopped and eyed Will. "You the one they say bedded the Sullivan girl?"

"That has been the rumor," Will said tightly. A rumor he would never live down.

The man nudged him in the ribs with a broad wink. "You have my vote then. I have to admire any man who can get inside the petticoats of these snooty upper-class ladies."

As he went inside, Will wiped his hand on his pants to shed his distaste. That kind of vote he didn't want.

As a miner approached, his clothing worn but well-mended, Will stepped forward to offer his hand. "I'm William Barclay and I would appreciate your vote today."

The miner merely looked at Will's hand until Will dropped it to his side. "Don't know as I could abide a man who treats ladies the way you do." Brushing past Will, he entered the courthouse.

Will sighed. The people he most wanted to help were the ones most offended by his liaison with Charisma. He should have resisted her charms, should have left her alone in her room at Mrs. Papadopoulos's, but he was, after all, only a man.

A man who had wanted Charisma with a desire beyond reason. Who still wanted her. Who missed her.

He was beginning to believe she wouldn't marry him even if he did have the opportunity to speak to her father. He should be relieved. After all, no matter what the outcome of today's elections, he would leave Colorado Springs and the last thing he needed was a wife.

Yet her adamant refusal mattered—more than he wanted to admit. Now that he'd convinced himself he needed to marry Charisma, he found it difficult to shake the idea.

"Well, I say Charisma Sullivan is getting what she deserves."

Hearing Charisma's name, Will turned to see Miss Mattingly and two of her friends ambling along the walkway in front of the courthouse. Miss Mattingly glanced at him from the corner of her eye and he realized she'd deliberately pitched her voice so he could overhear.

"I went to her house to offer sympathy," Miss Mattingly said.

More likely to see if more gossip could be found. Will knew Miss Mattingly's reputation.

The young woman paused below the courthouse steps to continue her farce. "When I told her about the rumor I'd heard, she laughed at me." She raised her hand to her chest. "Laughed. She said I must be in desperate need of entertainment to believe such a thing."

"What had you heard?" one woman asked, her eyes wide.

"Why that she and Mr. Barclay had been dancing naked down the street in that last blizzard. Can you imagine?"

Will tried to hold it in, but his laughter escaped in a loud guffaw that had all the women looking at him. He gave them a gentlemanly bow, then turned away to greet another voter.

Dancing naked in the snow. How ridiculous. No wonder Charisma had laughed at Miss Mattingly. If the rumor had deteriorated that much, would people actually believe it?

He glanced inside to where the votes were being gathered. Within the next day or two, he would know the answer to that question.

* * *

After a restless night he joined the crowd waiting outside the *Daily Gazette* the next day. His sleep had been disturbed by vivid dreams—not of the election but of Charisma: her smile, her laugh, her faith in him when he had needed it most, and through it all, the feeling that he was losing something very precious to him.

The only numbers posted in the newspaper's window thus far were so low as to be meaningless, and Will wandered away from the murmuring crowd. Somewhere during his sleepless night, he'd accepted that Charisma would not marry him. With the election over, marrying now wouldn't change anything other than her reputation, for which she showed a total lack of concern.

But her reputation mattered to him. He had despoiled her. He couldn't be so callous or uncaring as to desert her even if she insisted. She'd denied the possibility of a child, but how could she be certain? She *had* to marry him.

A loud murmur passed through the crowd and Will moved back to read the latest numbers. He was only slightly behind Mr. Howbert. This was much more encouraging than he'd expected. He just might win this election.

And as he'd learned over the past couple months, as a senator he would be expected to have a wife to host social functions, to stand by his side on all occasions, to support him in his political career. Therefore, if Charisma wouldn't marry him, he would still need a wife of some kind.

But what kind of wife?

Someone who believed in him, of course. Who understood and supported his endeavors. She had to have the right social standing, and the beauty and manners expected of a political wife.

But more importantly he wanted someone who felt as passionately as he did about his causes, who wouldn't hesitate to fight for what was right, who wasn't afraid to speak out if necessary, and take action. He didn't want a wife who was merely an accessory. He wanted an equal partner. Someone who worked *with* him, not *for* him.

He strode down the street. He wanted a woman who could make him laugh, with whom he could have intelligent discussions. A woman who shared his passion in the bedroom.

He wanted a woman he could love, who would love him in return. Will froze in mid-stride.

He had just described Charisma.

He wanted Charisma.

And he was going to lose her.

Sudden fear made his throat constrict. Without her by his side, his future appeared bleak. Lord help him. How could he fix this?

As a sign of fate, when he looked up he spotted Charisma and her sisters at the edge of the crowd by the newspaper window. Her face was wan and dark circles hung beneath her eyes, yet her stance was proud, despite the whispers that must be circulating around her.

He loved her. No wonder he couldn't imagine his future without her.

Moving with long strides, he made his way toward her. He had to make her understand, had to convince her that marriage was the only solution. Somehow.

Charisma spotted Will approaching and her

chest tightened. Did he mean to speak to her here? In this crowd which was all too willing to believe the latest gossip? He wouldn't be that foolish.

Yet he wove through the crowd until he stood before her, his gaze intense. "Miss Charisma."

"Mr. Barclay." She gave him a polite nod, nothing more.

"May I have a few moments of your time?"

"Now?" She glanced toward the window where the numbers were constantly changing. "They're about to declare the winner of the senatorial race."

"That's not important."

Not important? Charisma caught her jaw before it dropped. Will said this? "Are you feeling all right?"

"No." His gaze never left hers. "A moment only. Please."

Dumbfounded, she nodded and allowed him to lead her across the street, away from the growing crowd. "Don't you care who wins?" she asked. This campaign had been everything to him.

"I care," he admitted. "But not as much as I care about this."

"About what?" What could be more important to him than winning this election?

"Our marriage. I am asking you . . . begging you . . . to marry me, Charisma."

She closed her eyes against the pain. Every time she refused him, it tore at something inside her. Pulling her hands free, she turned away to return to her sisters. "We've already discussed this, Will."

She'd barely taken a step when his words froze her in place. "I can survive if I don't win this election, Charisma. But I can't survive without you."

Glancing back, she stared at him. The light in his eyes was different, deeper. "What did you say?"

"I have gone about this all wrong." Will closed the distance between them. "I don't want to marry you because of rumors or honor or because it's a good match."

"You don't?" Now he didn't want to marry her?

"I want to marry you because I cannot exist without you by my side."

Was she really hearing this? "But I thought you considered me too blunt, too unsuitable."

He shook his head. "I can't imagine you any other way than passionate, caring, and direct about all the things that matter to you." He brushed his hand over her cheek. "I love you, Charisma Sullivan. If you will agree to marry me, I'll spend the rest of my life trying to earn your love."

Charisma smiled and covered his hand with her own. "You don't have to earn it, Will. It's been yours all along."

His slow smile added to her erratic pulse. "Can I take that as an acceptance of my offer?"

His tentative tone made her laugh. "Yes. I accept your offer, Mr. Barclay."

He released a loud whoop of joy, then swung her in a circle, ending with a kiss that stole her breath. She stared up at him, unable to believe her good fortune.

"People will see us." Half the town stood across the street. What would they think?

As a loud cheer resounded, they both turned to look. Had they been seen? All eyes appeared to be watching the window. Moments later, Mr.

Howbert emerged, accompanied by hearty hand-shakes.

He crossed toward Charisma and Will and extended his hand. "A good race, Mr. Barclay. Better luck next time."

Will accepted the hand with a smile. "Thank you, sir. I wish you all the best in the senate."

"You don't appear too disheartened, sir. I find that encouraging."

Will wrapped his arm around Charisma's waist, tucking her close to him. "Miss Charisma has finally agreed to marry me. I could not be happier."

Mr. Howbert caught Charisma's gaze, then smiled. "May I be the first to congratulate you?"

"Thank you."

"In lieu of a wedding gift, I have a proposition for you, Mr. Barclay."

Charisma exchanged a puzzled look with Will. A proposition?

"What would that be?" Will asked.

"I doubt that you're aware Miss Charisma came to see me yesterday."

Charisma winced as Will shot her a quick glance. "I did not know about that."

"She very charmingly tried to persuade me to drop out of the race. She wasn't charming enough to make me change my mind, I'm afraid, but enough so that I started thinking." Mr. Howbert hesitated and Charisma held her breath. "I have need of a good assistant while I'm in office. Someone willing to work hard and learn about politics from the inside. In time, this person could probably become a senatorial candidate himself. I know you left the Republican party in order to run for the senate.

Miss Charisma's recommendation convinced me my best choice for an assistant would be you. Would you be willing to return to the Republican party and come work for me, Mr. Barclay?"

Will's smile filled his face. "I would consider it an honor, sir."

"Excellent. We can talk later about the details."

The men shook hands again, then Will glanced at Charisma and back to Mr. Howbert. "There is one thing you should know. Something I feel quite strongly about and may affect whether you want me or not."

"Yes?"

"I am very much in favor of equal rights for women. I believe Colorado should be the first state to offer them the right to vote."

Mr. Howbert said nothing, but tears welled up in Charisma's eyes. That Will would jeopardize this wonderful opportunity said more about the strength of his love than any possible words. "Will . . ."

"Well, Mr. Barclay, we'll have to see if we can't work toward that goal then, won't we?" With a wink, Mr. Howbert returned to the congratulations of the crowd.

Charisma wrapped her arms around Will's neck, uncaring if the entire world saw her. "I love you."

"And I love you." He stole a quick kiss. "I hope you realize you're far more charming than you think."

Mr. Howbert had called her charming despite her outburst at his house. When she cared about something, the right words did seem to come. "Maybe I am."

"There is something you should know, too."

Sudden trepidation filtered through her. "What's that?"

"You do make a difference. Every moment of every day you make a difference in my life."

Charisma smiled. That had been her unspoken wish that day at the Garden of the Gods. Maybe the Three Graces had been listening after all.

Epilogue

Thalia gave her sisters her most charming smile as she joined them. "That is settled now. Most satisfactorily, I might add. She not only has achieved her spoken and unspoken wish, but her heart's wish as well—a man to love her for herself."

Aglaia shook her head, her beauty illuminated by her teasing smile. "I must admit that there were times when I thought you would not succeed."

"Yes, mortals can be unpredictable." Thalia beamed at Euphrosyne as her sister served the tea. "Now it's your turn, dear."

"Ah, yes. Grace." Euphrosyne settled into a chair in one graceful movement. "She will be a challenge."

"But?" Aglaia prompted.

"I have an idea." A mischievous smile crossed Euphrosyne's face. "A very special idea."

Dear Reader:

Thank you for spending time with Charisma Sullivan and her quest to become charming. She was fun to write because I was never quite sure what she was going to say.

I especially enjoyed the chance to collaborate on this series with two other members of my critique group. We shared in the development of the Sullivan family and the residents of Colorado Springs.

While many people and events are lifted from actual history, anything involving my characters is purely fiction. There was one interesting bit of news I couldn't fit into the book, but I have to share with you. I learned that an earthquake—very rare for Colorado—hit just north of Denver on the day of the elections, November 7, 1882. People later said it was because James Grant actually won the position of governor of Colorado. A Democrat! Can you imagine?

Another interesting fact was that Colorado actually became the first state to approve women's suffrage in a popular election on November 7, 1893. I'd like to think Will and Charisma had something to do with that.

The first book in this series was *Belle of the Ball* by Pam McCutcheon and the next book is *Say Good*

Night, Gracie by Yvonne Jocks. I'm sure you'll enjoy reading about the other Sullivan sisters, too.

I love hearing from readers. You can write to me at P.O. Box 31541, Colorado Springs, CO 80931-1541 or e-mail me at *karen@karenafox.com.* To discover what other books I have coming out, visit my web site at *http://www.karenafox.com.*

See you between the pages.

Karen Fox